Schubert

Schubert

Twelve *Moments musicaux* and a novel

Peter Härtling

Translated by Rosemary Smith

HM

Holmes & Meier
New York / London

Published in the United States of America 1995 by
Holmes & Meier Publishers, Inc.
160 Broadway
New York, NY 10038

Originally published as *Schubert: Zwölf Moments musicaux und ein Roman.*
Copyright © 1992 by Luchterhand Literaturverlag GmbH, Hamburg-Zurich.

Book design by Sara Burris.

This book has been printed on acid-free paper.

Library of Congress Cataloging-in-Publication Data

Härtling, Peter, 1933-
[Schubert. English]
Schubert: twleve moments musicaux and a novel/
Peter Härtling; translated by Rosemary Smith.
p. cm.
Includes bibliographical references.
ISBN 0-8419-1347-1 (alk. paper)
1. Schubert, Franz, 1797-1828—Fiction.
I. Smith, Rosemary, 1942- . II. Title.
PT2668. A3S3813 1995   94-48451
833'.914—dc20   CIP

Manufactured in the United States of America

The greater my present insight into what he was,
the greater my understanding of what he suffered.

—Moritz von Schwind

Contents

1

Moment musical no. 1
(*Not too slow*)

*T*he scene used to be a picture, a drawing. Not any longer. Much time elapsed before they began to move, these figures sketched in fine pencil.

The small personage appears. Penciled-in light helps give him an undistorted outline.

He says, "Do sit down over there under the linden tree and wait until the ladies and gentlemen pause in their conversation, and I would respectfully ask that you not interrupt anybody."

He is playing in the far distance now.

I wish that Wunderlich were singing, or Patzak:

> The lark is swirling in the sky,
> And love is calling pain and sorrow
> Away from the depths of the heart.

> *Die Lerche wirbelt in der Luft;*
> *Und aus dem tiefen Herzen ruft*
> *Die Liebe, Leid und Sorgen.*

Anxious and confused, I turn to Herr von Spaun who has laid his walking stick diagonally before him across the garden table as a clearly defined boundary: "Excuse me, but do you find it as difficult as I do to decide whether we are out of doors or in a salon?"

"How so?" Herr von Spaun looks me up and down, mystified, then gazes back into the picture and listens to Schubert, whom once again I cannot hear.

I watch him. He puts his hand to his heart.

I seat myself farther back so that at last I can remain undisturbed.

I can no longer recognize anyone, not Schober nor Vogl nor Mayrhofer. The ceiling, as one might expect, has dissolved in light, and billows like a translucent sail.

And I see how Schubert, at his piano, drifts out into a meadow resembling a huge green basin, and I am overcome with fear that he might plunge over the edge, but a young lady, possibly Katharina Fröhlich, reassures me in passing: "There is no edge. Concentrate instead on the other gentlemen and their history."

I cannot interpret the charade.

"Would you be able to help me?" I ask the lady who happens to be sitting beside me. She laughs aloud, and puts her hand to her lips: "It is possible that you are hearing what you see," she says.

Hearing what I see?

She nods and looks straight through me. "Yes. Or that you are seeing what you hear."

Before I can reply to her, what she has just described takes place, or is it just in my imagination?

Although Schubert has left his piano and is bowing toward the horizon, the piano continues to play one of his waltzes, as if from memory, and Vogl is singing the Harper, and Therese Grob, who has dislodged a figure from the charade and now hovers on a puff of air, picks up his song:

> Bid me not speak,
> Bid me be silent.
> For I am pledged to secrecy.
>
> *Heiß mich nicht reden,*
> *Heiß mich schweigen.*
> *Denn mein Geheimnis ist mir Pflicht.*

Schober, at least I assume that is who it is, throws a letter into the air, up toward the hovering canopy, the paper unfolds, and there is an inscription to be read on it that remains illuminated whichever way the sheet of paper turns.

An officer is lowered from the flies. He must prohibit the performance until further notice in the name of His Excellency Prince Metternich.

He bows: "If you please, my name is Schodl, I am the censor."

There is nothing more to be seen of Schubert.

Spaun strikes a match and ignites the beautiful surroundings with a tongue of flame. Now are we out of doors or in a salon?

Before I turn away I realize with horror that an iceberg, high as a house, is advancing over the green border. It picks up the abandoned piano and deposits it on a ledge.

2

Births at School

*F*ranz Schubert came into the world in a schoolhouse. Not in one such as we would recognize, a public building, whose sole function is teaching and learning, but in a house where people lived and loved, were born and died, and where teaching took place as well. In which there were daytime noises and nighttime noises, sounds occurring to a fixed pattern, a rhythm of the hours.

The house in the Ninth District still stands, but it is no longer exactly like the one at the former Himmelpfortgrund.

What now appears like a museum in the large and inscrutable city was at that time, at the end of the eighteenth century, part of a suburban quarter into which three thousand people crowded in confined and meager dwellings, where artisans had their workshops in the courtyards, day laborers lived side by side with officials, teachers next door to servants. The confined space forced them all out into the street, where many of them not only worked and conducted much of their business, but also relaxed, played, and strolled about, spying on the activities of their neighbors.

The streets stank. At night there was practically no light.

The hustle and bustle of life warmed some, left others shivering.

Those who dreamed were soon disturbed by the cries of the day and the sighs of the night.

The summer sun dried out the alleyways and courtyards so that the garbage had no chance to rot. The rain heaped up the filth, and in winter everything that might rot and stink was quickly frozen.

Franz has not yet been born, and his parents still have no notion of where they will meet, or where they will begin their life together.

The region Franz Theodor Schubert, the father, comes from is one I know well. Neudorf is situated near Mährisch-Schönberg, in a hilly landscape that looms steep in the memory of my childhood. The Altvater mountains define the horizon to the east. There were, if my memory is not running away with me, streams in the valleys, lined with green, which cut through the forests, as in a picture book or a song:

> Downward and ever further,
> Always following the stream,
> A stream always rushing onward,
> Ever more fresh and bright.

> *Hinunter und immer weiter,*
> *Und immer dem Bache nach,*
> *Und immer frischer rauschte,*
> *Und immer heller der Bach.*

Perhaps Father Schubert sometimes told his children stories about this region. It is equally probable that he was silent, and wished to forget. After all, he had felt impelled to leave it, to follow Karl, his older brother, who was already working as a teacher in Vienna.

Franz Theodor arrived in Vienna during the winter of 1783. He had already taught in schools in Brünn and elsewhere, and so had no difficulty in being taken on with his brother at the Carmelite School. Without doubt he took time to adjust to life in the large city which at that time had over two hundred and fifty thousand inhabitants. He was ambitious, he wanted to be successful. For two semesters he attended lectures in philosophy at the University of Vienna.

A portrait still exists of Franz Theodor, a painting that shows him as a solid schoolmaster, and, upon closer examination, as a sinister figure. His facial features run together and yet in their expression convey a sense of strain. A peculiarly fleshy bridge of his nose pushes the eyes disproportionately far apart. His forehead, too, above the insignificant eyebrows, expands and loses shape. The cheeks droop and are slack.

The little mouth, biting back his sensuality, is above a thoroughly childish chin with a dimpled cleft.

This is someone who will not reveal himself for anything in the world, who plays the unobtrusive citizen and yet who unwittingly betrays much of what torments him, and from which his nearest and dearest suffer: that he presents himself as pious, although doubt and uncertainty constantly gnaw at him; that he insists on his own status; that he demands obedience to his authority to the point of ruthlessness, and yet curses his ever-crumbling self-confidence; that he is gratified to parade the qualities of honorable husband and Christian teacher, and yet is often scarcely master of the excesses and desires of his imagination; that he is surrounded by children throughout his life, but wants to teach them nothing but to become like himself and his kind.

It is true, music can touch his heart, especially simple Bohemian tunes, outdoor tunes that have become detached from anything truly idyllic and are heard by him merely as sentimental signals.

I do not mean to have presented Franz Theodor Schubert here as a philistine or a self-righteous scoundrel, but as a man who could only catch hold of one corner of his dream, and who in order to live a halfway comfortable existence declared it to be the whole dream. To be precise, he was more concerned with himself, his reputation, and his advancement than with the spiritual welfare of his wife and children. Because he was sparing with his love, he received little.

There is no picture of his first wife, Elisabeth Vietz. Yet I believe I know her better than her husband. Solely through the music of her son. Above all he was stimulated by his memory of her, and maybe even transfigured her.

Franz Theodor had only just gotten established, if this could be regarded as an apt description for the temporary situation, the time of waiting, in which they ran across each other, Elisabeth and he. How this happened has not been recorded, nor has it been communicated by the children.

For the beginning they could have imagined a fairy-tale that is always told anew and differently. But reality did not permit this, and so they kept silent about the passionate and breathless way in which they rushed upon each other. He, the assistant at the Carmelite School, twenty-one years old, and she, the maid from the suburb of Lichtental, three years older than he, well versed in the loneliness of the city and in the manifold but not always pleasant ways of escaping from it, those revels of a weekend.

They do not abide by the rules.

Is it he who sets the pace, or does she fear that time is passing her by? She tells much about herself.

He does not. He cannot. He cannot unmask himself even in a single moment of union. He has already taken possession of her, yet she still believes that she can make her own decisions.

She tells how twelve years ago her father, who was a respected gunsmith, had set out with them all, from their home in Zuckmantel in Silesia. "He had great expectations of Vienna," she says, "of everything. Back home things had not gone well for us."

Is he listening?

On the way her mother died, from what cause she does not know. "Now Father and we three children were bereft. It could still have turned out all right," she said. She is inclined to draw lines across the page, and to be constantly looking for fresh starts. In time she will let things be.

"We had scarcely taken quarters in the 'Golden Lamb' than Father passed away too," she continues. "Felix, my brother, took a job as a weaver in Lichtental, Maria Magdalena and I became housemaids. Always here in our suburb," she stresses, and indicates a large household, people whom she knows, to whom she is subservient, whom she likes and respects; houses where she goes in and out, which are hers while she is working there, the young rascals, the children, too, for whom she has to care, and when she shuts her eyes maybe one of the young gentlemen rubs against her hips like a tomcat and she permits it, not scratching as is her wont.

"I could imagine another life," she says. So could he. "A school," he says, "that could be a kingdom." Why, on only the first or second evening of their acquaintance, after they had fallen into each other's arms and were heavy as a lump of lead, he took her to his room in house number 152, he could not even in later times explain. In the ecstasy of their joint rebellion he proved himself bold, caring nothing for the gossip of the neighbors or of his brother. "If necessary, you two would have to get married."

He calms him down, he wants to look around, to see if there might not be a school available, a proper household. That takes two more years.

Long before this he has to marry Elisabeth. She is expecting a child. Does she want to tie him down, to force him? Perhaps. But—and this thought transforms Elisabeth, changes her character, tells the story of a rather different, more deceitful maid—but could it not also have been that she was already pregnant when she made Franz Theodor's acquaintance? They were married on January 17, 1785, in the church at Lichtental.

In the marriage register of the parish of the "Fourteen Holy Helpers" the profession of the bridegroom, "Franz Schuberth," is given as "instructor," an expression of his "better education": the six secondary-school classes in Brünn and presumably also his current studies in philosophy. In any case, he can teach Latin.

The bride, on the other hand, Elisabeth Vietz, has no profession in the register, not even that of maid, she is the "daughter of a master locksmith," and he has been dead for years.

The first two children, Ignaz and Elisabeth, were born in the bedroom of the Lichtental house, No. 152.

Franz Theodor does not give up, he wants his school. Elisabeth learns the right moment to keep silent and the best time to speak. She had in no way anticipated his grinding rigidity, nor how greatly he would value his reputation in the eyes of the world.

"Yes, Franz. No, Franz."

She responds fast. He likes that. Fast and businesslike, just the way in which many a night he makes love to her, then immediately falls asleep, gathering strength for his teaching and his search for a school.

I write: Franz Theodor Schubert is seeking a school. Just as at the present day someone seeks housing. Under similarly miserable conditions. And that is just how it was. He was seeking a school and at the same time an abode—for himself and his family, and not least for his pupils, who, he hoped, would soon come in sufficient numbers to provide for his daily needs.

His school already existed. It just needed a new teacher. The small family stayed in the same district, the present-day Ninth District, moving merely from Lichtental to the neighboring Himmelpfortgrund, into the house "At the Sign of the Red Crawfish" which was situated on "Upper Main Street by the Nußdorf Gate," and is now Nußdorferstraße 54.

There he is, reconnoitering his school. Or more precisely, he is examining the rooms where he will live and teach. Perhaps he is accompanied by his predecessor, Anton Osselini, who praises the school, its location and its children, and obscures the water stains on the wall by gesticulating in front of them, or throws open a cracked window so wide that the damage escapes the eagle eye of his successor.

Schubert himself must be responsible for the provision of furniture for the school. He, Osselini, has sold his own elsewhere. "Yes, yes, he had reckoned on that."

Reckoning is all he does now.

In the house there are sixteen apartments. Many of the tenants have already lived an eternity at Himmelpfort.

"At Himmelpfort, the Gate of Heaven," says Franz Theodor when he brings the good news to Elisabeth. He smiles again for the first time in a long while.

"Something could be made of that," she says quietly.

Franz Theodor rents two apartments from his landlord, the master-mason Schmidtgruber. The one on the ground floor will remain the school, somewhat refashioned. The family will move into the other one on the upper floor. Elisabeth takes charge of these arrangements.

In the kitchen there is room enough for the children to sleep.

She takes the measurements, making arrangements in her head.

He does the same for the two rooms on the lower floor by the courtyard.

On Christmas Eve 1787 his father dies in Neudorf. The small inheritance, ninety-six florins, enables Franz Theodor to acquire school benches and a blackboard.

On June 13, 1786, he had been accredited by the provincial government as the schoolteacher at Himmelpfortgrund.

To his annoyance the first pupils were mostly poor and their parents were not in a position to pay tuition. However, in time there were also children from families who were solvent.

With Schubert there is more singing than under his predecessors. This alone caused the daytime noise to change, that background of sound into which everything is woven that constitutes the banality of the human day: doors slamming, Herr Pospischil, the nightwatchman, whistling as he returns home, children screeching their way into the room, a baby crying who starts off a second then a third, a dog barking, Schmidtgruber, the landlord, shouting at his apprentice in the yard, and next door to the right Wandel, the good-for-nothing, decides to do it with his wife in the middle of the afternoon, and they hear his moaning and her groaning, then one of the children downstairs slams the door yet again so that the walls shake, and in the passageway an old woman is shrieking, "If you don't shut up . . ." for at least the tenth time, and her nagging voice makes quite clear how much she is enjoying it, then from time to time criers run past the house, and there are disputes and quarrels in the street, or just gossip among those who have nothing better to do than to steal the Lord's time or to bend the ear of the devil.

Elisabeth sits on the stool at the window feeding her little girl, who was christened Elisabeth after her, at her breast. The child will die soon.

She listens and is watchful. Always, when her husband mounts the stairs, she wants to go through his likely wishes or commands in her head and yet she gets completely bewildered.

She listens to hear if there is any change in the noises coming from the school down by the courtyard, if Franz Theodor suddenly shouts, if one of the children is given the cane and bawls, or if he lets the pupils sing more than usual. In this way she can prepare herself for his moods.

She scarcely has time to think of herself. Either she is pregnant or she has just brought a child into the world.

Before Franz, *the* Franz, is born, there is time for numerous pregnancies.

"Just yell, woman, yell," is what Franz Theodor is in the habit of saying by way of comfort when the birthpangs trouble her. He said that for the first one, Ignaz. Ignaz Franz is born on March 8, 1785, when they are still at Lichtental, as is Elisabeth, born on March 1, 1786. She dies on August 13, 1788, in the house at Himmelpfortgrund, of spotted fever.

In the meantime, Karl is born on April 23, 1787, and he passes away on February 6, 1788, before the weak and sickly Elisabeth.

"Just yell, woman, yell."

Franziska Magdalena is born on June 6, 1788, and dies on August 14, 1788, of colic, and while Elisabeth is still grieving for her two little pearls, Elisabeth and Franziska Magdalena, hers for so short a time, she has to expect yet another pregnancy, and she brings a little girl into the world on July 5, 1789, to whom she and Franz Theodor again give the name Franziska Magdalena, in defiance and in hope, but she cannot survive long, and dies on January 1, 1792, of bronchitis.

"Just yell, woman, yell."

She brings Franz Karl into the world on August 10, 1790, but he departs it again only one month later on September 10, and in less than a year, on July 11, 1791, Anna Karolina is born, whose name is entered in the Register of Deaths eighteen days later, on July 29, as having died of spasms and cramps.

"Just yell, woman, yell."

Petrus comes into the world on July 29, 1792, exactly a year after the death of Anna Karolina, and he dies not even two years after it on January 14, 1793, of the consequences of catarrh while teething.

He is followed by Josef, who is born on September 16, 1793, and is carried off by smallpox on October 18, 1798, aged five.

"Just yell, woman, yell."

However, from now on she seems to have gathered and husbanded all her powers of survival for the future, for the three who are recorded next in the register under "Births and Deaths in the Family of the Schoolteacher Franz Schubert" survive and grow up, brothers who are not alike, and eventually, when Elisabeth is gaunt with exhaustion, there is another girl, but before Maria Theresia, the fourteenth and last of the children, is born on September 17, 1801, Elisabeth brings into the world Ferdinand Lukas on October 18, 1794, Franz Karl on November 5, 1795, and Franz Peter, who has not yet fallen out of line, on January 31, 1797.

This Franz is baptized the day after his birth because Elisabeth has to fear, as with her other children, that he might depart this world again immediately. He is particularly small. After Franz, on December 17, 1799, the thirteenth, Aloisia Magdalena is born. She only lives for one day.

"Just yell, woman, yell."

Meanwhile, Franz Theodor applies for better positions and better schools. He applies at the Große Pfarrgasse in Leopoldstadt, at St. Augustine's, and at the Carmelites' in Leopoldstadt where he first started to work, with his brother Karl. After Karl's death in December 1804, Franz Theodor believed that he would be able to become his successor. The authorities passed him over, and chose another.

"Be quiet," he barks at the children, "for Heaven's sake, give us some peace."

3

Voices

He is almost three years old. The house has built itself up around him, and he knows his way around inside it. He knows who belongs in the house, who might come out of which door, whom to speak to, and whom to avoid. He knows all the people by their voices. There are dark voices and light ones, some gentle, some hard, voices that sing and voices that can only scold. He knows other voices that do not ring at all but seem muted, voices that always sound flustered. Sometimes he sits in the narrow passage on the first floor, which the apartment doors open on to, and just listens.

He knows Mother's voice best of all. This voice captures him, draws him to her side even if she has not called him. If he hears her voice, then he follows it and runs to her.

"Mama!" She holds him close for a moment, and he presses his face against her skirt and feels like rolling himself up in its soft folds.

"Get along with you, Franzl," she says, and her hands encircle his head like a cap.

Down below in Father's school the children are singing. Soon Father will come up the stairs and Franz will know if he is going to curse or to be silent, if he will talk with Mother or perhaps even laugh. The steps on the stairs will tell him. He listens for them. If their stamping signals Father's anger, then he makes himself scarce.

He can distinguish the voices of his brothers with no trouble at all.

Ignaz speaks a little like Father. His words seem to spit straight from his neck so that they bounce and ricochet. He loves Ferdinand because he often tells him stories and comforts him when he is hurt. Ferdinand can make his voice twitter like a bird. Karl, who is only one year older than himself but does not wish to have anything to do with him, snuffles between his words and is scarcely intelligible.

In one of the apartments there is a girl who sings so sadly that when Franz has been listening to her he has to press his thumbs into his ears.

"What's the matter?" asks Father. He has to go down to the school again. So does Ignaz, who is following in his footsteps. "What's the matter?"

"Nothing, Father."

He runs down to the courtyard and crouches against the wall of the house. It is warm. If he presses his head long enough against the wall he can hear the sounds it makes, dark warm stone sounds.

Now that it is summertime he stands in the gateway and watches what goes on in the street. Mother does not like him to do this. Under no circumstances may he leave the house. "Please, Franzl. Father does not approve."

He does not know most of the people who pass by. A few greet him. "Hello, Franzl," they call. He replies and is amazed how loud his voice sounds. He draws back into the shadows of the gateway when some people pass, but as soon as they have gone he steps forward again and watches them go. He would so much like to know where these strangers are going. He is so interested in them that he dares to ask Mother about them.

Irritated, she admonishes him. "They are wicked," she says, "terribly bad and wicked, wandering people."

He does not ask further, but puts his hands tight against his ears so that he can hear only the voices in his head, and then he sings: "The bad and wicked wandering people." It is singing in his head. No one can hear it except himself.

It is winter. The house smells of fire, wood, and burning dung. He may not go outside the door.

"Sing," begs his mother, who scarcely moves about any more, and holds her hands to her stomach.

"A little bird comes flying," he sings.

"Just like a little bird," says his mother.

Father says: "I shall take Franz into the school soon. He should learn the fiddle."

Mother is expecting a baby. "You will have a brother or sister," she tells him. She is not well. She leans out of the window and vomits into the street. "Watch out down there," she cries.

Ignaz, who is sitting by the stove and has a free period, calls out as if he were Father: "Shut that window. I'm freezing."

He is freezing too, but in a different way. The voices that he can usually control, which he can combine as he desires so that sometimes several begin together or sing against each other in a wonderful fashion, these voices shrivel and become small. "Aren't you well?" Ferdinand looks after him. He sits down beside him on the bench by the stove, puts his arm around his shoulders, and whispers into his ear: "Father is going to teach you to play the violin." He likes the word. It rings. It has its own voice. Violin.

"I don't feel well," says Mother with a sigh.

All four sleep near the stove. He is allowed to lie nearest to its warmth. Ignaz, as the oldest, must sleep farthest away. Karl and Ferdinand lie between them. Today Father does not close the door. It may be that the child will be born. He sleeps through the birth.

He wakes to hear Father talking to Mother.

"It's a girl," says Father.

"She cried like a girl," says Mother.

"You must rest," orders Father.

The sister is called Maria Theresia.

Aunt Maria comes to help, and shoos the two big brothers around, but she has to hold him close: "I wish I knew who I'm reminded of when I look at you, Franzl."

The new sister cries a great deal.

A little while before this Mother had brought another sister into

15

the world, who had died just two hours later. She had been called Aloisia. So that she will not be forgotten, they will sing for her in church on Sunday.

Father has called the priests and all the singers together, and the musicians too.

"Look, Franz," says Father, "they have violins just like me," and shows him.

A man waves his arms like a big bird and wakes the voices. Now they may sing out as Franz has always heard them in secret, all the voices together.

After the music Father leads him up to the man who is called the Choirmaster. He has to make his bow just as Ignaz taught him, and Father says, "Herr Holzer, I would like to present Franz to you, sir. I believe that he has a good ear and a beautiful voice."

"We will see," says Herr Holzer, and taps him on the head with a hard finger.

The music for Aloisia is called Requiem. It fills his head and pushes the other songs aside. It is not his own voice that he can hear on the stairs, clear and celestial: *Diesiraediesillasolvetsaeculuminfavilla.*

4

Moving House

*O*n May 27, 1801, Franz Theodor buys a house. He has to take out a mortgage, but as the money loses more and more of its value in the following years, this debt does not oppress him for too long. The house is particularly well suited for a school, with its spacious rooms on the first floor, and on the second floor there is sufficient space for the growing family. Franz Theodor did not need to worry about finding pupils. Most would move with him, as the new schoolhouse is only a stone's throw from the old one at Himmelpfortgrund. It is in the Säulengasse, "Sporkenbüchl Empty Ground, Registration No. 14," and bears the name "At the Sign of the Black Horse." Soon over three hundred children come to the schoolhouse in the mornings and the afternoons, some from distant parts of the city. Schoolmaster Schubert has a good reputation, and so he has little difficulty in finding suitably qualified assistants.

The house has no garden, just a courtyard as large as three rooms. This is considerably smaller than the one at Himmelpfortgrund. It could be, nevertheless, that it appeals to Franz at first sight.

Would that be correct? I am telling of a four-year-old, whose portrait I am making for myself by looking at later pictures of him and working the story backward. This is not the only reason why I imagine that I can recognize the face of the child in the features of the twenty-year-old, the child being taken for the first time by his eldest brother Ignaz to the house that they will soon be moving into. I can see in my mind's eye a short and sturdy boy with a round head a bit too large, who (and I am quite sure about this) prefers listening to speaking, and prefers to play by himself, though he does not like to be without company.

In almost all his pictures that have been passed down to us, the accurate contemporary ones and the imagined reconstructions, Franz is wearing glasses. When was he measured for these and fitted with them? When did he notice that he had poor sight? It would probably have been immediately after his father took him into the school. Since his father would certainly have insisted that he did not sit in the first row, he would have been unable to read the writing on the blackboard clearly. His father noticed this, and they decided to have a pair of glasses made for him. Children's glasses. Perhaps they were similar to those he wore in later life, and not even much smaller: thick oval lenses, exactly the same size as the eye sockets, set in a narrow metal frame, with a bridge holding them tight onto the nose close to the eyes, which is why in so many of the pictures it appears as if the eyes are sitting in the glasses like marbles.

For the moment he is not wearing glasses. He does not need to go to school as yet, though he does already know what goes on in the school. Many a time he has listened to the interplay of voices, those of the children and those of his father or his assistants.

But perhaps he avoided the new house too, barricading himself in the old one when his brothers were looking for him. He had finally, without any maneuvering on his own part, got the undivided attention of his mother. She told him stories of his grandfather, of the gentry with whom she was in service, of the great kitchens and huge public rooms, of marble staircases, and she sang him songs that had lightened her work.

He is now four. He sees her crying, not for the first time, but it is the first time he is alone with her. He snuggles up to her, strokes her tear-stained face, notices how catching crying is. Now she has to comfort him, which makes her cry again, at which point he can comfort her. In the end, when they are both exhausted, or when they hear someone coming, she bids him sing: "A little bird comes flying."

He cannot do this from her lap or in her arms. He must take up a proper position. He stands beside the chair, grasps its back tightly, and sings. He is pleased with his voice which sounds better than when he is speaking.

"If only I could sing all the time," he says, "and if you and Father and all the other people could too, that would be lovely."

She laughs and takes him in her arms: "I would like it if you did, Franzl, but not everyone else—that would be terrible."

Best of all he would like to have Mother entirely to himself, not to share her with anyone. Most certainly not with Father, who, since he has had the new school, has been even more bad-tempered and strict in the evenings, shouting at the slightest disturbance and striking out. He criticizes Mother above all. She is responsible for all this mess, she doesn't help, nor does she understand how to behave like a school-teacher's wife.

In September, shortly before they join Father in the Säulengasse house, Maria is born.

Franz has only ever seen his mother breathing with difficulty, expecting a child, her stomach protruding heavily—a massive, warm body of which he has to be careful when he snuggles up to her. Maria is the last child that Elisabeth Schubert brings into the world. She is forty-two years old.

We must assume that Franz Theodor, somewhat younger than his wife, was irritated by her growing tiredness and exhaustion. It may well be that it was to provide diversion for himself that he filled the little house in the Säulengasse with people. After the death of his brother Karl, he took in his widow, Maria Magdalena. Of their two daughters, one died soon after they moved in. Again they were living in very confined circumstances, they were constantly under each other's eye, and could only behave in a way that the others would tolerate.

Franz made friends with the young Magdalena. For a time Felix, Elisabeth's brother, moved in with his family as well, so that on the

19

first floor of the little house, above the ground-floor schoolrooms, there were a dozen people jostling together, children and grown-ups, the noisy with the quiet, the sick with the healthy. When they slept, their breathing blended and rustled like a breeze through the bedrooms.

He took a few days before approaching Magdalena. To begin with he avoided her. "Are you coming?" she asked.

"No."

"Come," she said.

"No."

Already questions and answers are forming the pattern of a game. He likes to be invited.

Down below in the courtyard they do not always choose the same place, but move with the sun, as if they were sitting together on the hand of a clock. Magdalena teaches him how to plait blades of grass.

"You do it this way."

"No."

"Yes you do. Look."

He does not have much time to play these games. Father wants to take him into his school soon. "You'll be a good pupil, Franzl," he promises him. Mother is convinced of this too.

In the evenings, after school, Father is incensed by a man who is waging war against Austria. He calls him Napoleon, sometimes Bonaparte. Recently he has been called Consul.

"Consul," says Franz to himself.

"What's that?" asks Magdalena.

He begins to sing the word Consul, sometimes stressing the "o" and sometimes the "u." Magdalena likes that. Their games come to an end before he is six.

First they all go together to church, then he remains downstairs with Father in the school. He learns to spell and to write. He learns fast, as his father had predicted.

Now that he is a schoolboy he has to listen to Father and Ignaz when they are playing music. As well as this, he accompanies his older brothers to choir practice in the Lichtental Church.

"You have a clear soprano voice, Franzl," notes Herr Holzer, the choirmaster.

Father teaches him the letters of the alphabet and how to read music. From the very beginning the notes are more important to Franz than the letters.

He is seven.

For the first time he sticks a violin under his chin. It is a smaller one than Ferdinand's, and the bow is not so long or heavy either.

He practices the piano too, but not as much as Ignaz demands. He doesn't need to. While he is sitting quietly in the corner of the court-yard he can see in his mind's eye how his fingers press down on the strings, or run over the keys. He can hear himself playing while the others think he is doing nothing. Sometimes music continues to play in his head, not the music from his practice book, but one that only he recognizes. If he lets this other music take over while he is practicing, then Father scolds him. He should look at the book and not improvise.

It bothers him that Father does not understand how the songs and pieces go on singing by themselves, repeating themselves and creating wonderful variations.

Mother often asks him to play to her. First he sings, then the violin repeats: "A little bird comes flying."

The first time that he was allowed to sing soprano solos in public during Mass he had rehearsed so fiercely beforehand with Herr Holzer, who was drunk and threatened him with the cane, that he was afraid his voice would fail.

He sang the Kyrie and the Agnus Dei. His parents, his brothers and sisters, and all his relatives from the house in the Säulengasse were sitting in the church. Their hugs afterward were greater than any he ever received on later occasions, even when he managed to acquit himself so well on the viola, playing quartets with Father, Ferdinand, and Ignaz that Father could not avoid praising him: "You did that well, Franzl."

On other occasions he deals with him differently. He makes him write properly, read well, both quietly to himself and out loud, calculate quickly in his head, and if he does not get it right, then he slaps his face.

"You can't fool me, Franzl."

He didn't intend to.

From time to time he manages to escape between supper and bedtime and to hide in the shed in the courtyard with Magdalena. He sits close up beside her and whispers in her ear that soon, or at any rate when he is grown up, he will compose a little piece for her, just for her.

"You won't really, will you, Franzl," she says.

He is ten.

Herr Holzer has advised Father to enter him for the chorister examination at the Court Chapel. Both of them prepare him for it.

He only meets Magdalena now at the common mealtimes. He has the impression that the house is constantly being filled with people, and he is being forced out.

Father accompanies him to the examination.

He is washed and scrubbed, and dressed in new clothes. Mother has sewed for him a light gray, almost white suit. It is striking, and people assume he is the son of a wealthy miller.

It is September 30, 1808. Since May he has been put through the mill by Father and Michael Holzer. That was when a notice had appeared in the *Wiener Zeitung*, which Father read out to him, as if it just applied to him. To him alone.

As there are two places newly vacant for choirboys in the Imperial and Royal Court Chapel, those who wish to apply for one of these positions should present themselves on the afternoon of 30th September at 3 o'clock at the Konvikt, to whit the Imperial and Royal Hall of Residence, No. 796 University Square, where they will be examined both in the progress made hitherto in their general studies, and in their attainment in and knowledge of music. They should also bring their school certificates. The applicants must be over the age of ten, and capable of entering the first class. The successful applicants who show themselves to be outstanding both in their behavior and their studies, may, in accordance with the Imperial and Royal regulations, remain at the Konvikt after mutation of the voice. In other cases, they will be required to leave the establishment after mutation.

He was not alone. There was a large group of applicants waiting outside the music auditorium. Suddenly it was immaterial to him whether or not he passed the examination, and he was indifferent when Father whispered into his ear that he had no doubts about his ability. "I believe in you, Franzl."

He lost all feeling in his head and his body. He was careful not to draw attention to himself, especially from the monks whom they had to follow in single file, who divided them into small groups, herded them into schoolrooms, questioning them one after another, sometimes singly, who dictated to them and for whom finally they had to sing.

To his astonishment, the clerical teachers were not nearly so exacting in their questions as Father and Herr Holzer. When he had to sing an Italian aria at sight, he noticed that the feeling was returning to his head and body. He grew hot, his hands were sweating, and he allowed himself another couple of coloraturas.

"That's Schubert," he heard someone say.

He learned that he had passed. From whom? From the Director of the leading center of music education in Vienna—the Konvikt School— from the esteemed Herr Lang, from Father, from Ignaz?

"You will move to the Konvikt School in the Inner City as early as next week."

Ferdinand announced very enviously a situation for which he was entirely unprepared, but which held no terrors for him, rather rekindling the equanimity with which he had faced and passed the examination, and which helped him now to take his leave. To take leave of this house, which had so often tormented him with its crowds of people, and which had never let him be alone.

Mother accompanies him to the Konvikt School. It is a good long way. When she kisses him goodbye at the gateway and gives him his little bag he says: "I would like to stay with you, my beloved Mother." To be more precise, he wishes that she would come with him, away from home.

"Farewell, Mama."

"Be good, behave yourself, Franzl." She waves to him.

He is still aware of her waving hand behind him. He mounts the staircase and pushes the heavy door, but he does not turn back to look at her.

5

Moment musical no. 2
(Fairly fast)

*O*ne day is sufficient for the Piarist Fathers to effect his metamorphosis and to turn him into a Konvikt student. He is to forget the person he was before he entered. He is to become a pupil of God and the Emperor. He is to sing like an angel. In praise and honor. He is to learn and to serve. He is to act in a pleasing manner.

"Can you see yourself, Schubert? Look at yourself!"

Father Pius, who is fitting him with his uniform, skips around him like a magician, twitching the cloth, angling his hat, pulling his coat straight, tightening his waistcoat, stroking his cheeks, patting him.

"Would you recognize yourself, Schubert? Take a look, now you're worth looking at!"

He is worth looking at, he bows low, doffs his tricorn hat, the old-fashioned headgear, as the brother indicates, presses his forehead fleetingly against the mirror:

"It fits," in Father Pius's opinion, "but you must turn around more so that you can see yourself completely."

Now he has been dressed and has moved into the Konvikt, Franz Schubert from the Säulengasse, ten years old, son of the schoolmaster Franz Theodor Schubert, a Konvikt student and choirboy, dressed in "low tricorn hat, white neck-cloth, cutaway coat of a dark brown color with one small golden epaulette on the left shoulder, plain shining buttons, old-fashioned waistcoat beneath it across the stomach, short breeches, and buckled shoes." But no sword. The Konvikt students may not wear a sword.

What would he use it for anyway. He will be singing. He has discovered a piano in the music room. He has passed the examination to become a choirboy, and if the assessments of the authorities had not been kept so secret, he would have known at least two phrases from the report of the great Salieri:

"Fra li soprani li migliori sono: Francesco Schubert, e Francesco Müllner."

"Be off with you, Schubert."

If only he knew where.

"No tears, boy!" orders Father Pius, and wipes Franz's face with a warm and comforting hand. "Thank the Lord God that you may join us."

6

The Prisoner Musician

he Konvikt School has no history behind it when Schubert enters. Emperor Franz I had founded it two years previously with the primary intention of educating the children of commoners for his service. There had been a Konvikt for the nobility for a long time in Josefstadt. The new establishment is situated in the former University next door to the Jesuit Church and opposite the New Auditorium. The Akademisches Gymnasium, in which the Konvikt students receive their instruction, is only a few steps away as well.

The ten choirboys at the Court Chapel all belong to the Konvikt School, but are not supported by scholarships as are the other musicians, being funded directly by the Court. The parents are responsible for small private outlays, such as any supplement to the meager meals. The choirboys are not allowed to appear in public, for they are to serve exclusively for the entertainment of the Court. Their chief supervisor is the Court Composer, Salieri. The Piarist Father Dr. Franz Innozenz Lang officiates as the first director of the Konvikt School. He is fifty years old when Schubert enters. He himself plays no musical instrument, but because of his love of music he has founded an orchestra, provided instruments and scores, and appointed the Court Organist, Wenzel Ruzicka, as conductor. Lang appears open-minded, and insists on proper discipline. His punishments are draconian, and he will not consider making exceptions to his established rules.

The students live together, but are divided into seven groups, or "chambers," each containing approximately twenty pupils. Each group has a study area and a dormitory, and is supervised, particularly at night, by a prefect who has his own room. The pupils are busy all day, learning and practicing. As options they may study Italian and French, drawing and calligraphy. They all receive instruction in religion, Latin, mathematics, natural history, and geography. In addition the choirboys are taught singing, violin, and piano.

He goes to Tranz for religion, to Strauch, whom they nickname Pius when he is not listening, for grammar and Latin, to Walch for mathematics and natural history, and to Rittmannsberger for geography. He studies piano and continuo with Ruzicka (whom he likes), violin with Hoffmann, and singing with Korner (whom he does not like).

Director Lang is everywhere, knows everything, and has a whole host of eavesdroppers and informers. He imposes punishments in a quiet, unctuous voice, usually when the whole group is assembled, so that they all knuckle under at the threat—it might just as easily be one of them as Senn, since the informers are inexact and partisan, and the Director chooses his miscreant as he sees fit: "Senn, you have talked back to Father Pius in the most impertinent manner." He makes the allegation as he enters the dormitory and before he pronounces punishment. Senn knows what is coming as he expatiates on the lack of culture and manners, the prevailing godlessness, and the blessings of music-making. "Senn, you will spend four nights in the detention cell. You will take part in lessons during the day."

Schubert tries to be as unobtrusive and invisible as possible in front of vindictive eyes, and finds that music is a help to him here. In the very first few days he volunteers for Lang's orchestra which is required to play every evening. For instance, at present they are rehearsing the Symphony in G Major by Haydn and Beethoven's Second Symphony.

Josef von Spaun plays the violin next to him. He noticed him because of his friendly strength of character, and his enthusiasm. The orchestra has him to thank for the score of the Beethoven. He bought it and gave it to the orchestra although, as he admits, he will now have to make do this month with the food and drink that the Konvikt provides.

"Hello, Schubert."

"Hello, Spaun."

Spaun has been studying for a long time, and is nine years older than Schubert. He makes friends with him, and with Kenner and Stadler and Randhartinger.

When they are discussing music, perhaps Mozart or Beethoven, then Schubert is inclined to get excited, showing transports of delight as he plays themes and motifs at high speed on the piano in the music room, where it is always cavernous and cold, and he is capable of infecting them all with his enthusiasm, so that the joy of being with them warms him.

As a matter of principle he passes no judgment on the teachers. He keeps silent.

Randhartinger, who quite possibly is one of those Konvikt students who act as Lang's informers, sometimes goads him to vent his anger at the Fathers and the court officials, and to take part in the political debates. But he prefers to voice no opinion, to be called "Cowardly Chocolate Curls."

"Leave him be."

"He's going to practice."

After lunch, which often enough causes his stomach to rebel, Lang permits him to go back to the music room to play the piano and to improvise, and he has no objection if Spaun and other Konvikt students go with him.

It is not only with his skill at playing the piano and his always faultless singing that he attracts them, but also with his jokes and his ability to mimic the teachers, and particularly by his enthusiasm. It sometimes happens that his veneration for Gluck and Mozart actually makes him stand up and harangue his friends like a preacher: "What do any of you know about Gluck's genius?"

Having given himself this cue, he pulls the chair up under his backside, and plays for them what he hears, what is going round in his head, both playing it on the piano and singing.

One evening before the daily symphony concert he asks Spaun to go with him to the music room for a moment. With short, swift movements he drags a chair to the appropriate distance from the piano. He ushers Spaun to this, while he himself, before taking his seat at the instrument, first bows to a large and imaginary audience on the other side, then turns to his friend too with a sketchy bow. He sits down and immediately begins to play from memory.

After Schubert has finished, Spaun jumps up: "Tell me who wrote that. I know it, and yet I don't know it."

He sings, tentatively. Schubert nods in agreement and joins in Spaun's singing. "That's it."

"Gluck?"

He beams and rubs his hands: "Yes. And then again, no."

Then he repeats on the piano what they had both been humming, continues it, finally breaking off and looking at Spaun with his head on one side:

"That's by me. That's my arrangement."

"Did you compose that?"

"No, only arranged it. Don't tell anyone. I want to work on it a bit more."

The next day the game is repeated. Again Spaun has to come with him to the music room before the orchestral rehearsal. Again Schubert places the chairs, but this time side by side at the piano, puts the music on the stand, and looks sideways at Spaun, testing him:

"D'you think you can?"

Spaun reads the title: "Overture to *Iphigenia in Aulis,* Arranged for Piano Duet by Franz Schubert."

Spaun starts playing, Schubert joins in, they play together, their hands touch, and their arms.

"It's a joy," says Schubert quietly. And Spaun repeats: "Yes, it is a joy."

Shortly after this, Spaun leaves the Konvikt. "I shall be back in Vienna soon," he assures him. "Don't forget me, Schubert."

Does it begin after this leave-taking?

It is a story of secret goings-on, of a week full of work in secret, hints to his friends, announcements: "Wait a while!"

He is thirteen.

It is April 8, 1810. He has been at the Konvikt for a year and a half.

Recently he has led the violins in the orchestra, sung first soprano in the choir, and occasionally, when the authorities are in a good mood, he has been allowed to conduct. He knows nothing of the complimentary but confidential report of his prefect, Mosel, to the Imperial Court Chamberlain of Music, Count Kuefstein: "Franz Schubert [is] to be praised for his exceptional application in the art of music."

"What do you actually do after lunch in the music room?"

"Why won't you play cards with us any more?"

"Are you writing poetry?"

Holzapfel asks questions. Kleindl looks worried.

He cheerfully leaves them in the dark.

He has invited his friends to a surprise in the music hall on May 7. Also the teachers, and Lang.

He had finished his work the previous day. At the end of the manuscript of the third movement, the finale, he wrote so heavily that the quill made a scratching sound: "Fantasia for Forte . . ." He could not continue immediately because the quill misbehaved. It left several heavy ink splashes before he could write "piano." "By Franz Schubert. Commenced on April 8. Completed on May 1."

He develops spots on his forehead just from stage fright. At first he had considered asking Ignaz to come to the Konvikt as his partner at the performance. Then he rejected that idea, because his father, who was absolutely insistent that he must prepare himself for a career as a teacher, and not be continually making music, might have become suspicious.

He takes Ruzicka into his confidence. During the composition of the first movement he shows him the manuscript and asks for advice. Ruzicka is not surprised. "I thought you were interested in how it was done, Schubert." He is prepared to play with him. He considers that it is a successful little piece, this fantasia, and there is no harm in its owing much to the spirit of Haydn.

There is a larger audience than he had expected. Ferdinand and Ignaz have come too. When he sees them his face flushes, and he suddenly feels secure.

Ruzicka gives him a little push. "You must bow, Schubert."

He sees Lang.

He begins to play, and so does Ruzicka. The introductory adagio came to him when he was arguing with Holzapfel over whether Klopstock had conceived his "Messiah" by the rules of poetry alone, or by those of a higher religion as well, at which point Holzapfel, somewhat taken aback, asserted his seniority, and told him that he should hold to the truths as given to him by Tranz in the religion lessons.

"How can you mention Klopstock and Tranz in the same breath, Holzapfel."

The first bars came to him while he was laughing. He could not write them down until the evening before he went to bed.

"Schubert, please!" Ruzicka taps the beat gently with his heel. "A bit faster," he whispers. "You should know."

The presto in the second movement is a splendid success. And in the allegro maestoso he forgets that he himself wrote what he is playing. The applause brings him to his feet. He bows. Ruzicka does likewise, but he has now moved several steps away and is applauding him.

Lang comes gravely up to him. As he is about to speak the applause suddenly ceases.

"I must commend you, Schubert," he says. "That is an excellent demonstration of your talent."

Schubert bows. Powerful laughter wells up inside him.

"That was a triumph, Franzl." His brothers shake his hand, and his joy overflows.

"If I can only show them," says Schubert, and after a pause, adds: "then I feel better."

"Show them what?" asks Ferdinand.

Schubert answers with a wild shriek of laughter.

"Now I can finally let it out," he sighs breathlessly, "what I couldn't say in front of Lang."

Ferdinand looks at him suspiciously from one side: "Whenever you should be serious, Franz, you play the fool."

"Goodbye!" Schubert hunches his shoulders, and runs along the corridor.

7

For Piano Duet

"For Piano Duet." He does not begin on his own, he neither can nor wants to. Music-making does not exclude, it unites. He had now released from their independent existence those voices which as a child he heard in his head, which he collected and grew accustomed to, and so he did not find it difficult to handle them.

He realizes that he can only free himself from his solitary state through music. He is alone when listening and composing. As soon as he makes music he leaves this solitary state behind him. He makes music both with and for others. Conversation, which frequently intimidates him because it forces him to speak of himself, to evaluate and pass judgment, loses its dull factualness in music-making.

"For Piano Duet," that is his program.

All that he is unable to experience in life, his innermost longings, he translates into music. This is his language and it absorbs the language of others, however paltry and banal may be the lines and verses to which it reacts.

"Go on, Schubert!" He begins with Ruzicka, with Ruzicka, praised by Lang in these words, "who has continued during this troubled half year, with his frequently commended zeal, to instruct the boys in the various branches of music during extra lessons, and to perfect their skills."

He can feel Ruzicka's left arm.

This "troubled half year."

This calm, gently uplifting response in G major.

Yes, he was afraid. More than the other pupils and teachers. Yet once again, as at Himmelpfortgrund and in the Säulengasse, he managed to disappear into the crowd, and while remaining with the others, to make himself invisible.

He remembers when Father first spoke the name Napoleon. When the General, who was also called Bonaparte, became Consul, transforming himself into a word which made him appear formless and menacing. Since then he had heard the name of the conqueror pronounced in many tones. Admiringly, contemptuously, with utter revulsion, with unmitigated fury, quietly or at full volume. "Bonaparte. Napoleon. The Consul. The Emperor. L'empereur. The Frenchman."

It did not start like that. Or did it? Was the name Napoleon not coupled with the word Peace? With the word Lunéville, which he had repeated because it sounded so beautiful and so strange: "Lunéville." Father had left the school and come home with the news: "Peace has been declared between our emperor and the French. At Lunéville."

He was three years old then.

He was four when Napoleon transformed himself into the Consul.

He was seven when he learned that Napoleon, not only sworn at by the grown-ups, but whom they also damned and feared like the devil, had become emperor, an emperor side by side with Emperor Franz.

He was eight when Father shed tears because the French had defeated the Austrian army at Austerlitz, and because Emperor Franz was emperor no longer.

The name came steadily closer. And now he, Napoleon, the long-expected, imagined, talked-of, feared, is standing with his army outside Vienna and finally wants to enter—Bonaparte, the conqueror.

He listens, he sees, and he astonishes his friends and teachers with his apparent equanimity. "Perhaps Schubert is daft" is the opinion of Holzapfel, who cannot understand how in moments of greatest danger, when the bombardment is coming close, Schubert still has a grin on his face, or even dares to continue practicing in the music room.

They are deceived. He deceives them unintentionally. He is afraid, terribly afraid. But it affects him differently, he reacts differently to it. Fear clears both his vision and his hearing. All the distortions in behavior that it causes amuse him. He cannot help smiling when he sees Lang turning pirouettes in his panic, or hears Stadler spluttering with fear.

"Lord God, what will happen to us, what will be done to us?" ask the Fathers at Vespers.

Just what none of them had thought possible now actually happens, something that really strikes at and touches the lives of both teachers and pupils: a cannonball hits the Konvikt, shattering a wall and causing enormous uproar—and nobody is in the slightest bit hurt.

"Now even Schubert finds this no laughing matter," states Holzapfel with relief.

They escaped unscathed.

Emperor Franz has ordered the choirboys to cancel all performances, and Lang expands the directive by canceling orchestral rehearsals as well.

The city recovers slowly from the terror. People have been killed. Rubble has to be cleared away. The conqueror can march in with his troops and occupy the Palace of Schönbrunn, where he takes up residence.

That was exactly a year ago.

"Go on, Schubert."

They have reached the allegretto in the second movement.

From now on Napoleon was the subject of their daily conversation. They argued and fought with each other, some cursing the Empereur, others daring to admire him for his power and his vision.

"And you, Schubert?" they asked him, closing in on him, wanting to know his opinion.

"Are you deaf? Does nothing excite you? Doesn't Napoleon deprive you of peace and quiet?"

Napoleon has for him a background significance that he just cannot communicate to the others. This is a sequence of words with varying meanings, a series of images in his memory, a chain of feelings in which not only fear and terror have a role to play, but also absurdity and incomprehension. And a magic that he would be incapable of explaining.

"He mesmerized me as the snake does the bird," is how Grillparzer described it, and it may have been that several Konvikt students took part with Lang or one of the Fathers in one of the magnificent displays put on for the Emperor, and Schubert would have had a memory of it similar to that of his subsequent friend: "With hatred in my heart and at no time a lover of military spectacle . . . I watch him run down the open staircase at Schönbrunn Palace rather than descend it, the two crown princes of Bavaria and Württemberg behind him as his adjutants, and now stand, stern as iron, with his hands clasped behind his back, to review his parading military forces with the dispassionate eye of the master. . . ."

Napoleon. Bonaparte. The Consul. The Emperor. L'empereur. The Frenchman.

He not only reviews parades and issues decrees, he also requisitions and billets soldiers, who pester the women and mock the men, who destroy and plunder.

Schubert learns from Ignaz that nothing has happened to his parents and family.

They have less to eat. All the more frequently Lang invokes the wisdom and sagacity of the Austrian Monarch and he turns out to be right. In October the Treaty of Vienna is concluded.

The Emperor Franz gives up Galicia, Fiume, Carniola, and Trieste, and in April Bonaparte marries into the Imperial family and takes the Archduchess Marie-Louise back with him to Paris.

Vienna is free. Hunger grows. Money has absolutely no value any more.

"That Schubert is daft. He laughs when we are worried."

In May, a year after Napoleon's entry into Vienna, he invites his teachers, fellow pupils, and friends to a concert.

Together with Ruzicka he plays his Fantasia in G Major.

They all had a collective memory of what had been going through his head while he was composing:

The departure of the Napoleonic troops;

the relief, the muted rejoicing;

the news of the death of Haydn—how the orchestra met afterward and played the Symphony in G Major, with its beating timpani, and how he could not stop crying the whole night through;

how they were told by Rittmannsberger in the history lesson that Andreas Hofer had been shot in Mantua.

"Go on, Schubert!"

He had waited for the allegro maestoso. It is some time now since he wrote it. He looks at Ruzicka's hands beside his own. They play what he heard. He is not alone.

Ruzicka taps the beat with his heel.

Yes, yes. He knows.

"For Piano Duet," that is his program. He cannot escape from himself, and yet when he makes music he is outside his normal self. In this way, he is divided, and yet remains within himself.

"Go on, Schubert!"

Ruzicka gets ahead of him by a tiny margin in the finale. Now he wants to call a halt.

"For Piano Duet": Much later, in April 1828,

> The ever turning years roll onward,
> on and on, you cannot check them.
>
> *Es rollen die immer kreisenden Jahre*
> *Hinunter, hinunter, du hältst sie nicht.*

he will compose a Fantasia for Piano Duet in F Minor and dedicate it to Mademoiselle la Comtesse Caroline Esterházy de Galantha. This is a recollection that he does not yet have, this boy, sitting beside his teacher at the piano.

"Bravo, Schubert."

The first piece. At some point somebody, for a reason best known only to himself, maybe it was Ferdinand or maybe his half-brother Andreas, gave this piece the title "Funereal Fantasy (*Leichenphantasie*) for Piano Duet."

8

The Voice

*N*ot everyone who knew him told their tale for posterity. Some kept to themselves what they knew of him, others were only asked when their memory had become unclear. Without doubt the story became changed in the telling, was put in the best light, or was flagrantly invented.

I am making a picture for myself from the pictures.

The total number of his letters is not great. Many exist only in fragments.

But I can hear him.

As soon as I hear him, I see him too. Not as a clearly outlined form, but in his essence, in his movements, I feel how he makes himself small or tall, how he grows heated with concentration, and loses himself in his work.

These are movements that become clear in music, in rhythms, motifs and themes, often in tiny variations. The longer I listen to his music, the more corporeal it becomes for me.

Whenever I hear him, I can see him, just as if I had known him in my childhood. He is one of those very small people, but not yet conspicuous. Strangely enough, one soon grows accustomed to his tiny stature. I know that he will not grow much taller, and in the end will scarcely top five feet.

The voice I can hear, his child's voice, is constantly singing, even in speech. In my memory this voice links sentences with melodies.

I am constantly overcome with the desire to take the child by the hand and to drag him down through the years to the place where I know the thirty-year-old to be with his music.

In the late afternoon they were rehearsing *a capella* to the shouting and bullying of Philipp Korner, while Schubert was annoyed at being spared by Korner and praised for his singing. In his head he had music of a different kind. Suddenly, as if summoned from the wings, there was Spaun standing in the doorway of the hall. Much older than he remembered him, much more sedate. That gave him a shock, but his joy bridged the unexpected distance.

Should he jump out of line, drawing Korner's anger down on himself, and run across the hall to greet Spaun? Should he wait until Spaun makes his presence known? They both wait. Spaun listens to them. Korner has scarcely dismissed them than he is at his old friend's side.

He would keep this evening free. Spaun begs off with a smile. He has already taken care of that. Of course Lang had given his permission. He plays the gentleman, leaning his chin on his high collar.

"Let's walk a bit first," begs Schubert. "I really can't tell you how troubled I am, Spaun."

He could not explain this disquiet, but he could play it on the piano, and then it would become clear that it was no disquiet at all, but a yearning, wandering melancholy. Something that is continually welling up inside him and does not know which way to turn. Like a thought without words.

"Have you exchanged your old money yet?"

They skip down both the staircases of the front schoolhouse, in step with each other.

"What makes you think of that, Schubert?"

Everyone is talking about money, about the new currency. The teachers, the Fathers. Yesterday Ferdinand came breezing in and told how with the currency changes, their father now had a new reason to be angry and torment Mother.

"Come on, Schubert."

When he had visited his family just a few weekends ago at the house in the Säulengasse and wanted to feel a warm glow, and to tell of his success in the orchestra and the choir, his father had bombarded him with reproaches. He knew that he was wasting his time with unnecessary musical fantasizing, and given half a chance would take up composing, instead of studying seriously to be a teacher.

He had not even tried to mollify him, but left it to Ferdinand to get the old quartet together, at which point Father gave in, but played the cello dreadfully badly.

Spaun tries another topical word: "Bonaparte."

Schubert does not pick it up. He is gone, his story belongs elsewhere. "Do you know, Spaun, sometimes I shiver for no reason. Although there is warmth around me, I feel cold."

"And at this moment, Schubert?"

He looks up at Spaun: "At the moment it is dreadfully cold around me. And I am growing warmer all the time." As if wanting to verify this, Spaun lays his hand against Schubert's cheek.

"If I could choose, we'd stop for a drink, just for half an hour."

Schubert cannot be persuaded. "You know that is forbidden for us choirboys."

Even in the little streets round the cathedral, they are saving on lighting. The March night lies heavy and black between the houses. As Spaun can obviously see well enough and is certain in his step, Schubert takes his arm. "I'd be no use as a night owl."

"I'm not so sure," counters Spaun.

At which point Schubert hunches himself up like a dwarf and begins to hop along on his friend's arm in order to keep up. "Would you like to see me as you have never seen me before, Spaun?"

"How?"

"Turn your back, if you please."

Here, in this place to which I have sent the two of them, perhaps in the Dorotheergasse, or on the Graben or the Wollzeile, anyway on some corner where a street lamp sheds a pool of light in the darkness,

I can tell the answer to my question of when the boy first wore glasses, just by the by, but in sufficiently pointed fashion.

The boy rummages in his jacket, pulls out a case, opens it carefully, takes out a pair of glasses, and puts them on. It is the glasses that we know, these exact glasses, just a bit too small, with oval lenses and with side-pieces sticking out from a hinged extension. Here I can put his glasses on him and let Spaun be the first person to see him wearing them.

"Please turn around!" Spaun hesitates, playing with the anticipation of the youngster who is holding his face to the light.

"Don't be difficult. I'm more excited than you."

Spaun turns on his heel and looks at the round childish face before him, as in a picture. It is that picture which may change over the years, but still has at its core this expectant, vulnerable childish face, peering into the light with twinkling eyes behind the thick lenses.

Schubert pulls a face. The glasses slip a little. With a touch of embarrassment and love, Spaun takes Schubert's head between his hands, holds him fast, and says gently: "There was always something missing in you. There was. Now I can see it. Now you're my Schubert."

"Are you lying so as not to shame me?"

"No, believe me, really I'm not."

Schubert pulls his face from between Spaun's hands and runs away.

"Time for me to get back to the Konvikt. If you like, do come tomorrow evening. I have a surprise for you."

Spaun's laughter echoes from the walls of the houses, and bounces after the boy.

"That's enough surprises for now, Schubert!"

Spaun does not come the very next day. He has to report to the Treasury to announce his return and his availability for future service, and he has to set up his apartment.

It suits Schubert that he is slow in coming. He needs more time than he had originally planned for his composition.

He is shuffling sheets full of notes that were written by somebody else, testing their idiosyncratic key structures, changing them, resetting them. For a long time now he has been occupying himself with Zumsteeg's "Hagar's Lament in the Desert of Beersheba," one of those sad songs that will not leave him alone, which he knows he could develop further.

He must begin in C minor.

Here on a hill of burning sand,
In the desert, devoid of humankind,
I sit.

Hier am Hügel heißen Sandes
In der menschenleeren Wüste
Sitze ich.

Everything must be made clearer than in Zumsteeg's version. It must be sung more. How God opened Hagar's eyes and she saw a spring of water in the wilderness, water for the small son who is in danger of dying of thirst.

But the poem does not get that far. It ends with Hagar's plea:

God, his Lord, do not scorn
The beseeching of this innocent boy!

Gott, sein Herr, verschmäh' das Flehen
Des unschuldgen Knaben nicht!

He only succeeds at the third attempt. His model is still evident here and there, and he perceives it like a faint echo in the distance.

Schubert, as Spaun recalls much later, had already composed quite a number of pieces, a sonata, a fantasia, a short opera. It may be that Schubert only talked about them, but that he had not written them down.

In any case, he invited Spaun, and only him, to an evening concert.

"His voice is not breaking yet," thinks Spaun, as the boy begins to sing with his clear soprano voice, and Schubert had never seemed so childlike to him. Even after his voice breaks, he will always have a high voice. All the songs that he writes, he hears first in his own voice. High and clear, almost without vibrato.

He jumps, singing "Hagar's Lament," from one key to another, and only at the close does he find his way back to C minor.

"Do you remember Zumsteeg's composition?" he asks. Without waiting for Spaun's answer he begins to play snatches of it, all bouncing echoes, and Spaun realizes how far Schubert has moved away from his model. It is no longer the choirboy whom Spaun sees sitting before him on the piano stool, but a messenger from Prospero.

Schubert jumps up, waving the manuscript sheets in the air: "I present them to you, Herr von Spaun. Do you remember how a long time ago I asked you who could have composed that piece? I've come a long way since then. Tomorrow I'll be even better."

He put his hand across his eyes in a gesture that touched Spaun with its helplessness and its fatigue.

"Is something wrong, Schubert?"

Schubert spreads his fingers and peeps through. "No. Yes, there is. Can you get me any manuscript paper? I badly need some. I would be so grateful."

"I then supplied him with enormous quantities of manuscript paper," remembered Spaun, "which he used at an unbelievable rate. He composed extraordinarily fast, and he continually made use of his study time for composition, so that his schoolwork suffered."

Lang had urged Spaun to impress on his young friend that he should pay more attention to his schooling. Spaun doubted that he would manage to do so, considering that Franz was so obsessed. He had also drawn his father's attention to this negligent attitude, said Lang. As far as he knew, his father had really hauled him over the coals, and even forbidden him to compose.

Spaun addresses Schubert on the subject. He in return angrily mimics his father: "Yes, Herr Father, the violinist who doesn't give a darn about music, dear Father, who'd beat the music out of my head. Well, I've set a few minuets already, so there!" He pushes the bridge of his glasses up against his nose with his index finger and walks on with his short steps beside Spaun: "My dear Father, dear Father!"

Since then he has not been back to the house in the Säulengasse. Ignaz and Ferdinand look in at the Konvikt occasionally, but very seldom. He begs them to give his love to his mother. He loves her very much, and she would not hold his music against him. He gives his minuets, universally admired both by Ruzicka and by Dr. Anton Schmidt, who used to play quartets with Mozart, to anyone who shows an interest in them, and the manuscripts disappear from sight and are lost.

"Do not permit yourself to be troubled about these bagatelles, Spaun. I shall think up many more."

Sometimes he speaks in a ridiculously precocious manner. From home he only receives a tiny allowance that is more a humiliation than a help. His father gives him to understand that since the new currency has come into circulation, he must be even more thrifty than before. At first he makes a joke of it: "I can manage on nothing," he boasts to his friends. And he is not bragging. He survives, although many a time he is gripped at night by a bad mixture of hunger and homesickness.

It is only in November 1812 that he finally decides to write to Ferdinand and not to beg, but to ask him for a small measure of brotherly help. It is the first of his letters that has survived, and straightaway we have one dictated by necessity. Yet he still writes with a light touch:

> Straight out with what is on my mind; this way I come to the point sooner and you are not detained further with pleasant circumlocutions. I have thought long and hard about my situation, and find that while in general it may be good, certain improvements could be made here and there. You know from experience that one is sometimes glad to have a roll or a couple of apples to eat, especially when, after a mediocre midday meal, one only has the prospect of a pitiful evening meal eight and a half hours later. This desire has often been manifest, but is now becoming more pressing, and *nolens volens* I finally had to find some solution to it. The few pennies that I receive from Father are gone to the devil in the first few days, and what am I to do for the rest of the time? "Those who put their trust in thee shall not suffer shame." Matt. 3:4.
>
> My thoughts entirely.—How would it be if you were to let me

have a few crowns a month. You would hardly notice the loss, and I in my cell would be happy and content. As I said, I rely on the words of the Apostle Matthew, who said: "He who has two coats, let him give one to the poor, etc." Meanwhile I wish that you would give ear to the voice which is constantly calling upon you to remember

Your poor loving, hopeful,

and doubly poor brother Franz.

He plays, plays with his own self, with his brother, with his poverty, with his anger, with his fear. Also with the biblical quotations, for it was not Matthew who taught that of the two coats one should be given away, but Luke. And he is recognized in his playing in a quite remarkable way. Salieri, the composer to the Emperor, asks him to come and see him.

Perhaps he had been expecting it. Ruzicka had prepared him: "His Excellency has great expectations of your talent."

There he is, standing before him, beside him, bowing, hearing the maestro speak, understanding nothing of what he says. He is required to go to the piano, to play and to sing. "Schubert, your voice is about to break. Do you realize this?"

He often reflects on that fact, not without some anxiety, for although he knows what is happening, he can conjure out of the phrase a transformation in which he loses his voice entirely, or one morning wakes up with a horrible bass.

In fact, his singing voice is still very expressive.

"Expressive" is the maestro's opinion.

"I have"—and while Salieri is speaking he is walking vigorously in circles around Schubert and the piano—"I have by chance been made aware of your exercises in composition. It is correct that you enjoy writing music?"

"Yes, Your Excellency." He is amazed how easily he can speak with the great Salieri. "Yes, Your Excellency."

"Would you like to study counterpoint with me?"

The boy jumps up, sits down, jumps up again. Salieri laughs, claps his hands, calls a servant. "The child is pleased," says the maestro to himself. The boy is delighted.

Schubert kisses Salieri's hand, bows several times, and withdraws. He can scarcely contain himself, and as soon as the door is closed behind him he skips along the length of the corridor like a billy goat, a Konvikt student released.

If only Father knew, runs through his head. The dear Father.

9

Moment musical no. 3
(Fast)

*H*e had wished neither to see nor to visit dear Father for many weeks now, yet he had met him, at his request, one Sunday after Mass in the Lichtental Church, after greeting Holzer, who was so pleased to see him, and who had enraged dear Father again, as Holzer had inquired about his progress in composition and whether Salieri had really taken him as a pupil and he in his pride had not held back modestly, whereupon dear Father had pushed him out of the church, where not so long ago he had sung and played the viola to Father's great joy, but now that lay long in the past, for dear Father was concerned with the near future, on which he, his son, should not cease to reflect, when he should be following in his footsteps: "Franzl, I mean it seriously, you can't do this to me, leaving me in the lurch, not coming to my school as an assistant, at least to begin with, you absolutely must study to that end, you must make an effort to earn a scholarship at the Konvikt, for you will not always be able to shine as a choirboy with your soprano voice, you must expect that your voice will break soon," whereby Father is horribly transforming him into a screeching larva, a roaring teacher-animal, who at the very most lets the children sing and hammers with disgust on the piano; "No, Father *sir*, not that," he wants to reply, but leaves it for the time being, as he accompanies dear Father home so that he can see Mother and his brothers, especially the youngest, who never visits him in the Konvikt School, only his dear Father has incapacitated the whole family so splendidly that they cannot move, cannot appear, not one of them, not even his aunt, and dear Father, in order to lend authority to his speech, even takes him into the schoolroom— "Hurry up, Franzl!"—he has to sit in the bench at the front, dear Father standing before him, his ringmaster, his schoolmaster, and to listen to him tell "you know, you know," how half a lifetime ago he followed his brother Karl, God bless him, to Vienna, after he had earned his credentials as an assistant in Brünn, how he had had to make his own way in the face of all kinds of opposition, in the face of incomprehension and brutality, official pressure and poverty, how the family had grown and his dear wife, "your mother, Franzl," had begun to suffer more and more, how he had eventually managed to buy his own house, but had to incur debts, how he was now relying on him, Franz, on his hard work that could benefit the family if only he were not such a scamp, dedicating his time to a penurious art; "But His Excellency, the court composer Salieri," he finally manages to interrupt dear Father, and slides backward and forward on the bench, "but Maestro Salieri expressly wants to further my career, dear Father, he is teaching me counterpoint and introducing me to composition, and he is a famous teacher, famous all over the world." "A damned Italian," his dear Father corrects him, and perhaps he is factually correct, if he is thinking of Mozart, Haydn, even more of Beethoven, who had his libretto for *Fidelio* written in German. None of this makes dear Father more favorably disposed toward his son, on the contrary, he demands that he stand up, beside the bench. "I ask you one last time," he says emphatically, "if you are going to persist in this obstinate behavior." He cannot do otherwise than to assure him: "Certainly, dear Father, I must compose, I want to, it is true, and Herr Ruzicka helps me with it." "That is of no interest to me," screams dear Father, "you are forgetting us, forgetting our concern, our love, our kindness to you, you will have to forget us completely, Franzl, I am telling you," and with his left hand he snatches the glasses from his nose while with his right he reaches out and strikes him on the cheek and forehead with a flat, hard and practiced hand, "I will teach you to obey your father," whereupon Franz ducks down, makes himself small and round, feels his sorrows like fetters on his body, "I don't want to upset you, dear Father, most certainly not, but just let me compose and I will try hard in school, I'll be diligent, dear Father," but he pushes him away and Franz smells, in a sudden last farewell breath, the atmosphere of the whole house, the smell left by the children's clothes, the steam from the kitchen on the first floor, the stink of the drain in the small courtyard, the laundry soap, he breathes in deeply and smells what he was, that from which his dear father is expelling him, from his childhood, his home, as dear Father likes to call it, or what constituted his childhood, his shelter beside Mother, nestling in her skirts, her hands on his head, "Sing for me, Franzl, you sing so beautifully," but dear Father does not allow another breath, he tells him "I will take care of the absolute necessities, so that no one may speak evil of me, but I will have no thought of giving you any further attention or fatherly love," a quality with which dear Father had been sparing enough in the past, thinks the boy, even when he was not composing, "Farewell, Father dear, and remember me to my beloved Mother," he says this by the door, which he opens without turning back, he jumps into the street with its dirty snow, and thinks he can hear Father dear speaking behind him, full of rage at his fleeing ill-bred son, Franzl . . .

10

Salieri's Pupil

*S*chubert was fifteen years old, and had already composed many pieces, but he had never heard an opera,"
Spaun remembered, and he makes Schubert older
than in fact he was on his first visit to the opera. I am no longer surprised at these inaccuracies. In Spaun's memory he has already assumed
that ageless quality which is his characteristic. The old child. It is open
to question whether or not he had already composed so much, even if
Spaun is counting in the lost minuets.

When did Spaun invite him to the Kärntnertor Theater, to the
Court Opera? They sat in the fifth gallery to hear an opera by Josef
Weigl, either *The Swiss Family* in July 1811, or *The Orphanage* in
December 1810. It was probably in the summer of 1811, since Spaun
only returned to Vienna in March 1811.

He did not have to explain to Schubert the importance of Weigl.
For many years Weigl had been the conductor at the Court Opera and
each of his works had also had its premiere there. Schubert had even
been permitted, accompanied by Ruzicka, to look around the opera
house beforehand, on an afternoon when there was no rehearsal and no
preparations were being made for the evening performance. They
stepped into a brilliant, sparkling world that was waiting to be animated by people, to ring with voices.

"For an opera by me," he whispered. And old Ruzicka had run his
hand quite roughly through his hair. "Why not, Schubert, you can do

it, you will be able to." In his use of the future tense, his comment assumed the power of a prophecy.

Now the white and golden horseshoe is humming with people's voices. The lights dance. He and Spaun, with the entire fifth gallery, are all ready to be spirited aloft, enticed by events which are waiting behind the curtain, waiting to be set in motion by the conductor and his orchestra.

He sees Weigl as an old man. He is not that. He is just forty-four and is at the pinnacle of his fame as the protégé of the Emperor and Salieri.

They have found seats right by the balustrade. Schubert presses against it as if he could release it from its anchorage and set the balcony flying.

Spaun watches him from the side, just as I would like to observe the boy at this moment in his anticipation and eagerness, and with the tiniest hint of superiority, or premonition: "I know a couple of Weigl's overtures. I've written one myself." Secretly he even allows himself the thought: "It's just as good as his." And out loud he tells Spaun, like a young scamp laughing at family connections: "I'm one of Maestro Salieri's pupils too, just like Weigl."

The title page of his magical opera *The Devil's Castle in the Air*, composed a year after his first visit to the Kärntnertor Theater, was not the only place that he wrote "By Franz Schubert, Pupil of Salieri, First Imperial and Royal Court Conductor"—he will repeat it several times.

I see him as Spaun saw him, excited, impatient and yet tiny in his Konvikt uniform, his tricorn hat on the balustrade in front of him, absorbing everything both on and off the stage as in a trance.

"How can I thank you for taking me, Spaun," he says.

When Spaun asks him during the interval for his opinion of Weigl's opera, he answers as if he is quite accustomed to strolling in foyers and passing comment on what he has just heard: "I like Weigl's music. It is popular and elevated at the same time. It must be wonderful to bring a stage to life with music, to transform people through singing."

(*Ritardando*. I accompany him, but I cannot hear with him the first opera he heard. It is no longer performed anywhere. He hears in a different way from me, already knowledgeable but learning. He considers, and I would probably not share his opinion, that Weigl's music is stimulating and successful, and proves thereby that even he, with his own individual values, is in bondage to his time, and is enmeshed in aesthetic conventions. But he counts himself with Weigl as one of the elect, "a pupil of Salieri." He will make his acquaintance when the maestro celebrates the fiftieth anniversary of his arrival in Vienna. Salieri still only speaks broken German. He still insists on "Italian" music, and still considers the songs of Zumsteeg and others to be crude. Schubert will honor him, alongside disciples of varying ages such as Beethoven, Weigl, Moscheles, or Hüttenbrenner, and he will compose a trio for male voices with piano accompaniment and write a text for it that is a word-by-word genuflection expressing his devotion in childlike form. I realize that the nineteen-year-old cannot do otherwise, being shaped and bent by the spirit of his age and his unfavorable situation.

He is already sitting at the piano. Three singers have grouped themselves. They are performing to the best of their ability Franz Schubert's "Offering for the Fiftieth Anniversary Celebrations of Herr von Salieri, the First Imperial and Royal Court Conductor in Vienna":

> Most Kind and Best One,
> The Wisest and Greatest,
> As long as there are tears in my eyes,
> And I refresh myself at the fount of art
> May both be dedicated to you
> Who have endowed me with both.
>
> Both Kindness and Wisdom flow gently
> From you, O likeness of God,
> You are an angel for me on earth,
> I wish to express my gratitude to you.
>
> The Granddaddy of us all,
> May you remain long with us.

Gütigster, Bester,
Weisester, Größter!
So lang ich Thränen habe
Und an der Kunst mich labe,
Sei beides Dir geweiht,
Der beides mir verleiht.

So Güt' als Weisheit strömen mild
Von Dir, o Gottes Ebenbild,
Engel bist Du mir auf Erden,
Gern möcht ich Dir dankbar werden.

Unser aller Großpapa
Bleibe noch recht lange da.

For the last two lines, with their ridiculously gushing child's wish, he had devised a Canon with Coda that makes one oblivious to the words, and I know that no one in the knowledgeable audience laughed, that they all listened reverently and were moved to tears, and Schubert had demonstrated with his own text that even the fatuous was able to kindle his musical imagination. But at present he is still listening to Weigl's music in the opera house, and another five years must pass before Salieri's pompously choreographed celebration. It may be that he determined during the performance to conquer this resonant house with his own opera, but he still has first to make the acquaintance of Mozart, with either *Figaro* or *Don Giovanni*.)

On the way home he hums and talks, both together. Spaun reminds him in no uncertain terms that he must make great efforts with his schoolwork, particularly in mathematics.

"I will try, I will."

"Don't be angry with me for insisting so much on it. I would just like to see peace between you and your father."

"Yes, yes."

He nods, pushes his glasses up on his nose, pulls his hat over his forehead. He skips. He giggles.

"You are not taking my warning seriously."

"Oh yes I am."

Spaun is deceived. Schubert is utterly serious about it, but he just does not see how he can resolve the conflict with his father without giving in. This he cannot do. Whenever he can see no solution, when he is caught in the vise, as now, his reaction to his dilemma is to play the fool.

"You know that Lang has asked me to speak to you."

"Yes, yes."

Neither of them has any idea that Lang is only giving a warning as director of the Konvikt School. For he maintains absolute silence on what Count Kuefstein, the man responsible for the choirboys, has written to him, to the "Most Excellent, Reverend Government Counselor," on the subject of the singers, musicians, and pupils of Ruzicka and Salieri: "Concerning Franz Schubert . . . to express especial satisfaction with his excellent progress in all subjects. . . ."

"You can't help me, Spaun. I have to grieve you."

"It is not me whom you grieve, dearest Schubert, but your father."

"Might that not be the other way around?" asks Schubert, his voice rising to a falsetto pitch.

They walk on silently side by side until they take leave of each other at the Konvikt gate.

"You will usually find me in the music room during the late afternoon, Spaun. Come if you have time. I beg of you."

Spaun assures the boy that he will, and Schubert turns abruptly away, and stumps step by step up the staircase like a muffled-up old man.

"Farewell, dear friend," Spaun calls after him. Schubert does not reply.

He is hearing in his head what he heard just now in the Kärntnertor Theater, is already trying to respond to it, and at the same time the anxiety over the quarrel with his father threatens to paralyze him.

Ferdinand comes to visit him and tells him that his mother is not well. For the time being she is incapable of doing his laundry.

This brings him criticism that he stinks, that he is not changing his clothes frequently enough, or not at all. One of the boys he likes, someone younger, who has only been at the Konvikt School for a year, comes to his defense saying that his stink is better than the presumed perfume of some of the others. Without taking breath he half speaks, half sings: "The perfumed and the stinking are not the same to me . . ." He is called Nestroy. "Scram!" This hurts Nestroy's feelings, and drives him out of his company for a while.

He does not respond to the Weigl opera at such length as he had intended, merely with an overture in D major, "completed on 26 June, 1812."

He learns from Ferdinand that his mother is confined to bed. She has no more pleasure in life.

He runs through the city on Sunday after Mass, with Lang's permission, almost as far as the Himmelpfortgrund, but before he reaches it he turns back, for he does not want to be turned away by his father. From Ferdinand he learns that his father is occasionally meeting another woman, and his mother is on her deathbed.

He cannot accept it. She is not dying. That cannot be.

Although the teachers are understanding of his anxiety and his distress—Lang is informed about his mother's condition—they still frequently call him to order and their reprimands and rebukes form a drumming rhythm in search of a melody.

"Pull yourself together, Schubert!"

"Pay attention, Schubert!"

"A bit more concentration, Schubert!"

"That won't do, Schubert!"

"Come on, Schubert!"

"You are late, Schubert!"

"Help Chimiani make a fair copy, Schubert."

"Are you coming out into the garden with us afterward, Schubert?"

His mother dies.

"Tell Father I want to visit Mother."

"Your father wishes to inform you that your presence is not desired."

From Spaun he receives the scores of Beethoven's Second and Third symphonies. He studies them so carefully that he could soon conduct them from memory. He should really write a symphony, and transfer the drumming disquiet to manuscript paper. "It could take the form of an allegretto, preceded by a short introductory adagio, an attempt at a song, but not the song itself, not yet. What do you think, Spaun?"

"I can only offer you my encouragement."

Naturally, the Konvikt orchestra would perform his symphony. He has that in mind with his instrumentation, and he also considers the way in which Ruzicka conducts, which tempi he prefers, which he does not find comfortable, which he cannot handle. Perhaps Ruzicka will allow him to conduct it himself at a subsequent performance.

"Sometimes, Holzapfel, I think I'm mad. Do you sometimes feel as if you are outside yourself, I mean that you simply leave your body standing and you take off? Everything in and around you pulls you this way and that, and you want to fly, to be invisible, to have a voice that can divide into five or six parts, a sextet. That would be happiness. Only I'm unhappy, you know, I really am."

"Don't let yourself go, Franz."

"That's just it. I can't let myself go. If only I could, then I'd be far away, right outside myself. In a major key, anyway."

"What d'you mean?"

"The symphony must be in a major key."

On the evening of the Feast of Corpus Christi, that is on May 28, 1812, Ignaz brings the news of Mother's death, and that she will be buried on May 30 at the Lichtental Cemetery.

She died of typhus, of "nervous fever." The shivering frost forced its way into her feverish and overheated body and turned it black.

"May I see her?"

"That is no longer possible."

His fellow pupils leave the dormitory. The brothers stand alone, and embrace. "I didn't know you could cry like that, Franz," Ignaz says, amazed.

"I would so much like to have seen Mother, to have taken leave of her."

"Sing, Franz, sing," she had always bidden him, when he perched on her foot like a swing or a little branch. "A little bird comes flying."

In the Register of Deaths for the City of Vienna there is an entry for May 28 which reads: *"Schubert*, wife of Herr Franz, public schoolmaster and Imperial and Royal tutor of the poor, née Vitz, born in Silesia, at the Sign of the Black Horse, Himmelpfortgrund No. 10, of nervous fever, aged 55 years."

After the funeral, back home again, Father takes him into his schoolroom, his attitude friendly and emotional, and begs him to come home whenever he can and would like to, as they all miss him, and they are also missing a viola in the quartet.

"I thank you, Father." He does not trust this man, suddenly somber and yielding in his mourning, on whose country features is printed the effort to try and achieve victory through severity.

As in former times, the family sits close together round the table. Aunts, brothers, nieces, nephews. They reminisce about Mother in what are often silly but all the more painful anecdotes.

Elisabeth.

Father bids him farewell outside the house. "Do not take it amiss when I implore you to be a good student, Franz. I know that music is important to you. But you need a profession too."

Once again there is a crack in his friendliness.

Recently he has been permitted to visit Salieri twice a week to learn counterpoint. He writes on a sheet of exercise paper, with pride in his hand: "Commenced counterpoint on June 18, 1812. 1st Form."

Six days later Napoleon's army marches into the vastness of Russia—but his winter music has not yet been written.

11

Frau Anna

I am gathering up what he scattered. It is a sort of paper chase, where I don't run behind, but frequently overtake him. I don't have to keep to the chronology of events, and I know things that he cannot know. That is a dubious advantage, often a painful one. Does he have any idea how much or how little time he has left? He must not know. He makes plans. He still has everything ahead of him. At the time of his mother's death he is fifteen years old. Almost as many years again are left to him. It is half a lifetime for him.

"I'm not the same as I was any more," I have him say to Spaun. "I've no home any longer, I've lost my mother and my voice all at once. My voice is breaking, and I don't want to go on being a pupil at the Konvikt, and I don't want to become a teacher. Where should I go, what should I do with myself?"

Yet he does not really have to pose these questions. He needs no home, he will yield to his growing restlessness and make the city his greater dwelling place, leaving it to his friends to provide him with shelter. He needs time for composition, a few hours each day when he can shut himself away, far from any distractions. And afterward he has even more need of friends to free him, at least for a short time, from the voices in his head, to drown them out with the cheerful or riotous din of the tavern. They all find that he is extraordinarily gifted as a friend. He is, because he has to be.

The four choirboys whose voices are breaking, including Schubert, are given scholarship places at the Konvikt. So he is to remain there and continue his secondary education at the Gymnasium. He is successful in all subjects except mathematics. His doubts about religion also make themselves felt.

Two days after the Battle of the Nations at Leipzig, Emperor Franz issues an edict from Rötha in Saxony that concerns three pupils at the Konvikt in Vienna, namely Franz Schubert, Johann Geraus, and August Gment: "If after the vacation these pupils do not progress beyond the Second Class, or in the next term's examination regress to a Second Class, they must immediately be dismissed, since singing and music are subsidiary subjects, and good behavior and diligence in their studies are of primary importance and an obligatory duty for those who wish to be beneficiaries of a foundation scholarship." Schubert is not aware of the reports carried to the Emperor, and the hackneyed replies carried back to the Konvikt Curator, Count Dietrichstein, who in turn allows Lang to apportion praise and censure, for all these are authoritarian noises in the background of his school career. He is busy, inspired by Salieri, composing trios and canons, and he has begun writing his first symphony. He is searching word by word, note by note, for a language that can contain all that troubles him. "Franz, you're letting your grief drive you mad." His friends try to divert him, and he plays along with them, goes out and drinks with them, "croaks" with his breaking voice, showing off, and he stinks, because it's an eternity since he changed his clothes.

No, he won't talk of Mother any more, nor write of her. She has become part of his memory, a silent, unchanging image. He could bring it into his music. But he realizes how little he has succeeded in that as yet.

In April 1813 his father marries the "'Good Citizen,' Spinster Anna Kleyenböck." She is twenty years his junior, has three sisters, and her father owns a silk-weaving business. She brings "a considerable dowry to the marriage," and her stepson Franz has his first sight of her on the day of the wedding when she stands beside his father before the altar of St. Giles in Gumpendorf, a delicate figure, but with a stately presence.

How should he address her. She will be coming up to him in a minute, together with his father. He has squeezed himself in between his brothers, a clown with a glittering pair of glasses. It is not difficult for him to play the clown.

The new mother moves prettily and without complacency. "You must be Franz," she says. "Good morning, Frau Anna," he replies.

"Good morning, Frau Mother," says Ferdinand, correcting him.

Although he intended to keep his distance, he likes the woman at first sight. There is no question that she could replace his mother. She does not need to do that. He has long since given up living in the house, has distanced himself from it, is already making his own way.

Moritz von Schwind made a drawing of Anna Schubert, a profile which with its gentle outlines immediately leaps from the paper and in a wondrous way maintains a smile.

She for her part takes a liking to him, perhaps because she has heard from Franz Theodor that he is obstreperous, and wants to be independent.

At the table during the meal she assesses him from time to time with an inquisitive glance. She sees him as everybody sees him from now on when they paint or draw him, by himself or in a group, listening and making music: the round, too pale and somewhat bloated face beneath the shock of black curls, the childish forehead, gently arching but not particularly high, which does not go with the bushy eyebrows, themselves parted by a rather short, stumpy nose. Little button eyes sit behind the thick glasses, and their reflecting game of hide-and-seek is quite contradicted by the unabashedly lusty, well-fleshed mouth, set off by the defiantly jutting chin with its little dimple.

She asks Ferdinand across the table whether he could not persuade his brothers and father to give her a serenade. The Schubert Quartet is legendary.

How can that be, when it is scarcely ever heard now?

Ignaz agrees, and even Father can be persuaded. Only the one for whom the request was really meant, whose heart should be warmed by this request from his second mother, is reticent. He has not touched the viola for a long time, always playing the violin in the Konvikt orchestra. Or the piano.

Ferdinand gives him a nudge: "Don't make a fuss. How noble you look in your Konvikt uniform."

Schubert laughs. "As if you'd never seen me wearing it."

"At school, of course, but not at a festivity such as this."

They pull the chairs together. Ignaz puts out the parts, a Haydn quartet. He knows that. They had practiced that one very carefully in his former, domestic existence.

They had not forgotten it at all, in the opinion of Aunt Maria, after the assembled company had finished applauding heartily, and the new mother had kissed Father on the forehead. "That touched my heart," she said.

It was noticeably different, said Ferdinand later, somewhat drunkenly, to Franz, the way he had played his part this time. Wilder and freer, and certainly in a more virtuoso manner. "You've learned a lot, Franzl."

He could not have explained how much.

Sometimes, in the midst of the daily routine, during schooltime, or at evening recreation, he disturbs them, is transformed and looks old, is off with his music, over the hills and far away. And so he shocks his friends, in particular Spaun, with a poem that Holzapfel preserved. He wrote it in May, a month after the marriage celebrations, and gave it the title "Time":

> Inexorably rolling, ever onward,
> The Beloved may never return,
> A constant companion during life's course,
> Who sinks with us down into the grave.
>
> Only a breath—and it is Time
> A breath, make haste, be worthy, you below,
> To the Throne of Justice!
> Bring songs of virtue forth from your mouth!
>
> Only an echo—and it is Time
> An echo, make haste, be worthy, you below,
> To the Seat of Mercy!
> Pour prayers of penitence before him!

Inexorably rolling, ever onward,
The Beloved may never return,
A constant companion during life's course,
Who sinks with us down into the grave.

Unaufhaltsam rollt sie hin
Nicht mehr kehrt die Holde wieder
Stät im Lebenslauf Begleiterin
Senkt sie sich mit uns ins Grab hernieder.

Nur ein Hauch!—und er ist Zeit
Hauch! schwind' würdig ihr dort nieder
Hin zum Stuhle der Gerechtigkeit
Bringe deines Mundes Tugendlieder!

Nur ein Schall! und er ist Zeit
Schall! schwind' würdig ihr dort nieder
Hin zum Sitze der Barmherzigkeit
Schütte reuig Flehen vor ihm nieder!

Unaufhaltsam rollt sie hin
Nicht mehr kehrt die Holde wieder
Stät im Lebenslauf Begleiterin
Senkt sie sich mit uns ins Grab hernieder.

"Where do you get such ideas, Schubert."

"I don't know."

"Always your melancholy moods."

"Why, Holzapfel? I'm fine. I feel happy."

There we have an old man playing a sixteen-year-old, or a sixteen-year-old playing an old man.

Three years later he lightly jots down this tension in his diary. In the entry for June 14, 1816, he writes: "For the first time in several months I took an evening walk. There can be few things more pleasant than walking of an evening, amid the fresh greenery after a hot summer's day, and the fields between Währing and Döbling seem especially made for it. I felt so happy, in the capricious light of the dusk, in the company of my brother Karl. How beautiful, I thought, and I called out, and stood, rapt in delight. The proximity of the cemetery reminded us of our dear Mother. And so we came in sad and intimate conversation to the point where the Döbling road forks. . . ."

I can watch them both here, the younger brother who in the meantime has grown taller than the older, and I begin to hear the sentences
that he wrote down. They resemble his music, as the words of one sen-
timent spring directly into another.

12

Moment musical no. 4
(*Fairly fast*)

When they learned in school that Napoleon's great army was defeated, Moscow was burning, the soldiers were crossing the Berezina in dreadful conditions, the frozen Berezina River in Russia, and in crossing the Berezina many were frozen, overcome by the snow and buried by the snow—

When they learned, however, that the Austrian contingent had been spared the worst since Prince Schwarzenberg was negotiating with General Kutuzov and the Czar—

When they read in the newspapers how the troops of Europe had humiliated Napoleon's Guard at Leipzig, and the returning invalids had begun to beg around St. Stephen's Cathedral—

When, according to rumor, Napoleon had had to abdicate and had taken his leave of the Old Guard with these words: "If I have made the decision to survive you, it is because I wish to serve further the cause of your glory. I wish to commit to paper the great deeds that we have brought to pass together"—

When finally it became known that Bonaparte, in order to escape the raging mob, stole away in an Austrian uniform on the ship to Elba, then

The Konvikt students celebrated,

The seminarians celebrated,

The school assistants celebrated,

And he wrote a song, eight verses long, "They are in Paris," and when Emperor Franz I returned from Paris and paraded in triumph

through the evening city, the Himmelpfortgrund was not just extrava-
gantly illuminated but on the house of the schoolteacher Schubert there
was fixed a sign that read:

> O could I but do as I would wish,
> I would honor, as is most fitting,
> Franz the best of Emperors!
> Mere candles may be burning here,
> But from my heart are sprouting
> Sprigs of laurel.

> *O könnt ich, wie ich wollte*
> *Ich ehrte, wie man sollte,*
> *Franz den besten Kaiser!*
> *Es brennen hier nur Kerzen*
> *Allein aus meinem Herzen*
> *Sprießen Lorbeerreiser.*

13

Take-off

*A*gain he laughs too often and without cause, surprising his fellow pupils and teachers with unexpected questions and dubious jokes, and when silence and concentration are called for, while they are preparing written work for instance, he hums absent-mindedly to himself. If he is admonished, he laughs, and thus draws disapproval and wrath down on his head.

His friends regard the laughter as a premonition. They are not comfortable with it.

They have long become accustomed to the fact that in the afternoons he "expresses his thoughts" at the shaky little desk that has been assigned to him in the recreation room. This is how he describes his composing. To the astonishment of all, he does not need a piano, and it is for this reason that most of them did not at first notice that he was writing on manuscript paper.

He tells Holzapfel, "The piano merely distracts me when I am composing. It stops my concentration, and I can't hear my voice."

"You are a strange bird, Franz."

So he plumps himself up like a little bird, pecks with his head and taps as he sings "A little bird comes flying."

With much ado on the part of the curator and of the rector, one of the Konvikt students is expelled. He had behaved in an unacceptable manner.

"Senn behaved like a swine, you know."

"Why? He expressed his own opinion."

"Don't let it upset you, Franz."

But he lost the thread long ago. Why does he need biology and mathematics? Why doesn't he give up? Why doesn't he just break out? To bring him to his senses and to divert his mind from the perils of the school system, Holzapfel and Stadler beg Schubert to play the piano more than ever, even before the orchestra meets after supper.

Perhaps one of the minuets that were lost because he was careless with them. He didn't need them any more. Later he simply forgot songs that he had written the previous month. They were overlaid and replaced with new inventions, which were themselves the old ones in new form.

He gave the remaining minuets to Ignaz. In any case he could play them better than he could himself.

Stadler liked his piano-playing: "It was a real pleasure to hear and see him perform his own piano compositions. Good touch, calm hands, clear, nice playing full of spirit and feeling. He still adhered to the old school of good piano-playing where the fingers had not yet learned to attack the keys like predatory birds."

I imagine that he played like a gifted accompanist, always ready not only to support the voice, but to spur it to greater heights, to make it shine and celebrate it.

On this particular day he was playing for a few friends. They soon noticed that his heart was not in it.

"You've played that better." Stadler spoke in jest, but deep down he was reacting to the restlessness in Schubert's playing.

"What are you planning to do, Franz?"

"I'm not happy at the Konvikt."

They know this complaint, and don't take it seriously, haven't done so for some time. They are certain that he will reach the secondary level, with a little effort, and will afterward be permitted to study as a scholarship student.

He does not like to talk about it. He changes the subject. "I want to dedicate my symphony to Director Lang," he says, and he might have added—possibly it has not reached that stage yet, possibly indecision itches like a sore under his skin, and causes him to break into laughter, this unholy giggle—and he might have added: "as a farewell to the Konvikt."

He seems disturbed, distracted, to them all. On the contrary, however, he is quite on the ball, making plans that his father, his teachers, and even most of his friends consider out of the question. He proceeds step by step. Not always consciously. Sometimes he playacts, taking himself in hand, in parody or disguise.

For some time now he has been working on the text for a cantata "For Father's Name-Day." He is busy with this throughout September. Writing the poem bothers him so much that he becomes silly in his rage. Then suddenly it goes smoothly. The tone of it creates the music. Is it imbued with childlike gravity, or with the irony of the son who while not wishing to submit in any way, would still like to win his father over? Anyone listening to the cantata, as his father and the birthday gathering heard it, would be touched by its fresh sincerity, and only later discover the bold underlying meaning.

He plays the guitar himself. It is the only time that he chooses this as an accompanying instrument. With it, and on it, he demonstrates how he can jest while remaining serious, as he honors his father, and at the same time measures out the distance between them. Ignaz, Ferdinand, and Karl sing. It is the name-day not only of the father, but also of the son:

> Sing out, lyre,
> For the feast of celebration!
> Apollo, descend,
> And inspire our songs.
> Long live our Father Franz!
> Long may the Chorus of his days endure!
> And may the garland of his life
> Bloom in everlasting beauty.
>
> May joy hover smilingly
> Over the course of his quickening fortunes.
> Ever held free from mournful pain,
> May the Shades of Elysium uplift him.

Resound, fair lyre, eternally,
When the yearly round brings Time back,
Gently, beautifully, at this festive celebration,
May Father Franz's happiness last forever.

Ertöne Leier
Zur Festesfeier!
Apollo steig hernieder,
Begeistre unsre Lieder.
Lange lebe unser Vater Franz!
Lange währe seiner Tage Chor!
Und im ewig schönen Flor
Blühe seines Lebens Kranz.

Wonnelachend umschwebe die Freude
Seines grünenden Glückes Lauf.
Immer getrennt von trauerndem Leide
Nehm ihn Elysiums Schatten auf.

Endlos wieder töne holde Leier,
Bringt des Jahres Raum die Zeit zurück,
Sanft und schön an dieser Festesfeier
Ewig währe Vater Franzens Glück.

Before the performance begins, the brothers set the assembled company in motion.

"Take your seats!"

"No, not here."

"Not there."

"Leave us enough space if you can."

Schubert distributes the parts and the brothers pull faces as if they are seeing them for the first time. But with Lang's permission, they have rehearsed a few evenings before this at the Konvikt, to the amusement of the Konvikt pupils.

"Schubert's playing the guitar!"

"Does he know how?"

"I'll say he does!"

He plays like a guitar player who plays a guitar player.

Now in the family circle they are all in thoroughly festive mood, and fall naturally into two groups, the audience and the musicians, and they resemble the representations we have of Schubertiads, Schubert Evenings, I cannot picture it any other way: ladies and gentlemen listening and applauding round the piano and the pianist, artistically arranged, sitting or standing, just as now, if somewhat more informally, and we have the two of them, father and son opposite each other, suppressing and overlooking their differences for an hour of happiness, while the son makes an attempt at reconciliation, in which he does not quite succeed, for in the third verse he hesitates almost imperceptibly in the guitar accompaniment so that the trio loses its tempo for a moment at the line which, while not reproaching, still betrays its painful target in that it raises the subject of mourning, and adjures the father to be "ever held free from mournful pain . . ."

Does the father notice the loss of tempo? Or does he already have a premonition that this son, whom he entrusted to the Konvikt for a time, would soon preoccupy him in quite another way?

When he sits down on the stool in front of his brothers and plucks his guitar in virtuoso style, has he already taken leave of the school? Or does he just know that there is no other course left for him?

Before the school year came to an end he had been awarded a scholarship.

He would have been able, if he had made a greater effort, to finish his secondary schooling and he would have had time enough for his profession.

But it is time that he is lacking, one way or the other. The time that is left to him, which he often seizes in both hands, he needs for his work.

Spaun tries to persuade him to persevere. Holzapfel and Stadler also support Spaun: "Don't throw it all away, Franz. What'll you do when you're out there?" What would he do?

He manages to appease his father by saying that he wants to resign himself, to limit his horizons, and to enter the teacher training establishment on the Annagasse immediately.

How does he go about this?

Not long after the name-day celebration he visits his father. He appears to have already guessed the reason for the visit, and sends Frau Anna from the room as he must discuss something with Franz, which causes the latter some anxiety, for he is suddenly afraid that his father might lash out again as he had done just a short time before.

"It is about school." He hesitates already. His father leaves him little room for maneuvering. He cannot avoid the issue, cannot fool around.

"It is about school. I have to leave."

"You have to? The teachers have not complained to me."

"They may do, Father. They probably have only refrained so far because Maestro Salieri and Director Lang are favoring me. They will not be able to help me."

"I have your best interests at heart, Franz."

The father stands up, towering over the son, who takes off his glasses as a precaution, and peers up at him. It is not that he has found unexpected courage. He cannot take any other course of action. He must hold on, for if his father forcibly ejects him from the house, denies him shelter, he has no idea how he will finance his education and living expenses.

"What's going to become of you, Franz?"

"I want to go to the teacher training college, Father."

"And leave the Konvikt?"

"Yes. Even my friend, Herr von Spaun, shows his understanding of that." Which was not true. He calls on his friends for support, as he always will from now on, he needs them as in the present situation he needs his father. They will all provide him with accommodation from time to time, a temporary refuge. No more than that.

"How else can I live?"

"Are you asking me, Franz?"

"I will not be able to improve in mathematics."

He can feel how his father is scarcely able to contain his anger, and fears that he may yet strike out at him. But he turns away, goes to the door, and says, without turning around: "Let me know when the time comes," and leaves the room, banging the door behind him, which is

71

the signal for the others to come storming in asking questions, and once again he cannot control himself, bursts into giggles, then calms down, telling them that he will soon be coming home, but not quite yet because he must attend the teacher training college first, but that will not prevent him from assisting Father, and what is more, the Konvikt orchestra will be performing his symphony, which he is dedicating to Director Lang, but not in farewell, as he will not be losing his friends, particularly not Spaun, but not Stadler or Holzapfel either.

"You're getting quite out of breath, Franz." His second mother lays a calming hand over his.

"No, no, I'm fine."

And so he is. For he has finally taken the step that will turn things his way, and he is not letting himself be manipulated by others, by Father or by his teachers, but is pursuing his own desires and plans.

"Whereas it has been made known by the Curator of the Konvikt that the Meerveld Scholar Franz Schubert will be renouncing his studies, his place is therefore to be assumed vacant, and proper measures will be taken to fill this vacancy . . ." This appears in a decree of the Provincial Government of Lower Austria for November 23, 1813.

By then he has left the Konvikt. He proceeds to attend the teacher training college.

He has already quarreled with his father, and they do not speak to each other for a time.

Then his second mother is delivered of a girl, Maria Barbara Anna.

He keeps winter at bay by composing, meeting Spaun and his other friends, making music at the Konvikt and at home, and occasionally visiting the theater.

Then he sells his schoolbooks, as he has no further need of them, in order to go to the Kärntnertor Theater, to hear and see *Fidelio*. It is the premiere of the final version. From a distance he watches Beethoven, whom he reveres above all others.

And he continues to endure the silence of his father, with difficulty.

Since the house still smells as it did before of pupils' perspiration and cooking aromas, he escapes to the street, despite the cold.

Then he writes under the first movement of his B Major Quartet, the allegro ma non troppo, "Finished in four and a half hours. September 5th.," expelling thereby the thing that has him in its clutches and is making him ill, and he is already at work on the second movement, the andante.

14

Image of a Love That Might Have Been

He first became aware of her when she sang. He had met her on many previous occasions, and he knew her name from conversations with his parents and brothers. She was one of the Grobs. There were two Thereses, mother and daughter, her brother Heinrich and her aunt Wilhelmine, who was married to the coin engraver Leopold Hollpein. They all lived together, close by. His second mother sometimes went to make purchases at Therese Grob's silk-weaving shop. Since he is back living at his father's schoolhouse he regularly attends Sunday Mass in the Lichtental Church, and he has resumed his musical discussions with Michael Holzer, the choirmaster, just as if he had not been away for six years. He often takes part in choir practice in the evening, and if they sit afterward over a glass of wine he enjoys the encouragement of his former teacher.

He should practice counterpoint and continue his lessons with Salieri.

"I am allowed to go to him twice a week, although I am no longer at the Konvikt."

Would he be confident enough to compose a Mass?

"A Mass?"

It would be a commission for a special anniversary, explains Holzer. A hundred years ago, on September 25, Mass had been celebrated for the first time in the Lichtental Church. He would like a Mass from him in commemoration.

He did not really know a great deal about the church.

He had not meant the Church in general, but his own church. "Your church, which you have known since you were a child, where you began to sing, Franz." Holzer talks, persuasively, but little persuasion is needed, since his table companion at the inn already knows how it might sound, for in the meantime he has found one of the voices, the most important one, has heard it singing at choir practice, that of his neighbor, Therese Grob.

"I'll try."

Holzer jumps up, wanting to throw his arms around Schubert's neck, more intoxicated with his own powers of persuasion than with the wine, but Schubert is already on his way.

I can date this: it must have been one evening in May, presumably quite a warm one, and they might well have sat outside in the garden of the inn, and there would have been stars hanging amid the leaves of the great chestnut tree. "He said it begins with the Kyrie," reports Holzer. Above the Kyrie he writes: May 17.

To begin with, it is her voice alone that assumes life and breath, as he settles down to compose.

"I ought to ask her," he says.

"Whom?" asks Ignaz.

"Therese. Whether she would like to sing the first soprano part in my Mass."

"Therese? In your Mass?"

He is already speaking of the work he has done, and assumes that they are all automatically involved.

"Yes, Therese Grob."

"Are you writing a Mass?"

"Yes." He waits most impatiently for the confirmation of what he had already settled long ago in his own mind. Naturally Therese will sing the soprano part, she really should already know that herself. When it comes down to it, he doesn't need her agreement, since her voice is already woven into his Mass.

Does a love story begin like this?

Certainly not one that can be told chapter by chapter. Or one that has an ending, be it happy or sad. But this one has no ending, it drags on and peters out.

He accompanies her home after the rehearsal.

The walk seems much too short to him and after a few days to her as well. She is not beautiful. Later he will recall her pock-marked face. But he likes her nevertheless, finding her attractive. She has a pretty, well-developed figure. And she has her voice with which she captivated him. He surprises himself how effortlessly he can talk to her without stammering or being embarrassed. He is so full of ideas. That is how he can win her.

He is seventeen, she is one year younger. Sometimes when they are walking together—she is a little taller than he—he touches her with his elbow or shoulder, pretending that it was accidental and not to notice, but each time he shivers in a combination of ecstasy and misery, for he remembers the smutty innuendos of his friends at the Konvikt, the sort of things they used to say about women, and how they boasted about their various experiences with them.

The June weather makes them hot. It becomes difficult for them to repress their longings. For her perhaps more than for him, as he can turn to his music, pouring out what he feels, what he is suffering. Did he tell Therese on one of their evening walks that he loved her? Did he say it out loud: "I love you."

Most probably he did not go so far. In his music he went much further.

They are observed. The Himmelpfortgrund is an open stage. The parents watch, Therese's mother, the brothers and sisters, the neighbors. There is talk. Sentences are strung together like garlands: What a lovely pair; look how he's courting her; quite the gentleman, such a lady; how beautifully she sings; and that's the lad who's composing the Mass for the Lichtental Centenary.

That lad, small and a bit on the chubby side, deceives them all here. He has grown accustomed by now to being a different person when he is alone. Here he jokes with his friends, joins in all the fun, raves to

Therese about the power of Beethoven's imagination, astonishes the musicians at rehearsal for the Mass with his cheerful self-confidence. There, on his own, he can only overcome his bouts of melancholy, his stumbling, stuttering consciousness, when he can lose himself in composition. There his wild fantasies have free rein, and he stands wretched and bowed in the courtyard at night and gratifies himself. There, he has only one wish, to escape. But here, he acquiesces of necessity to the wish of his father, that immediately after the examination he should begin teaching in the school as his assistant. Sometimes he cannot separate "here" from "there."

His second mother is afraid of his helpless rage. "That is not the real you, Franz." It is one side of him, and not the other. Right at the end of his life he will succeed, with Heine's help, in reconciling this division:

You my double! You pale companion!
Why do you mimic the pain of my love,
Which tormented me here in this place,
So many a night, in time long past.

Du Doppelgänger! Du bleicher Geselle!
Was äffst du nach mein Liebesleid,
Das mich gequält auf dieser Stelle,
So manche Nacht, in alter Zeit.

For the time being, the "time long past" is his present.

In this little courtyard where he used to play with his cousin Magdalena and where he sometimes comes secretly to relieve his desire, in this little courtyard he kisses Therese for the first time. All the shadows from which he had escaped during the course of his life converge at this moment and overwhelm him. The childhood years, the death of his first mother.

"You seem far away, Franz."

"I am thinking of you."

She draws him close, presses up against him.

"No, you are certainly not thinking of me, Franz."

"Yes, I am."

He likes her laughter, with its hint of resentment.

"If only the musicians were at the church right now we could try out the Gloria."

He escapes with her from the darkness of childhood and takes her into Father's schoolroom, where he immediately throws open the windows. "We are in the school, Therese and I," he calls up into the house. He receives the answer that Father is on his way, and may they listen while the music is going on, and should the brothers bring their instruments, and would it disturb them if Mother came to join them later?

No, they should just bring down the new composition that is lying on his table, the Matthisson song.

Could she sight-read that? Therese reads the manuscript, expresses doubt, acts coy.

That puts him in a good mood, he plays along with her. He outlines the melody, trilling away. An allegretto, in six-eight time. But she shouldn't listen to him. His voice isn't right for it.

"I know the poem," she admits.

He giggles. This giggle makes her anxious.

"Yes, I read it to you."

"I know." Her answer is to sing, without waiting for his accompaniment.

Past spruce trees on the hillside, past alders by the stream,
Your image, my beloved, follows me constantly.

Durch Fichten am Hügel, durch Erlen am Bach,
Folgt immer dein Bildnis du Traute! mir nach.

She breaks off. "But it's your song, Franz, not mine."

"Please sing it."

Her voice is like one of the sounds of Nature, in Ferdinand's opinion, when she has sung the song through to the end.

She has to go home, her mother will be waiting.

He accompanies her the short distance.

On the way it begins to rain. As soon as the water softens the dried refuse by the side of the road, it begins to stink.

"It is wonderful that you can have such dreams, Franz." After pausing for breath, she adds: "For you."

He bids her farewell at the door of her house: "Until tomorrow, at the rehearsal, Therese."

On September 18, 1814, a second high altar is dedicated in the Lichtental Church. This inaugurates the weeks of celebration for the congregation.

On October 9, a Sunday, the poet Zacharias Werner preaches the sermon. They discuss him at the Himmelpfortgrund. After an encounter with Satan in St. Peter's Square in Rome he had fallen to his knees, forsworn his Protestant beliefs, and been converted to Catholicism. A short two years later, he had been ordained a priest, either in Munich or elsewhere. Most recently he had been appealing to the consciences of the diplomats at the Congress, and that he should preach at the Lichtental Church was a great honor for the congregation. Schubert finds a poem by Werner in a magazine, and puts it aside. That might become a song:

> Only one who knows love
> Can understand the longing
> To be eternally bound to the beloved.

> *Nur wer die Liebe kennt,*
> *Versteht das Sehnen,*
> *An dem Geliebten ewig fest zu hangen.*

He is amused by the echo of the first line: "Only one who knows longing" ("Nur wer die Sehnsucht kennt . . .").

He has a continuing disagreement with Holzer over an omission in the text of the Mass. He insists that he will not compose a setting for one sentence in the Credo. It is the acknowledgment of belief in the Catholic Church: "Et unam sanctam catholicam et apostolicam ecclesiam." It will be missing from the Credo.

Holzer battles with him. He cannot do that to the Church.

He refuses in such a friendly and even-tempered way that he appears almost uncanny to Holzer.

"Is it really so important to you, Franz?"

"Yes."

"Don't you believe, then?"

"Oh yes, I do."

"But why this then?"

"I believe in God, in Jesus."

"And the Church?"

"Belief in the Church is not mandatory."

"A good thing that no one can hear you, Franz."

"There you are wrong." Schubert puts his finger to his lips as if he wanted to keep silent about what would otherwise become public: "They will all hear it, Maestro Holzer. Because they will not hear it."

Ferdinand will play the organ and Holzer take charge of the choir. He himself is allowed to conduct.

On October 16 the church fills with people while they are still rehearsing. Salieri has announced his arrival. He waits for him at the great door. Full of pride, he conducts him to his seat.

Therese has transformed herself into a great lady. He looks at her repeatedly, admiringly, and gradually the blood rises to his face.

He is excited, he hears his father say, as he sits with Ignaz and Karl in the orchestra.

Spaun greets him from a distance. He is accompanied by a young man who is flaunting his own elegance. After the Mass they are introduced. His name is Franz Schober.

Go on, he hears Ruzicka say, as in the old days "for piano duet."

Go on. Ruzicka has not missed the opportunity of hearing Schubert's Mass either. They all crowd round him like a protective shield.

The Kyrie.

Sing, little bird, sing.

Therese has never sung so warmly and so lithely as now. He loves her very much. How, he asked himself, or I imagine that he asked himself, how is it that I cannot manage to convince her of the depth of my feelings so that she no longer mistrusts me?

The Gloria.

The Credo. Even the choir pauses for a moment at the place where the article of faith is missing, as if they wanted to breathe it into being.

The Sanctus.

The Benedictus.

The Agnus Dei.

That's not the end of it, he says, as Salieri offers his congratulations and his brothers fall over him in their glee, Therese takes his hand and does not let go, and Holzer reminds him of his first lessons with the choir: "You have come a long way, Franz." And his father amazes him by promising him a piano, not just for instruction in the school, but for himself. It arrives a few days later, one built by Konrad Graf, with a range of five octaves.

This beginning, which constitutes at the same time a return to the Himmelpfortgrund, could not have been more resplendent. It casts light ahead. But there is something that the others, the parents and the friends, the love who might have been, do not see, that torments him all the more: That there cannot be this light without darkness.

He takes up his position at his father's school, but has scruples about it. He is given the youngest pupils. And he is not up to the task. He fights against their noise, their stink. They grate against the melodies in his head. He slaps them and bullies them. But sometimes he forgets their tormenting, sinks down behind the desk, disappears, writes, composes, and the pupils leave the classroom on tiptoe.

Therese counters his complaining and persuades him of the benefits of a teaching career, he must just understand the comforts it can bring. He finds this touching and at the same time it inspires him with fear. In the long run, he is sure, he could not endure this miserable existence. In that case there would be no future for their love either.

Winter comes early and spreads an icy mantle over the city.

Since the stove in the classroom cannot heat the room adequately, the children keep their coats on, and their caps. He treats them like a horde of trolls.

"Quiet, quiet, calm down, just calm down! I beseech you!"

"Go on trying, Franz," says his father soothingly, "it is your profession."

He does not yet contradict him, because he has not quite given up hope of a life together with Therese. In any case, it lasts longer than a few songs.

Sometimes he just cannot manage to teach any longer, so many ideas are proliferating in his head, taking hold of him and putting him beyond reach.

"May we go, teacher, sir?"

"Don't disturb me—or shall I play something for you on the piano, a song that I have just written?"

It is immaterial to him whether the children listen or not, but he does in any case have more control over them with music than with the cane. They sit still for a few verses. "I don't have much of a voice. You should hear Fräulein Therese sing."

> My peace is gone,
> My heart is heavy.
> I will never, ever
> Find it again.

> *Meine Ruh ist hin,*
> *Mein Herz ist schwer.*
> *Ich finde sie nimmer*
> *Und nimmer mehr.*

Why is this Gretchen so upset and sad, the children want to know. "She is in love, of course."

"What's the name of her beloved, teacher, sir?"

"Heinrich Faust." The children burst out laughing, and think that name is quite unsuited for a beloved.

Therese sings it to the assembled family. Her mother and her brother are also invited. She has to sing it a second time.

"That takes guts, to set Goethe to music!"

All of them are so much under the spell of the song that they treat Therese as if she were Gretchen, sick from love. But in the song he had been visualizing not her, but himself. He projects. It is something that he will do again and again. His songs are like entries in a diary, often only slightly veiled. Sometimes they become the expression of something that could happen, sometimes the embodiment of a desire or of new and unexperienced realities.

The Gretchen song came into being before the bright winter of Therese, on October 19, 1814, three days after the performance of the F Major Mass, but it really belongs to the next year, with its wealth of songs. Spaun immediately grasps what is happening. "You're surpassing Zumsteeg, Franz, you've come further than he did."

Schubert is less touched by the praise than by the fact that Spaun had unexpectedly addressed him in the familiar form, "du," as a friend and equal.

The answer came easily to him in the same form: "I thank you, Spaun."

There is many a day when he cannot cease to "express his thoughts" in composition. In the space of a few hours three of Goethe's poems become songs. Spaun begins collecting them. "We could present them to the great man." That won't happen for a while.

News of the Congress is brought from the city by Ferdinand, Spaun, and also Mayrhofer, who has joined the group in the meantime, and they immediately discuss and debate it; they argue about who is intriguing against whom, or who has danced and flirted with whom.

"Have you heard, sensational news, Napoleon has landed in France, back from exile."

He listens.

He pictures the Emperor as he saw him at Schönbrunn. In the image that he makes in his mind he conjures the distant ruler far away from the flight of steps, placing him on the top of a rocky cliff, absolutely isolated, and imagines that in the shimmering light and swirling air he will quite simply dissolve.

When Mayrhofer relates how the Austrian army has defeated King Murat of Naples, Schubert stares so concentratedly down at the surface of the table that Spaun taps him gently on the arm and asks if he has music going round in his head again, but he is imagining tiny troops on the smallest surface, in vivid colors, ridiculous battle-crumbs, and he starts to giggle, as he so often does. In the Konvikt they used to say to him: "You're daft, Franzl."

He celebrates the closing of the Congress of Vienna with his friends at the "Red Cross." "Now we'll go dancing, Franz."

He goes with them, but doesn't dance. If Therese had been there, he might have tried.

In the summer, when they had put the table out in the courtyard, Spaun brings news of the defeat of Napoleon's army at Waterloo. A song or a ballad might be made from that. For him this song had begun, not with a defeat, but with a peace treaty. Lunéville was the childhood word.

"Will there be peace?" His question surprised the group.

"Of course."

"Quite certainly, Franz. At last!"

His song doesn't turn out that way. He looks at Therese, who has come with her mother to the Schubert house, beseeching her.

"I could sing a song," she says, "a new one."

For my own amusement I picture such scenes in my imagination. They might have taken place, but they are not recorded in any reminiscences. We are here, in the courtyard of the schoolhouse, in the little courtyard. He leaves the assembled company and goes into the house. When he opens the window they can hear the piano. Therese is standing in the doorway, framed by it. All their eyes are on her. The sky appears just as a starry backdrop. The crescendo of the introduction sounds from the piano like the radiance of moonbeams at an opened window:

> I think of you when the beams of the sun
> Glimmer on the sea;
> I think of you when the beams of the moon
> Shimmer in the brook.

I see you when on distant pathways
The dust rises;
In deepest night, when on the narrow footbridge
The Wanderer sways.

Ich denke dein, wenn mir der Sonne Schimmer
Vom Meere strahlt;
Ich denke dein, wenn sich des Mondes Flimmer
In Quellen malt.

Ich sehe dich, wenn auf dem fernen Wege
Der Staub sich hebt;
In tiefer Nacht, wenn auf dem schmalen Stege
Der Wandrer bebt.

Is this her song? And is he already the Wanderer?

In January 1815 he writes Holzapfel, who is still at the Konvikt studying law, a long and explicit letter about his situation. He loves Therese Grob, whom his friend had heard singing in the Mass. She may not be particularly beautiful, but she has the sweetest personality, and of course the voice that he knows. In his prompt answer Holzapfel is not minded to encourage him, although in his own way he gives a portrait of the girl that is not at all unfavorable: "Good figure, rather well developed, a fresh and childish round face, with a beautiful soprano voice (right up to high D)." He should not tie himself down too early, is Holzapfel's advice in a parenthetical sentence. "I beg you, Franz, do not lose your head, think of yourself, and your art."

Probably he will have given in to his desire one last time and begged her to love him, "Theres', I am yours, you know that."

With every sentence he made her anxious. "I don't know," she replied. "We must be patient. My mother, your father," she said.

His father would have approved the match. The Grobs had a good name, and even though there was no head of the family, Therese had had a good education and lived a sheltered life.

Perhaps Franz did not appear manly enough for her, he was too gentle, too absent-minded. The one thing that marked him as exceptional, his incomparable talent, frightened her more than anything else.

"Love me, Therese, wait for me."

She is no longer waiting for him even while he is still her neighbor, accompanying her on the piano. And he is moving away, involuntarily. He plays the piano at her side and is far away, off "on the narrow footbridge, the Wanderer."

They gradually lose sight of each other. He keeps her image in his mind. In his dreams he conjures it up, desiring it, as did the boy in the schoolyard at night, forlorn and without hope. There is no letter from him to her, nor from her to him. Only the poems by Goethe that he set to music in these two years of his love can be read as his messages:

> My weeping must always be in secret,
> Yet I can appear to be cheerful,
> Even well and rosy-cheeked;
> If these sorrows were fatal
> To my heart,
> Ah, then I should have died long ago.

> *Heimlich muß ich immer weinen,*
> *Aber freundlich kann ich scheinen*
> *Und sogar gesund und rot;*
> *Wären tödlich diese Schmerzen*
> *Meinem Herzen,*
> *Ach! schon lange wär' ich tot.*

In 1820 Therese, his first singer, his first love, married the master baker Johann Bergmann. Therese, "not exactly pretty, with a pock-marked face, but so good, so good-natured."

15

The Wanderer

*D*uring the years 1815 and 1816 the assistant schoolmaster, working under his father's supervision at Himmel-pfortgrund, writes approximately two hundred and fifty songs. These alone should have been enough to occupy his musical imagination day and night, but there are in addition four symphonies, several singspiele, cantatas, oratorios and masses, string quartets and compositions for both piano and violin, and for piano solo, and this is by no means the complete list of everything taking the attention of this nineteen-year-old, tormented by his daytime profession, of everything that consumes his time, takes possession of him and drives him on. As a general rule he composes songs as the poems fall into his hands, a pile of Matthisson, Schiller, or Körner, a pile of Goethe: On August 19, 1815, alone he composes "Heidenröslein" ("The Meadow-Rose"), "Bundeslied" ("Song of Fellowship"), "Der Schatzgräber" ("The Treasure Seeker"), "Der Rattenfänger" ("The Rat-Catcher"), and "An den Mond" ("To the Moon"). He sets poems by fellow students at the Konvikt, Joseph Kenner or Anton Stadler, texts that he finds in almanacs, and sometimes he can win friendship in this way, with Johann Mayrhofer for example, or Franz von Schober, who simply puts one of his poems on Schubert's table.

He seems always ready to compose. The stimulus might be a poem, a single line, even the situation of the moment, a mood or feeling. Individual words might be sufficient. They may be paltry, naive, inane words, or words that shine, powerful in themselves. When he composes he does not choose words for their quality. He leaps from one linguistic realm to another, according to his mood, the sway of his emotions.

So he reads and discards, responding in song to the color in a turn of phrase or a sentence, to the mood or content of a poem, and he creates a fantastic anthology that can hardly be called a collection of poems, but can rather be read as the curve of his moods, a hodgepodge of the soul, which he arranges and expresses in melody:

A lady looks out of a high tower,
Into the snow, the rain and the wind.
Leave me, leave me, I must grieve.
There is a maiden whom I see in my
    mind's eye, both early and late.
Can I not hear the gate opening?
Bury the body in a deep grave.
The oak forest thunders,
    the clouds race by,
Sister, reach me down my harp.
Silent and wild I creep across the field,
    my gun ready to fire.
He died for the Fatherland, a sweet
    death in the battle of liberation.
Who are you, Spirit of Love, who
    is at work throughout the firmament?
A boy saw a little rose
    growing in the meadow.
I found her in the spring garden,
    I bound her with ribbons of roses.
I am a German maiden.
Have you not seen Liane—
    I saw her walking to the pond,
Rose, do you think of me?—
    I think fervently of you.
Only someone acquainted with longing
    can know what I suffer.
Today I will be joyful, so joyful.
You do not disturb us, O Night.
Let yourself be touched with gentle strokes.
Let me appear like an angel
    until I become one. . .

Ein Fräulein schaut vom hohen Turm,
Dem Schnee, dem Regen, dem Wind entgegen,

Laßt mich, laßt mich, ich will klagen,
Ein Mädchen ist's, das früh und spät
mir vor der Seele schwebet,
Hör ich das Pförtchen nicht gehen?
Begrabt den Leib in einer Gruft,
Der Eichwald braust,
die Wolken ziehn,
Gib Schwester mir die Harf herab,
Im Felde schleich ich still und wild,
gespannt mein Feuerrohr,
Er fiel den Tod fürs Vaterland,
den süßen der Befreiungsschlacht,
Wer bist du, Geist der Liebe,
Der durch das Weltall webt?
Sah ein Knab ein Röslein stehn,
Röslein auf der Heiden,
Im Frühlingsgarten fand ich sie,
Da band ich sie mit Rosenbändern,
Ich bin ein deutsches Mädchen,
Hast du Lianen nicht gesehn—
Ich sah sie zu dem Teiche gehn,
Rosa, denkst du an mich?—
Innig gedenk ich dein,
Nur wer die Sehnsucht kennt,
weiß was ich leide,
Heut will ich fröhlich, fröhlich sein,
Du verstörst uns nicht o Nacht,
Laß dich mit gelinden Schlägen rühren,
So laßt mich scheinen,
bis ich werde...

It is a confusion of beautiful sentences, inane phrases, a melodic universe.

The friends who witnessed this explosion of creativity were quick to understand what a miracle was transpiring, and they assumed the world too would be amazed. Here they were wrong.

From the start Spaun aimed high. He would like to send Goethe a selection of the songs. "If he acknowledges anyone as his equal, it will be you, Franz."

First he has to bind the sixteen songs together, including "Gretchen am Spinnrade" ("Gretchen at the Spinning-Wheel"), "Erlkönig" ("Erl-King"), "Heidenröslein" ("The Meadow-Rose"), and must persuade his friend over and over again to give his permission, for Schubert does not necessarily want to be compared with a model like Zumsteeg.

Spaun spends a whole long evening writing the accompanying letter:

Your Excellency,

The undersigned ventures to deprive Your Excellency of a few minutes of your precious time with these lines, and only the hope that Your Excellency might find the enclosed collection of songs a not unwelcome gift can excuse the great liberty that he presumes to take.

The poems contained in the present volume have been set to music by a musical artist, aged nineteen years, by the name of Franz Schubert, endowed by nature from his earliest years with the most pronounced talents in musical composition, which were brought to the finest fruition by Salieri, the Nestor of our composers, with the most altruistic love of art. . . .

The artist now craves permission to dedicate this collection humbly to Your Excellency, to whose magnificent poetry he owes not only the creation of its greatest part, but also the essence of his development as a German Singer. Yet being himself too modest to consider his work worthy the great honor of being adorned with the name of one so highly celebrated wherever the German tongue is spoken, he has not the courage to make this request of Your Excellency himself, and therefore I, one of his friends imbued with his melodies, venture to request this of Your Excellency in his name. Arrangements will be made to produce an edition worthy of this honor. I will refrain from further acclamation of these songs. . . .

Should the young artist be so fortunate as to obtain the approval of one whose approval would signify more to him than that of any other person in the entire world, then I would dare to request to be graciously acquainted in a couple of words of the desired permission.

I remain, with infinite respect, Your Excellency's most obedient servant,

Baron Josef von Spaun

The "couple of gracious words" were not forthcoming, and the volume was returned without any accompanying letter. It is doubtful whether understanding or indeed praise would have kept Schubert as an assistant schoolmaster, and whether his departure from the Himmelpfortgrund might have been postponed. In any case he had found with the help of Goethe the underlying motif for his existence and his art: The Wanderer. On July 5, 1815, he had set "Wanderers Nachtlied" ("The Wanderer's Night Song"), Goethe's first poem of that name:

> Ah, I am weary of life's struggles!
> Why all this pain and joy?

> *Ach! Ich bin des Treibens müde!*
> *Was soll all der Schmerz und Lust?*

During the second of these two years of song composition he found a poem in which many a line is weak, many a rhyme faulty, but which attains the status of a deeply and inwardly felt hymn through his music: "The Wanderer."

Originally the poem was entitled "The Unfortunate One." He found it under this title in the little volume *Poems for Recitation*. The author is given here as "Werner." Schubert must have assumed that this was Zacharias Werner, the poet and preacher to the Congress of Vienna. It was not so. The indifference of the editor to his authors resulted in the suppression of the name of the real writer. It was Georg Philipp Schmidt, called Schmidt of Lübeck, Schubert's contemporary, who had an amazing career far from Vienna, dividing his time between Altona, Lübeck, and the Danish island of Fyn, as physician, alienist, secretary to a Danish minister, bank director, and head of the Imperial Bank. He died twenty years after Schubert.

However, he gave his poem to the twenty-year-old at Himmelpfortgrund without knowing of his existence, donating the basis for the melody in which the Stranger and the Wanderer are intrinsically united. The music, as ever, absorbs and carries the words even where they are poor and stumbling, right to the last sentence of the fifth verse, which rises, spare and precise, above the banality of the rest.

I come from the mountains.
Mist rises in the valley, the sea roars,
I wander silently, I am seldom joyful,
And my sighs ask repeatedly—Where?

The sun seems so cold to me here
The flowers faded, life seems old,
And their message seems a hollow sound—
I am a stranger everywhere.

Where are you, my beloved land?
Sought for, dreamed of, but never known,
That land, that land, so green with hope,
That land where my roses bloom,

Where my friends wander,
Where my dead arise,
The land that speaks my language
And has everything that I lack?

I wander silently, I am seldom joyful,
And my sighs ask repeatedly—Where?
The answer comes back to me in a ghostly whisper,
Happiness is in the *place* where you are *not*!

Ich komme vom Gebirge her:
Es dampft das Tal, es rauscht das Meer,
Ich wandle still, bin wenig froh,
Und immer frägt der Seufzer—wo?

Die Sonne dünkt mich hier so kalt,
Die Blüte welk, das Leben alt:
Und, was sie reden, leerer Schall—
Ich bin ein Fremdling überall.

Wo bist du, mein geliebtes Land!
Gesucht, geahnt, und nie gekannt,
Das Land, das Land, so hoffnungsgrün,
Das Land, wo meine Rosen blühn;

Wo meine Freunde wandeln geh'n,
Wo meine Toten aufersteh'n,

92

Das Land, das meine Sprache spricht,
Und alles hat, was mir gebricht?

Ich wandle still, bin wenig froh,
Und immer frägt der Seufzer—wo?
Im Geisterhauch tönt mir's zurück,
Dort, wo du nicht bist, ist das Glück!

16

Double Application

*I*t is not only the son who seeks to escape from the confines of the Himmelpfortgrund, but the father too. Both attempt to secure a better future for themselves, and both persuade themselves of their good prospects.

In April 1815, the second mother had brought Josefa Theresia into the world. Another reason for the father to wish to improve his situation.

They are all sitting round the table one Sunday lunchtime, the brothers and sisters, and the parents. This has not often occurred recently, and Father takes the opportunity to voice his long list of grievances yet again: the trouble he has in running the school; his helpers who do not help; what troublemakers there are among the pupils; with all this drudgery he can hardly make ends meet; and so he has come to the decision that he will apply for the vacant position as teacher in the school at the Abbey of the Scots in the Inner City— which they had all been expecting in any event. Father's demand that they should all make more of an effort is aimed only at Franz, who wants to find time for his music. Ferdinand and Ignaz, both of them by now experienced teachers, are held up to him by Father as examples, and now Karl, too, who has successfully trained as an art teacher.

"Take a leaf out of your brothers' book, Franz."

But the brothers mollify him. "He's as good a teacher as we are, Father."

He will not concede: "Where d'you think your music's going to get you? You can't live by it and you can't die by it."

"Yes," replies the son, I make him reply, for I think it possible that such paternal wisdom at once set a train of thought going in his head to avoid the hassle it caused him. "Yes, Father," and he might have replied, "if I only knew, Father, where between living and dying I could settle on this piece of wasteland between the 'Here' and the 'Not-Here,' no longer in the one place and not yet in the other, but if I'm not mistaken, you are mistaken about the nature of this territory, this region of the soul, for in my experience, Father, it is certainly possible to live in insufficiency, for that is where the inspiration which is nourished both by life and by death, runs wild in a nonexistent wilderness, dear Father." "Where have your thoughts led you Franz?" "Nowhere, Father."

"That is obvious."

"I beg you, Father," interrupts Ferdinand, "do not be too harsh with him. You were very pleased when he was so successful with his Mass."

"Yes, yes, but . . ."

Now he will declare that sacred music will not earn any money for Franz, only the blessing of the priests and with it the admiration of Holzer and Salieri.

"You received nothing for it."

"Yes I did, Father, a piano."

And so there is peace again for a while, and he can ask his bemused and gently vanquished father if he may leave the table.

"Off you go, then."

In fact in his application he had praised his gifted son for his own advantage. But he had said nothing to him of that. With a touch of self-aggrandizement, which was at the same time deferential, he had spoken of himself as a teacher and a father:

Most particularly it is the situation of his four sons, all of them already employed in the German schools, that makes him desirous of this gracious preferment, for one of them is concurrently Drawing-Master to the Institute for Girls at the Court, and attends the Academy of Drawing (at which he last year received the first prize in life-drawing), and the other, at the same time, has devoted himself to musical composition with happy results under the gracious direction of the First Imperial and Royal Court Conductor, Herr von Salieri, and so each of them would in his own fashion be greatly furthered in his education and ultimate career.

In all of which he ignores the two sons Ferdinand and Ignaz, who, as they cause him no trouble, are incomparably dearer to him than Franz, but whom he omits, as too unimpressive, from his self-glorification.

The father waits. His impatience and bad temper are vented on his family and pupils.

"You haven't learned much as a teacher, Franz."

"I will make an effort, Father." Two casualties are talking together, here, where the elder has the advantage of being allowed to reprimand the other. They carefully watch each other, and each has already, in his thoughts, escaped to success and to fame. In their everyday world they move like prisoners, without much hope of grace.

In September 1815 the father finally receives a notice of rejection. It is a normal schoolday. He beats fear into his pupils with his cane. "How dare you take such liberties," he screams, and means himself: Had he taken too great a liberty?

In conversation with Spaun and Mayrhofer, Schubert distances himself from the Himmelpfortgrund, not all at once, but gradually, for he suspects that such a refuge will not be available any longer.

In his imagination he has not yet given up Therese. They are still making music together, more often now in the Grobs' apartment than in the schoolhouse.

He will be able to make a life as a musician too, he insists.

She is doubtful. At some point during one of their walks, on the staircase, or when they are left alone for a moment in the room by Mother Grob, he makes another attempt, takes her hands, tries to kiss her, promising to try as hard as he can, but she reacts with gentle derision: "You're just a poor wretch, Franzl."

He has to show her, and not her alone, but his father. And himself. In the Vienna newspaper *Wiener Zeitung* of February 17, 1816, the Government of Lower Austria advertises a position for a music instructor at the German teacher training institute in Laibach.

By order of the High Central Court Commission for Organization of December 11, 1815, notice is given of the establishment of a public School of Music within the German Teacher Training Institute in Laibach, for which a teacher is sought herewith, who will be able to demonstrate exemplary conduct, and will in addition be a thoroughly trained singer and organist and an equally good violinist, and will not only possess the necessary knowledge of all the common wind instruments, but will also be competent to give instruction therein.

He has no problem in fulfilling any of these qualifications, except for the didactic capability, about which he himself has ever-growing doubts. Yet he is sure that he would find teaching music much easier than general subjects.

He applies. Spaun, well versed in official jargon, helps him. He must not be too expansive, nor too humble. After all, he has proven capability, and his talent is already acknowledged.

Before he sends off the application, they meet often at Schober's house, where he lives with his mother and his sister Sophie in the Inner City, and they debate among themselves, do not remain serious for long, and think up the maddest, most abusive, and stupidest letters of application. Josef von Spaun is there with his brothers Anton, Franz, and Max, and so are Schober and Mayrhofer.

When Schubert has enough of this nonsense he withdraws to the piano and he can bring peace and quiet to the mad circle of friends within the space of a few bars. "I know that *écossaise*," says Anton Spaun. "Josef brought the manuscript to Linz recently."

"So, Franz, let's write," suggests Josef von Spaun.

"Most Highly Esteemed Imperial and Royal City Governor's

Office," he writes, and I copy down his letter, telling myself that he resisted these expressions of humility, but this may not have been the case, for my repulsion is based on the temporal distance, and he may not have been surprised at all at expressions such as Central Court Commission for Organization, since being obsequious was an everyday state of affairs at that time. Certainly they sometimes gave vent to their feelings, got silly, and exaggerated to extremes, but now, when he composes this attempt, he is serious, deadly serious:

"Most Highly Esteemed Imperial and Royal City Governor's Office," he writes,

The undersigned beseeches most humbly that the vacant position of music director in Laibach most graciously might be accorded to him.

He supported his request with the following arguments:

1. He is a graduate of the Imperial and Royal Konvikt, a former choirboy at the Imperial and Royal Court Chapel, and a composition pupil of Herr von Salieri, the First Imperial and Royal Court Conductor, at whose most kind suggestion he is applying for this position.

2. He has acquired such knowledge in every aspect of composition, and such capability of performance on the organ, violin, and in singing, that according to the accompanying testimonials he is declared to be the most qualified of all applicants for this position.

3. He vows that he will apply his talents to the best of his abilities so as to justify completely the gracious granting of his request.
Franz Schubert
Presently assistant teacher at
his father's school in Vienna
Himmelpfortgrund No. 10

It is doubtful whether, without the persuasion of Schober and Spaun, he would have declared himself "the most qualified" of all the applicants.

"My" Schubert has not appeared in this light before. But it could well be that with this letter he has changed, and I must tell now of yet another Schubert, of that Schubert who forgets himself at social gatherings, but who steps forward with great assurance where music or his position as a musician are concerned, whether or not he is successful.

Salieri writes an excellent testimonial for him. It does him as little good as any other reference. There were twenty-one applicants. Those on the short list were Franz Schubert, Franz Kubick, Cathedral Choirmaster at Görz, and Franz Sokoll, Composer from Klagenfurt. Sokoll was chosen.

Therese learns the devastating news from Anna, the second mother. She is unable to comfort him. You're just a poor wretch, Franz.

In the diary that he began in June 1816 his feelings skip inconsistently this way and that from sentence to sentence. He cannot yet succeed in breaking free from Therese by writing. He loves her as a better, perhaps the best, opportunity in his life, and at the same time realizes that she, and he with her, are already lost:

"Happy the man who finds a true friend. More fortunate still the man who finds in his wife a true friend," he writes, or: "A fearful thought for the free man in these times is marriage; he mistakes it either for melancholy or a coarse sensuality . . . ," or, and here he speaks both about and against himself: "Light in feelings, light in heart. *Too* light a feeling most often hides *too* heavy a heart."

He bids no farewells, he seeks no further altercation with his father—he just steals away. He reduces his presence imperceptibly. At first his father scarcely notices the apologies, the excuses.

He has had to hand his class over to Ignaz. He does not even fabricate a reason for doing this. He has to—and this course of action cannot possibly be postponed—he has to go to Hartwig again at the Schottenhof. His father can hardly object to this meeting since Hartwig is one of his old group of friends with whom he used to play quartets and who had subsequently founded a small orchestra. Hartwig, an excellent performer on both the piano and the violin, was a member of the Burgtheater orchestra and had recently moved to the

Schottenhof in the Inner City, where he wanted to continue their joint music-making. He was currently planning to perform Schubert's Third Symphony. "I will make arrangements to have the manuscript copied, Father. It is important to me."

One day during the summer of 1816 he goes down the stairs of the house in the Himmelpfortgrund, bids a casual farewell to his second mother and his little brothers and sisters, asks them to inform his father that he is moving in with Herr von Spaun, and therefore, at least for the time being, will be unable to serve as an assistant schoolmaster. It is a sore point that his father conceals from the school authorities for a while. He is ashamed of his deserter son, of whom he cannot even state what profession he follows.

Schubert has to share a room with Spaun. At least this is in elegant and peaceful surroundings. Spaun, who is looking for an apartment, is lodging temporarily with his law teacher, Professor Heinrich Josef Watteroth, in the suburb of Landstraße. Watteroth's circle is made up of officials, courtiers, middle-class professionals, musicians, and men of letters.

"Play the piano whenever you like," he tells Schubert encouragingly. "It disturbs no one in this house." His daughter, Anna, might learn a little more about piano playing from him. Anna is seventeen, much better-looking and more open-minded than Therese. But he does not see her because he cannot hear her. Unlike his lost love, she has no voice.

He composes the cantata *Prometheus* for Watteroth's name-day. Its performance in midsummer of 1816 in the garden courtyard of the Watteroth house becomes a great occasion that unites the honored professor with his students. Schubert conducts the orchestra.

The score has been lost, but not its echo. For the first time—even if it was a year after the performance—Schubert's name is officially quoted in the *Wiener Allgemeine Theaterzeitung* in a poem by the Konvikt student Franz von Schlechta: "To Herr Franz Schubert upon the performance of his cantata *Prometheus*":

> With the deep trembling of the tones,
> When the strings rang out in joy,

An unknown life
Arose in my breast.

In der Töne tiefem Beben,
Wie die Saiten jubelnd klangen,
Ist ein unbekanntes Leben
In der Brust mir aufgegangen.

It could be that the "unknown life" "arose" in Schubert's breast on that evening. True, it was not the first time that he had been at the center of a musical performance, but never before had he been so surrounded by fellow feeling and friendship. He perceives this new departure as a good fortune and an act of rebellion. A turbulent sense of community spirit warms him for a moment. He can expand his horizons, gain in self-confidence.

The new-won freedom has its rewards as well. In his diary for June 17 he records: "Today for the first time I composed for payment. Namely a cantata for the name-day celebrations for Herr Professor Watteroth von Dräxler. The fee is 100 florins in post-devaluation money."

In the late autumn he moves in with Schober, who has returned from Sweden, and their friendship quickly establishes its own pattern of unrest and high spirits, closeness and lack of understanding, decorum and meanness.

Schober, like Schubert, has dropped out. To be sure, he can afford to do so. His family fortune places him in a position where he need not earn a living, where he can write for a time, listen to music, and push the career of a musician like Schubert. It is he who persuades Schubert not to continue as his father's teaching assistant, and who encourages him to renounce such banal security. He becomes the Wanderer at Schober's side.

Schober shared with his mother a spacious apartment in the First District, the Inner City, in the Landskrongasse. The house was called "At the Sign of Winter"—another of those ambiguous coincidences.

Furthermore, to celebrate his new beginning he was presented with a poem. On one of their walks, Johann Mayrhofer and one of the Watteroth sons, Hermann, found their conversation continually coming back to Schubert, that strange genius, and the rhythm of their feet aided Mayrhofer to anticipate a Schubert song in words:

Tell us, who teaches you songs,
So beguiling, so gentle?
They conjure up a Heaven
From our present gloom.
The land lay shrouded in mist
Before us—then
You sing, suns gleam,
And spring is near.

You do not see
The old man, crowned with reeds
Who is emptying his urn, you only see
How the water flows through the meadows,
So it is with the singer
Who sings and marvels to himself.
The silent creation of a God,
Is as strange to him as to you.

Sag an, wer lehrt dich Lieder,
So schmeichelnd und so zart?
Sie rufen einen Himmel
Aus trüber Gegenwart.
Erst lag das Land verschleiert
Im Nebel vor uns da—
Du singst, und Sonnen leuchten,
Und Frühling ist uns nah.

Den schilfbekränzten Alten,
Der seine Urne gießt,
Erblickst du nicht, nur Wasser,
Wie's durch die Wiesen fließt.
So geht es auch dem Sänger,
Er singt, er staunt in sich;
Was still ein Gott bereitet,
Befremdet ihn wie dich.

Schubert is not embarrassed to accept this praise, and composes an incomparable setting for this astonishment at his person, his gifts, and his aloofness.

"I have already set your song, Mayrhofer."

"What?"

He runs ahead of Schober and Mayrhofer into the room where the piano stands, excuses himself to Frau von Schober for the disturbance, but might he just quickly play through a composition.

"You sing, Schober, you have the best voice."

Schober cannot help it, he is so overcome by the first phrase that he has to stop. "Tell us who teaches you songs."

"Well, start again, Schober, and then, I beg you, sing it right through."

17

Moment musical no. 5
(Not too fast)

*I*n 1815 Spaun had witnessed how the "Erl-King" came into being, one afternoon, as it were, between the Himmelpfortgrund and the Konvikt (for it appears that at that time there was no piano available at his father's school and Schubert could play over at the Konvikt whatever he had composed in his head, or noted down in manuscript). He saw how at the Konvikt Ruzicka had played the piano part and clapped his hands in delight, particularly taken with the dissonances it demanded—and now Spaun is intent on having this particular song (which in the meantime had been sung by the great singer Vogl, who sang the song exactly as Schubert imagined it, and whose acquaintance he had made through Schober, this song that was making a reputation for Schubert in Vienna)—on having it printed for publication. Shall we say by Breitkopf and Härtel. With Schubert's permission, Spaun sends it to Leipzig, and they hear nothing for a long time, then receive, very tardily, a letter of rejection. There is a reason for the delay. There is a second Franz Schubert, also a musician, a double—"You my double! You pale companion!"—who is a composer of church music, living in Leipzig, and who has been connected with Breitkopf and Härtel for many years. Now, to his surprise he has returned to him a composition that he never wrote, which he could never have conceived, a setting of Goethe's "Erl-King." He lays the sheets of music to one side and writes to his friend Gottfried Christoph Härtel: "I also have to inform you that about ten days ago I received your esteemed letter together with a manuscript, Goethe's 'Erl-King,' purporting to be written by myself, and to my great astonishment I must note that this cantata was certainly never composed by me; I will keep the above in my possession in order that I may perhaps learn who sent you such an abomination, and in such an impertinent manner, and also to discover who this scoundrel may be who is misusing my name in such a way."

Regrettably there is no way of concluding how the submission came to be "impertinent," since Spaun's accompanying letter was presumably kept by the publisher while a careless assistant returned the manuscript of the "cantata" to the wrong Schubert. He was thirty years older than the Viennese composer, but he had a son—and a doppelgänger situation like this cannot but have consequences—who made the acquaintance of Schober and became his friend after the death of both his father and the great Schubert. In this way scores written by the Viennese Schubert came into the possession of the Dresden Schubert family, but not the "Erl-King," for this found its way back to its composer, this "scoundrel," though without the accompanying letter from the Dresden Schubert from which the Vienna Schubert could have learned what Goethe himself probably thought of his "Erl-King" cantata, accustomed as he was to the settings of Zumsteeg and Zelter, namely that this composition was quite simply an "abomination."

"You my double! You pale companion!"

18

To the Castle

nce more he returns to his father's schoolhouse, probably working again as assistant teacher. He can find no other lodging. But he does not have to prostrate himself and beg his father's humble forgiveness. His father has finally found a better position, a few streets nearer to the Inner City but still in the area of Lichtental and the Himmelpfortgrund. A position as school director in the suburb of Roßau was offered to him. His predecessor, who had founded the school only half a year previously, proved himself unsuited to the profession in that he had misappropriated funds or committed some other offense that made him fair game for informers.

They move to house No. 147 in Roßau, and he is quite simply counted as part of the large family, which is described in a census form dated January 1818, stating not only names and dates of birth, but also the most peculiar personal details.

No further details are given of the "public teacher" Franz Theodor Schubert nor about his wife Anna; it is said of the teaching assistant Ignaz, however, that he has a hunchback, of the orphanage teacher Ferdinand that he is married, of Karl that he "is reported to be a landscape painter," of the music master Franz that he measures "four feet, eleven inches, two hairs," that is approximately one meter fifty-five, in height; there are no details of the daughters Therese, Marie, and Josefa, nor of the late-born sons Andreä and Anton.

It is a large family.

Once more they will suffer from the close quarters.

Franz is no longer listed as a teacher. Although he assists his father, he has made his way. His profession is music master. His size is noted not with malice, but for official reasons: youths who measured less than one meter seventy-five in height could not be called up for military service. He would not be staying long, of that he was sure. The circle of his friends and admirers was growing larger, the number of voices speaking about him and around him increased. His compositions were copied, and were played and sung in many houses in Vienna. The special quality of his "intuitive expression" had become known. Wherever he was a guest, there was a space cleared where he could compose. When he had finished, his friends arranged for his diversion and entertainment.

As a general rule he wrote in the mornings. If he was disturbed, he lost his temper. From time to time he would ignore habit and pursue his own inclinations, sitting down just for a moment, dashing down what was already in his head, as happened on February 21, 1818, in the middle of the night at the home of his friend Anselm Hüttenbrenner.

He had already made two settings of Schubart's poem about a trout. Now suddenly the lines begin to jump around in his head once more. It is as if they were knocking for attention. He begs Hüttenbrenner for some manuscript paper, makes an apologetic face, draws his chair up to the windowsill, and is beyond reach of his friend. No sooner is the work finished than he jumps up, darts about the room, asks Hüttenbrenner for a glass of punch, and suggests that he send the song without delay to Hüttenbrenner's brother Josef in Linz who is so fond of his songs, and he writes a letter to go with it, stressing that it is "at 12 o'clock midnight": "I am extremely pleased that you like my songs. As a token of my sincerest friendship I am sending you another herewith which I have just . . . written. I wish that I could toast our closer friendship with a glass of punch. Farewell." Somewhat befuddled still from the effort of composing, and from drinking, he is clumsy: "Just as I was rushing to blot the thing with sand, I absent-mindedly picked up the inkwell and poured it all over the letter."

Hüttenbrenner had no choice that night but to put his exhausted friend into his bed beside him.

"I will curl up small," Schubert assures him, and laughs to himself.

But before this happened, he had had to take his leave of Schober, with whom he had been living, and to move into the schoolhouse at Roßau. He had prepared for a longer stay with Schober.

"So that you can compose in peace, Franz," his friend had promised. But he often has to adapt to Schober's restlessness, which he is not unwilling to do.

They meet friends. He drinks more than he can handle. In the evenings they prefer to meet at inns than in the autumnal cool of private houses.

The circle of friends makes plans and distributes Schubert's music to ever-increasing acclamation.

When in February and March 1818 the time comes for the first concerts, in private establishments, Schober will no longer be among them, and Schubert will be living in the suburb of Roßau.

Schober had departed very suddenly. He has to travel immediately. "I cannot keep my brother waiting, Franz. I have to ask you to find some other accommodation. I need the room for Axel."

Schober had received a message to say that his brother, a first lieutenant in the hussars and stationed in France, had been taken seriously ill and was on his way home. He wanted to go to meet him. In addition he was planning, if he found his brother to have recovered, to continue his journey on to Sweden.

Schubert felt torn by the unexpected farewell.

"Come back soon."

They embraced many times. He liked the strength with which Schober, so very much taller than he, held him close.

"Farewell, Schubert."

"Farewell, Schober."

He wrote a poem for Schober in his autograph book:

Farewell, dear friend!
Departing to a foreign land!

Take the trusty bond of friendship
And preserve it with a loyal hand!
Farewell, dear friend!

Lebe wohl! Du lieber Freund!
Ziehe hin in fernes Land!
Nimm der Freundschaft trautes Band—
Und bewahr's in treuer Hand!
Lebe wohl! Du lieber Freund!

Schober comes back earlier than expected, accompanying the body of his brother. He had died en route.

His compositions were performed in the hall of the "Roman Emperor," including one of his two overtures in the Italian style, and the sharp-eared critic of the *Wiener Allgemeine Theaterzeitung* characterizes in words what the young musician was striving to create. He finds the overture "wonderfully lovely," and its theme "strangely simple."

Things could have continued in this pattern. This is not what he wants. He complains to Spaun that he cannot escape from the city. His father is continually seeking confrontation.

Spaun introduces him to Karl Unger, the father of the singer Karoline Unger, and he in turn approaches Count Johann Karl Esterházy of Galántha on Schubert's behalf.

Unexpectedly a door opens for him to the outside world. But only after a complicated and not particularly pleasant prelude. He is requested to call on the count at his city residence in the Herrengasse. He wishes to make his acquaintance and to assess his capability as a musician and also as a possible music teacher for his two daughters, Karoline and Marie.

He enters the salon and tries to make a good appearance. Although this milieu is new to him and he feels overawed, he has no intention of adopting the role of the lackey.

I shall withdraw and view this scene from a distance, from the back row in an old-fashioned theater. The curtain has just been raised, the air is still disturbed. The figures on the rather small stage, built to represent a salon in the Empire style, seem disproportionately small, almost weightless. It is as if they were hovering a hand's breadth above the stage.

I cannot hear them.

I am watching a pantomime:

An older man, tightly buttoned into a cavalry uniform of exaggerated neatness, looks across at a young man standing beside a bureau, who comes toward him with small steps and is continually pushing his glasses up against the bridge of his nose. On reaching the older man, he bows. With a sweep of his hand the older man gestures to his guest to be seated, and is about to sit down himself when just at that moment two girls are ushered in by a maid. The older man remains on his feet, and the younger one, who is no longer standing but has not yet sat down, straightens up, kisses the hands of both children, which the older man watches with some amusement, shaking his head and rocking back and forth. Now one of the girls is permitted to sit down, while the other runs to the piano, turning round frequently to look at the diminutive gentleman, holding her hand to her mouth, and obviously stifling a giggle. She pulls a chair up to the piano and plays something that I cannot hear. The older man listens, and observes how the younger man listens. He nods, then takes some music out of the folder that he has been holding so close pressed to his body that I only just noticed it; he goes up to the girl and places the sheets on the music stand, shows her, points, looks at her inquiringly, she nods, he nods, she smiles at him, he smiles back, turns to look inquiringly at the older man, who makes another gesture of approval or encouragement, as a result of which the younger man draws up a chair beside the girl. They begin to play a duet. I can see their backs. They stretch and move in rhythm together. I can hear nothing, yet I am listening. The older man applauds. The girls run out of the room, and each is holding her hand up to her mouth. The two men sit down. The older one takes the hand of the younger. That must be a signal that the curtain should fall. It comes down slowly from either side and leaves to the imagination of the audience what happens next, or how the story should unfold.

Count Esterházy engages Schubert for the summer as music teacher to his two daughters. Naturally he would also be expecting a considerable amount of musical entertainment. He himself sings, as does his wife. At Zseliz Castle there would constantly be guests talented in music. He would be especially pleased to meet the Baron von Schönstein: he has an outstandingly rich tenor voice.

These are the promises made. He is suspicious of them, but whatever happens, he will be financially secure for the summer, away from Vienna, from his father and from Therese.

The two little countesses who will be his pupils seem to him to be highly musical. They not only play the piano in a most accomplished way, but Marie sings an excellent soprano, and Karoline likewise. Marie will be sixteen this summer, and Karoline thirteen. Their mother, Countess Festerics de Tolna, whom he has not yet met, is reputed to have a good alto voice.

On July 7, 1818, a passport is made out for him as the "Music Master to Johann Esterházy" for five months to travel to "Szellesz in Hungary." It is his first long journey.

Summer overtakes the city with its heat and storms. He packs, and unpacks again. He has repeated arguments with his father, who accuses him of bowing and scraping to the nobility for their pleasure and entertainment but nothing else.

"No, Father, Count Esterházy is offering me the freedom that I need for my work."

Spaun is in Linz for the summer.

Schober puts him in a suitably agitated frame of mind: "Take advantage of what you are given, Franz, time and mood, pleasure and love."

Oh, Schober.

In the last weeks his inspiration seems to have dried up. His head rings more than it sings. The poems he reads cannot find their echo.

"I'm in a bad way," he complains to Ferdinand. "Perhaps I'll soon be finished as a composer."

Before Spaun left for Linz there had been some minor disagreements. Spaun's brother Anton, together with Mayrhofer, Kenner, and others, had founded a magazine, *Contributions toward the Education of Youths,* which in Spaun's opinion was both too free-thinking and too frivolous. This angered Schubert. Following the demonstration by students at the Wartburg for freedom and national unity, Metternich had clamped down on public opinion. The publishers of this magazine were soon made aware of this. They received a visit from the police and were cautioned. This was not really necessary, since the magazine failed for lack of interest.

A few days before his departure, when his place in the post-coach is already reserved, he happens to meet a friend from the Konvikt School who tells him that his mother has died on the previous day. Schubert comforts him, and is overcome with a sadness that is not of sympathy but remembrance. "Your mother," he says; "My mother," he thinks. He promises his school friend that he will compose a funeral song. He may even collect it from him the following day at the school in Roßau.

> Blow more gently, evening breeze,
> Lament more softly, Philomel,
> A beautiful and pure angelic soul
> Sleeps within this grave.

> *Hauche milder, Abendluft,*
> *Klage sanfter, Philomele,*
> *Eine schöne, engelreine Seele*
> *Schläft in dieser Gruft.*

This was echoing in his head as the coach left Vienna. He hoped that his imagination would be recharged by the constantly changing surroundings, the beautiful scenery day and night by the Danube, of woods, fields, and villages which grew ever more foreign-looking. The road followed the course of the river through Preßburg, Komarom, and Gran. Keep watching, he admonished himself. He was affected by the strangeness of it all. In amazement he decided that even the landscape had a different language, and expressed itself as unintelligibly as the people. In time he came to enjoy being a stranger.

From time to time on the journey, and later at the castle, it seemed to him as if the summer's pictures, bright and beautiful but distant images, acquired a black border.

In the coach, and again at the nightly rest stops in the coaching inns, he avoided conversation with the other passengers. He withdrew into himself.

In this way, excited and at the same time exhausted, he arrived at Zseliz and was immediately gripped by a turbulent atmosphere that banished the melancholy of his journey, if not for long. The count greeted him, and Marie, Karoline, and their younger brother Albert rushed up to him. The countess came out of the house and stood at the top of the flight of stairs. A lackey took charge of his baggage and the castle inspector, Johann Már, undertook to introduce him to all the domestic staff in a noisy and cheerful procession, faces that he could not immediately remember, but which gradually became familiar to him during the following weeks, Anton and Kaspar, the two grooms, Johann, the factor, the ladies' maid Pepi, and the nursery-maid Barbara.

"How d'you do," he nodded. "Pleased to meet you."

He also learned that there were two doctors who were unavailable, and a musician, Herr Fröhlich, who was attending the count.

The girls danced along in front of the inspector and him as they crossed the courtyard to the servants' quarters. He was speaking, to himself:

"Our castle is not as large as some but very prettily built. It is surrounded by a very beautiful garden. I am living in the inspectorate building. All the people around me are thoroughly nice," as he told his friends in Vienna, Schober, Spaun, and Mayrhofer, and he described them in a way that conjured up again the feeling of strangeness that he had had throughout the journey: "The inspector, a Slav, is a good man and makes much of his former musical talents," he wrote, and credited him with "blowing two German dances in three-four time" on the lute. "His son, a philosophy student, just arrived on holiday," he wrote, and added from a great distance a child's wish, "I want him to be my friend." The wife of the inspector "is typical of the sort of women who wish to be called gracious." And so he would persistently address her as "gracious lady," "Your Grace," "Gracious Madam Inspector"—would never abandon the fundamental coolness underlying his high spirits. "The steward is exactly suited to his position, a man with extraordinary insight into his bags and sacks. The doctor is very skilled, and at twenty-four he is as ailing as an old lady," he wrote, and he included his employers in his descriptions: "The count, rather crude, the countess, proud but more sensitive, the countesses, good children." And further on, "I have so far been spared a roasting," by which he was making a play on his position at the bottom table in the servants' hall, and finally, "The cook, rather lax, the ladies' maid, thirty years old, the housemaid, very pretty and often sits next to me, the nanny, a good-hearted old woman, the factor, my rival."

He had already spent two months in Zseliz before he sent this report to his friends, drew for them this distorted genre picture.

On the edge of it appears someone who is unexpectedly described as a rival. It is the factor Johann Röhrer. He enjoys the privilege of living in his own little house in the park and is courting the favors of the very pretty housemaid who, as Schubert wrote, "often sits next to me."

Josefine Pöckelhofer, universally known as Pepi, was promoted to the role of ladies' maid in the year that Schubert came to Zseliz. She was on her way up.

It could be that he first noticed her when he was trying to pull himself together, his problem again being love.

It all began with laughter, while they were playing.

Yet it was as serious for him as it was for her.

"I beg you, Countess Karoline, to play the triplets in the left hand a little more firmly."

He pulls his chair closer to hers and guides her hand. She laughs aloud and puts the fingers that he has just touched to her lips.

"Couldn't we play duets, Herr Schubert? The German dances that you composed recently, and the trios and the country dances?"

"Try them with your sister, countess."

His eyes rest on the the girls' backs, he is hardly listening, and is tempted to pass his hand over the narrower, more childish one. He does not wish to acknowledge the fact, but his dreams, free and unbridled, though they weigh on his conscience, know better: he has fallen in love with the thirteen-year-old child, Countess Karoline. "Look, Herr Schubert, I'm almost there"—and she puts her hand to her hair—"just that much more and I'll be as tall as you."

He pulls a face, as if he has had to swallow a bitter medicine: "Perhaps I shrank in the night."

He likes to see her laugh, clap her hands, throw her arms around Maria's neck. He applies all her actions to himself.

He must not allow himself the luxury of this love.

"I am employed by the count to perfect your technique at the piano, and that of Countess Marie also."

"The way you express yourself, Herr Schubert."

The three of them walk together in the park. Fröhlich, the musician, joins them on the way. He is an old man, who plays the violin as well, or as badly, as he plays the piano. He maintains that in his younger days he composed with great success. He launches straight into a story about a groom who had started an affair with a lady from Gran, on the quiet, of course, when he pretended that he was bringing her firewood for the kitchen stove, which seemed quite innocent to the head of the household, and the two of them grew so brazen that they carried on in broad daylight—Schubert interrupted him in some embarrassment: "Please, Herr Fröhlich, you must not tell that in front of the countesses." Marie, who had been overcome with giggles at the last sentences, broke in firmly here: "Herr Fröhlich often regales us with crude stories like that. He probably tells even worse ones to Papa when they are alone together."

"That's no reason . . ."

Fröhlich shakes his head, feigns agreement with Schubert's misgivings: "Let's leave it there, Herr Schubert, but the countesses are quite used to selecting the parts of my stories that they are allowed to hear."

"Please, Herr Fröhlich, finish the story."

The old musician, embarrassed and thoughtful all of a sudden, takes his leave with a bow: "There is no ending apart from the usual one, murder and death." He turns resolutely on his heel and leaves the girls and their music teacher standing in the shade of a chestnut tree.

"Now you have spoiled it all, Herr Schubert." In the evening, when he can return to the confines of his room, he wrestles with his own feelings. He finds it unthinkable to desire a child, although she is not really much younger than Therese. And although he assumes that she is being deliberately provocative, is aware of her body. He knows that it is absolute madness even to dream of a relationship with the countess. A Schubert from the Himmelpfortgrund and an Esterházy! He lies on his bed and stares at the ceiling, raging at thoughts such as these, and that although he spends half the day making music with the children, their mother, and occasionally with the count himself, and is constantly talking about music, he is incapable of composing. "I'm not worthy of it," he tells himself, striking his head against the end of the bed. Then he changes his mind again, and asks himself, "Why not? Why may a Schubert from the Himmelpfortgrund not declare his love for a Countess Esterházy?" And he realizes immediately how little this gifted, spoiled child knows about him, or wants to know.

In the middle of August a guest arrives who is delighted to make Schubert's acquaintance at last as he has heard Vogl singing his songs, and he himself has a bold tenor voice, or as he would put it, a high baritone. Many who hear him sing maintain that he is "one of the best, perhaps the best Schubert interpreter." Later he will state in proud remembrance, "Schubert liked me, and enjoyed making music with me on many occasions, and he told me repeatedly that from then on he mostly considered only my vocal range for his songs."

Schubert might have put it somewhat differently. Schönstein's voice is the one he hears in any case; it is the same as his own. For this reason it is unnecessary, when the count introduces them, for the baron to refer to their common acquaintances, such as Vogl and Spaun, since they got along together and trusted each other from the beginning. Now, just before Schönstein and Schubert perform at a small soirée to which Esterházy has invited friends and neighbors, they are standing side by side for a moment, Schubert's new friend and the child he loves: Schönstein concentrates, Schubert is already at the piano, and Karoline eagerly turns the pages of the music.

It could be a picture.

There are portraits of both Schönstein and Karoline. Schönstein is a good head taller than Schubert, and remarkably gaunt; his manner is generous, he is a man of the world. His face is narrow, expressive in every feature, and dominated by very bright and ever-watchful eyes. He sports a cavalry moustache on his upper lip, and the curls of his hair frame a high brow and rather hollow temples. When at this moment Karoline looks up at him a smile lights his eyes, a direct and yet strangely melancholy reaction to the glance from the girl. "Won't you be seated, countess," he asks gently.

In the pictures that we have of her, it is remarkable how far apart the eyes are placed, very large eyes separated by an almost coarse nose with a powerful bridge. Thus the gentle face, childlike even in old age, constantly wears a look of amazement that calls for protection.

With studied obedience Karoline goes to join the audience, sitting between the countess and Marie.

What should he play, what should Schönstein sing? Perhaps "Auf dem See" ("On the Lake"), or "Mahomets Gesang" ("Mahomet's Song"), and certainly "Der Liebhaber in allen Gestalten" ("The Lover in All His Guises"):

> I wish I were a fish,
> So nimble and fresh;
> And if you came to catch me,
> I would not fail you . . .

> *Ich wollt' ich wär' ein Fisch,*
> *So hurtig und frisch;*
> *Und kämst du zu angeln,*
> *Ich würde nicht mangeln . . .*

And certainly he would finish with the first of the three songs that he wrote that summer and autumn at Zseliz, a lean harvest that terrifies him. Yet this cantata speaks note by note, bar by bar of what affected him in Zseliz, and what Mayrhofer had enjoined on him, not as prophecy but simply as stimulus: "Give me the Fullness of Solitude," "Give me the Fullness of Bliss"—a song of life.

At the time of Schönstein's arrival in Zseliz, Schubert had already turned to the pretty Pepi in order to banish thoughts of Karoline.

At first in great secrecy. He was afraid that Karoline might be jealous. He was mistaken. The little countess found the rumors of his amorous adventures amusing rather than anything else. She simply was not yet ready to fall in love.

So he courted Josefine all the more resolutely. She was slightly older than he, and quite experienced in her dealings with men. She knew how to look out for herself, but was touched by his attention and wooing—he was, after all, the music teacher to the countesses, and as she had heard from Fröhlich, quite famous in Vienna, certainly an artist.

"He's too short for you."

"He looks like nothing on earth, a shrunken schoolteacher."

"He doesn't know how to flirt."

"He has a soft spot for the Countess Karoline," that much she did know.

In his embarrassment when he chanced to meet Josefine in the park he had kissed her hand and made her ashamed: "That's not proper, Herr Schubert, I'm only a chambermaid, and you"—he took refuge in his shy and dangerous small boy's giggle. She only put up with that for one moment, then she held his mouth shut: "How horrible, when you know how to make such lovely music."

"Yes," he said.

"Do you have a sweetheart in Vienna?" she asked.

"No," he replied.

"But you did have one," she retorted, unrelenting, not so much to hurt him as quite simply to explain away his timid behavior and his strangeness. "And wasn't that painful?"

"No," he said.

"And Countess Karoline?" she knew that she must ask about her in order to reach his feelings. He had to speak of her so that she herself could then speak with him.

"She's a child."

"She plays the piano wonderfully. And you like her so much, don't you, Herr Schubert?"

"Just as much as I like Marie. I like both the countesses. They are my pupils."

She did not give up. With every question she made him a little less inhibited, a little more secure.

"She's noble-born, is Karoline."

"Yes," he replied, "she's Countess Karoline."

Josefine linked her arm through his. "We could . . . ," she thought. "It would be . . . ," he promised. It did not take her long to catch him, to take him down to the meadow, to the barn, to creep into his bed in the dead of night, with the soundless steps of experience.

"I'm your first," she whispered, and on another occasion: "I'm not surprised at anything."

(*Ritardando.* At this point I shall interrupt myself and air my own views. Not to be tactful, but to contradict a rumor that is actually a slander. I am stepping outside the chronological sequence of Schubert's life and anticipating. The meeting with Pepi, this relationship, is supposed to have had consequences. Schubert contracted syphilis. It is not known exactly when this happened, probably toward the end of the year 1822. The course of the "French Disease," which was at that time a fast-spreading and highly contagious sickness, could not be halted before the discovery of penicillin. In the hospitals the sufferers were treated with mercury, or to be more exact, they were poisoned. The illness develops in three phases. A few weeks after the initial contact, sores develop on the sex organ—Moritz von Schwind calls them in a letter "the rash"—and the lymph glands swell. All these phenomena disappear, and the patient appears to be cured, but twelve weeks later the same symptoms recur in a more acute form, the swellings discharge, the patient feels wretched and exhausted, and his hair begins to fall out. This is the con-

119

dition described by the doctors as "lues." At this stage again there is spontaneous recovery and apparent cure. In a further three, or maybe even thirty years, the disease enters its final and terminal phase, that of progressive paralysis. The patient is gradually consumed from within— tissue, nerves, liver, heart, and last but not least, the brain as well. Schubert was spared all this. He left Josefine, his courageous beloved, for the space of one summer, with his health intact, and remained so for more than four years. Six years later they would meet again in Zseliz. At this point, however, he intends to press that other suit which he had not dared in that first summer, even though it is to experience the pain which he had been spared with Josefine's assistance.)

Schönstein reminded him of his duties, recalling him to music. "I beg of you, dear Herr Schubert, do not abandon us. You are our orchestra and our conductor all in one." He sang arias by Mozart and Rossini with Marie, whose soprano voice was becoming ever more strong and clear.

The countess, who seldom missed one of these impromptu concerts, encouraged them to marshal all the available musical forces in the house and to perform larger-scale works, Haydn's *Creation* and *Seasons*, and also Mozart's *Requiem*, of which she was particularly fond, and in which she sang, adopting a pose as if she were the countess in *Figaro*, sorrowing for her wasted life.

Now he goes walking on his own whenever he gets the chance, going farther afield, often following the course of the Gran, which winds along in its narrow bed until it joins the Waag. He wanders from summer into autumn, but cannot shake off his melancholy which stifles him, almost silencing him. He recites the names of the three women, Therese, Karoline, Josefine, as if he were making a sort of litany of them to break the bonds with which they constrict his thoughts. Only in moments when he is very tired do his eyes widen to take in the surrounding scenery, a group of trees on the distant horizon, the trellis-work of tall grasses and flowers between the path and the stream, farmers working in the fields, and the black wall of clouds building up over the darkening green of the forest.

Schönstein departs. He will bear greetings to all the friends, in particular Vogl, with whom he will be singing Schubert's duets. "Look, my friend, you will never, ever, be able to escape from us."

He stands in the doorway of the inspectorate building and watches the count's family taking leave of Schönstein. Karoline throws her arms round his neck. "She still looks rather like an ugly little duckling," as Schönstein confided to him quite casually and innocently one day. "But the beautiful swan can be imagined. Don't you agree?"

In his embarrassment he had not replied.

When the coach drove past the servants' quarters he waved to her.

The days grow shorter. Pepi still comes to visit him. Their lovemaking is silent, cautious, and almost as if it were already a memory.

"When are you going?"

"In November, with the count's family."

"Soon," she said.

The house is freezing. The heating stoves are not all lit.

"Will you come back next summer?"

"I don't know."

"Might you?"

"I doubt it."

She is walking along the edge of the drive, as if by coincidence, when the two coaches depart through the gates in the direction of Gran. The previous night she has bidden him a lingering farewell. "Look, there's Pepi," remarks the count in surprise.

"She wants to wave him goodbye," says Marie.

"Who?" asks the countess.

Karoline replies instead of Marie: "Us."

At long last—after the countess had chided him for his silence and he had virtually flown into a sunset at a stopping place by the Danube—he managed to fulfill the count's wish and to compose a song for him. He had been carrying the poem around with him for quite a time. It had just not begun to sing.

Quite the contrary—he had been struggling against its images. Now they opened up.

O Sun, ray from God, you are never
So magnificent as when you flee.
You would love to draw us after you,
To the fount of your glory.

O, Sonne, Gottes Strahl, du bist
Nie herrlicher, als im Entfliehen,
Du willst uns gern hinüberziehen
Wo deines Glanzes Urquell ist.

He dated the manuscript "November 1818." And for place he wrote, as if to sum up the months spent at the Castle: "Zseliz." The count thanked him for the gift. He would invite him and Schönstein to visit him soon in Vienna, and they must perform it for him. He later gave the sheets to Karoline, and she kept them all her life.

To the count's question as to where he would be living and could be contacted, he could not answer. "Perhaps at my parents' house, or with Herr von Schober."

"You can live a free life, Herr Schubert."

He said nothing. This freedom, however crazy it might sound, could become a sort of prison. It admitted him, and would not let him leave. Only in October Ignaz had written him a letter expressing his envy and admiration: "You lucky man! How I envy your lot! You are living a life of sweet golden freedom, you can give free rein to your musical genius, you can cast your thoughts wherever you wish, you are loved, admired, revered, whereas the rest of us must put up with all the brutality of undisciplined youths like the wretched school donkey, subject to a quantity of abuse, and what is more, we must humbly submit to an ungrateful public and to idiotic bosses. You will be amazed when I tell you that things have reached such a pass in our house that no one even dares to laugh if I tell a silly story about superstition from my religion class."

No, he would not go back to the Roßau schoolhouse for all the world. He is lucky. In Vienna a servant of the Esterházy family hands him a note from Mayrhofer. He is waiting for him in the Inner City, in house No. 147, on the third floor.

He moves in there. "Good evening, dearest friend."

"How was the summer?"

"Like any summer spent in a castle. You must know."

"I don't know, Franz."

19

Moment musical no. 6
(Rather fast)

O nce upon a time there were two brothers, Franz and Ferdinand. They were both teachers, both instrumental- ists, both played music, and both composed. But their talents were unevenly divided. Franz heard the most beautiful melodies in his head day and night, while Ferdinand had to slave over every bar. He considered this unjust. So he began to steal his brother's music. He did this in the strangest of ways. He promised the school where he was employed—it was called by the sad name of "Orphanage School"—a "German Requiem Mass" for an anniversary. Then without delay he asked his brother to compose such a piece. He would see that it was performed at the school as his donation. Franz was at this time work- ing as music teacher for a count in Hungary, and his musical output was, to his chagrin, not as great as it might have been. Nevertheless, he immediately set to work, and within a few days he sent the Mass to his brother. He was overjoyed, and performed it, but under his own name. This was not the last time that he enriched himself in this way. But the borrowed glory weighed so heavily on his conscience that he confessed the substitution to his brother. He expected a rebuke and a scolding, and was all the more amazed at the self-assurance of his younger brother: "The sin of appropriation was forgiven you in the first letter. . . . The Requiem Mass pleased you, you shed tears over it, maybe over the same word as I did. My dear brother, that is the great- est recompense I can receive for this gift, and I will hear of no other."

And since his fraternal cupidity has been blessed in this way, Ferdinand, the older brother, immediately follows it up with a further request. He desires something that is closely connected with a triumph on the part of the younger brother. The one large gift that his father had ever made him: a five-octave piano. He had received it following his first Mass, which had been performed in the church where his parents were married. Now Ferdinand writes boldly to Franz. "One more thing: My fortepiano has been sold, and I would like to take over yours. If you agree, name a price, and payment in cash will follow." Once again the younger brother surprises the older with his generosity, which one might almost consider indifference: "Do take over my fortepiano, I should be pleased. . . . But I do not like the way you always speak of payment, recompense, and gratitude to a brother— that's disgusting!" and Ferdinand reads the sentences out loud when he receives this letter from his brother, as if he could punish himself with them. He still has no idea that he will eventually have to take his younger brother in for charity's sake. And at that stage he will be writing music of a kind that he can no longer pretend is his.

20

Mayrhofer

*H*e hoped to be creatively stimulated by Mayrhofer, despite his innately inhospitable manner, and he finds the opposite. Mayrhofer is in a black mood, although, as he continually assures Schubert, he is pleased to have him stay. And his father issues a summons.

It is snowing and raining all at the same time. The rows of houses huddle together, shivering. He goes on foot. Mayrhofer had offered to order a cab for him. "You'll have turned into an icicle before you get to Roßau."

"That's what Father wants."

"You're a pessimist, Schubert."

"What about you, Mayrhofer?"

They exchange their moods of gloom and part, laughing. "Goodbye. Don't let them hurt you, Schubert."

He views the city through the eyes of a *flâneur*, cast out by the Hungarian summer. The city rejects him. How far removed he is from both, from Zseliz and from Vienna.

The facades of the buildings in the whirling snow seem even taller and more menacing.

He will have to have a fight with his father. The old man will be incensed that he has not returned to Roßau, but has moved in with Mayrhofer—without giving prior notice of his intention.

Ignaz catches him outside the house. "Be careful with him. I beg of you, Franz." He puts his arm round his brother's shoulder as if he wanted to tame him with friendliness. They enter the house together. As always when disagreements lie ahead, he assumes an attitude of indifference. "It's really all the same to me, Ignaz," he says, and shrinks down under the arm of his brother.

Therese once accused him of not actually possessing any "real feelings." When he asked her, in amazement, how she came to have that idea, she answered him in embarrassment: "Perhaps you need all your feelings for your music, and there are none left over for me."

His father greets him in a surprisingly amicable fashion. "Why didn't you come and see us straight away, Franz? We were expecting you. I had assumed that you would want to come back and live in the schoolhouse. You surprised me with Herr von Mayrhofer."

He sits down on a school bench, pushes the frame of his glasses up against his temples with the palms of his hands, and looks out the window at the courtyard.

"I got used to being independent in Zseliz, to being able to compose as I please, Father."

"You could have had that time to yourself here, too."

"But I need not have a teaching obligation any longer."

"I must ask you yet again, Franz, how you are going to support yourself."

"I have savings left from the summer, and I am composing a singspiel. Herr Vogl is going to arrange for it to be performed at the Kärntnertor Theater."

"Even if that is the case, Franz, it just seems like castles in the air to me."

He recognizes the tone colors, can attune himself to the volume of sound. This crescendo might lead to force, and he cowers down as a precaution.

"I don't know what better I can do, Father."

"But I do. I have made arrangements for you." The father runs to his desk. Anger speeds his steps so much that he has to continually slow down, applying the brakes. To make matters worse, he cannot immediately find what he is looking for in the drawer. Finally he pulls out a sheet of paper and casts a fleeting eye over it. "I applied to the school authorities to reinstate you as a teacher."

Schubert faces the man who suddenly looks oversize, the man who is his father, whom he has often made music with and whom he loves, when he permits him to do so. He is silent, waiting.

"You should add your signature, Franz." Now the paternal voice has adopted an almost pleading note, but the undertone of menace remains.

He had often sat or stood like this, waiting, anticipating the punishment, the shouting, and the beating, an anticipation that did help, as he noted with satisfaction each time when the storm had passed. It's all the same to me. It will pass. I can leave. I can leave the house.

"I will not sign, Father, it would be contrary to my plans. If I have to become a teacher again I will go under."

"You'll go under in a different way. I swear you will. I can see it coming." He is already standing over him. Schubert hurriedly takes off his glasses, raising his hands to protect his head, because he remembers how his father strikes, first at the back, then in blind rage, at the protective hands, and at the head. He does not want to hear what he is shouting, all the names he is being called. No sooner has the old man finished with him than he dodges out of the bench, runs to the door, turning in farewell. "You know where I am staying, Father, and with whom."

Once more he hears the curse that he should never again show his face in this house, and again the shadow of his second mother brushes past him: "Don't hold it against him, Franz!" Once more he breathes in the smell of the schoolhouse, and asks himself why, when it revolts him to the point of nausea, he should still be addicted to it.

Mayrhofer had welcomed him in an excited and effusive manner, talking endlessly and enlarging the little room in which they would both be living, with his gesticulating hands, into a salon. It had seen better days, its wallpaper was hanging down in strips, its bookshelves threatened to break, and its piano, when he ran his hand over the keys, was hardly stimulating. This is echoed in Mayrhofer's words: "Both house and room showed evidence of the passing years: the ceiling had sunk somewhat, the light was restricted by a large building opposite, there were an outworn piano and a narrow bookshelf. . . ."

The landlady, Frau Sanssouci, "Gracious Lady," who has humorously gone along with Mayrhofer's mood of stormy enthusiasm, is prepared for Schubert to work in the mornings. He will not disturb her if he uses the piano.

"I will not need to use it so often."

"But you compose, don't you?"

"For just that reason, dear Madame Sanssouci."

Such verbal exchanges are just what Mayrhofer likes. Could she offer him a welcoming cup of coffee?

He would be very grateful.

From experience he notices how his feelings relax, how he is impervious to pain for a short while. He must wait and see, test out how it will be, living with Mayrhofer. He is a friend of his, he reads the poems that he writes as letters addressed to himself personally, but he does not know much about Mayrhofer. He has some idea of his idiosyncrasies and is a little fearful of the timidity that makes him seem almost invisible in society, and of his bouts of melancholy that appear to cripple him. On the other hand, he can also be cheerful and overpoweringly affectionate.

"You're a bit like Mr. Punch, Mayrhofer."

"D'you think so?"

"Take a look in the mirror. The long, thin nose, the bony face, the button eyes. But the regular Mr. Punch doesn't have the demonic nature."

"Which I have?"

"You know you do, dear friend. Sit down and write a poem so that I can compose."

They throw their arms around each other, hold the other close, rest their foreheads together.

Maybe he has never before felt moments of being so well cared for, and thus he is all the more fearful that they will soon be frittered away.

"We mustn't go to extremes in our little room, Mayrhofer, otherwise the walls may cave in, or we shall get on each other's nerves." Mayrhofer, on the other hand, seems to be intent on these points of contact, he begins to play with proximity and distance.

"You pimp."

"You prick."

"You shrimp, fatso."

"You clown."

They have organized their day strictly. Schubert's appetite for work and Mayrhofer's sense of duty are in league here. Mayrhofer leaves the room in the morning with a "Goodbye," once in a while putting out a poem for Schubert, or a book that he had been reading: "I have to go to the office, my auditing office."

Schubert will compose into the early afternoon, without making much use of the piano, but sitting at the table, leaning forward, tapping the beat with his fingers, as if glued to his chair, only pacing up and down when he breaks his train of thought.

During the afternoon he keeps appointments, writes letters, lies down, sometimes sleeping until Mayrhofer wakes him.

They go out almost every evening, to an inn, to a private reception, to a concert, to the theater. Schubert is often invited by Vogl. New friends seem to appear of their own accord, and old ones fall by the wayside as they leave Vienna. Anselm Hüttenbrenner is working this year, 1819, at the local government office in Graz, but Josef, his brother, is living in Vienna for the time being and finds a room during the course of the year in the Wipplingerstraße one floor below Mayrhofer and Schubert.

When they get home, often late at night or in the early morning, drunk, their heads buzzing with conversations whose course and drift they have already forgotten, they throw themselves down, fully clothed, on their beds, leave the lamp unlit, and stare into the darkness, talking to each other in ever shorter breaths, unburdening themselves about others, their love affairs, and their lives. But not about themselves.

They whip up their feelings with whole sentences. Individual words act like soothing hands, protecting and stroking.

At some point, but not in the first few weeks, Mayrhofer creeps across the room, remains standing by Schubert's bed, waiting for a word from his friend, who stays silent, stiff as a board, holding his breath, thinking no thoughts, until Mayrhofer retreats, step by step:

"Schubert?"

"Yes."

"Didn't you notice anything?"

"No."

"You're lying."

"Yes."

"Why?"

"For your sake."

"Pal."

"Be quiet, Mayrhofer."

They both lie down again and feel how their thoughts are touching, craving, and fearful at the same time, because they want more than they will permit themselves at this time, how they both give up, almost with the same breath, how they are overcome with a melancholy that excludes everything but the trembling, helpless self. In the morning, before Mayrhofer leaves the room, letting the door fall shut behind him with an intentionally loud bang, he positions himself beside Schubert, looking down at him. The first time he did this he was completely amazed: "Do you sleep with your glasses on?"

"What?" Schubert feels over his face with his hand. "Yes, I sleep with my glasses."

"Don't you notice them?"

"Yes, I do. I can see better when I'm dreaming."

Mayrhofer sits down, laughing, on the edge of the bed. "Look, you're not just a great composer, but a notable philosopher into the bargain."

Schubert sits up, a child who has not slept enough, fighting off the day: "And you, Mayrhofer, you're not just an efficient auditor and a gifted poet, but also a dear friend."

And by the next day he could be disputing this. There they are, fighting like two old washerwomen, bickering and scuffling, and

Schubert, undoubtedly the stronger of the two, frequently hits hard at his friend.

In the first months he is unable to compose a setting for even one of the poems with which Mayrhofer presents him. Vogl is pressing him to complete his singspiel, a farce with the title *Die Zwillingsbrüder (The Twin Brothers)*, which he does not find particularly inspiring. The barren period at Zseliz is still making itself felt.

"What's worrying you, Mayrhofer?"

"That you're giving Vogl preferential treatment. Are you serious about that?"

"No, of course not."

Feeling awkward, they grasp for each other's hands, timidly at first, and begin to dance around in a circle like children, finally crashing about, giggling and laughing: "Now if only someone could play for us, Franz! But even you can't dance and play the piano at the same time, can you?"

"Hang on, Mayrhofer."

"Usually you just tuck yourself away behind the piano."

"And you, Mayrhofer, disappear into a dark corner."

The noise had alerted Frau Sanssouci, who would like to know what was amusing the two gentlemen. They ask her in, to take a seat and watch their show which they had just interrupted for a moment.

"Because we were out of breath."

Then they set themselves revolving again, a long thin bear and a short fat one.

Just like children! Madame Sanssouci claps her hands, but she's not quite sure if these two old boys aren't acting a bit inappropriately.

None of Schubert's songs has yet appeared in print. The manuscripts begin to make their way round the city.

Franz Jäger, a tenor at the Theater an der Wien, pays him a visit accompanied by Vogl, and persuades him to set "Schäfers Klagelied" ("Shepherd's Lament") by Goethe in a new arrangement for him. It is one of those songs that he had set at the schoolhouse at Himmel-pfortgrund, and which Spaun had sent to Goethe. He didn't wait to be asked twice.

For the first time one of his songs is performed at a public concert, and receives critical discussion. "A beautiful composition, sung with depth of feeling by the delightful voice of Herr Jäger."

While he is sitting in the concert hall listening to Jäger, he remembers the table at which he sat on the previous occasion, on November 30, 1814, and the rush of emotion that shot through him as the shepherd halted at the top of the mountain and looked down into the valley, from which his love was departing. He remembers how he felt the urge to hurry through the key modulations, from C minor to E-flat major, and then through A-flat major, A-flat minor, C-flat major back to E-flat major.

Out into the distant land, and beyond,
Perhaps even over the sea.
Onward, sheep, move onward!
The shepherd is so wretched.

Hinaus in das Land und weiter,
Vielleicht gar über die See.
Vorüber ihr Schafe vorüber!
Dem Schäfer ist gar so weh.

He read, and what he was reading was already singing in his head. Now, in the "Roman Emperor," listening to his song, he notices that in the last verse he inserted one extra word, which, so he thinks, belongs there because the inner rhythm of the song demands it: "Onward, sheep, only move *ever* onward!" ("Vorüber ihr Schafe, *nur* vorüber!")

(*Ritardando*. I think that he might have thought like this. Just one "only." A few letters that, when placed here, make the phrase more bitter and more emphatic. Here is the Wanderer at an early stage hastening over the horizon.

133

Further, then, only further
My trusty walking staff.

Nur weiter denn, nur weiter,
Mein treuer Wanderstab.

The shepherd's crook becomes the walking staff. Even at that stage, the seventeen-year-old had changed Goethe's line by two syllables, expanding it. Again a few more letters that imperceptibly assume dedication and power.

Up there on the top of that hill
I have stood a thousand times,
Leaning on my staff,
And looking down into the valley.

Da droben auf jenem Berge
Da steh' ich tausendmal,
An meinem Stabe gebogen
Und schaue hinab in das Tal.

He set the line as "Leaning *over* on my staff" ["An meinem Stabe *hin*gebogen"]. This was certainly not just because the rhythm dictated it.)

There has been more and more talk of "the prince," and not just since Schubert has been living with Mayrhofer. In fact, recently "the prince" has been turning up in all their conversations, an evil spirit inciting conflict between them. "Shit on the prince."

"Will you be quiet, you daft musician. What on earth d'you know about it."

"Only the mischief that the prince makes."

"You know nothing at all."

"I can tell by looking at you, Mayrhofer, he's destroying you, he's chewing you to pieces, your prince."

"He's my master, Schubert."

"Leave his service, then."

Mayrhofer jumps to his feet, runs to the piano, opens his mouth to speak, gasps for breath, shakes his head in despair, grabs his jacket from the peg, looks questioningly at Schubert, who has been aware for some time how meanly he is behaving toward his dutiful friend, and storms from the room.

Schubert runs after him. "I went too far." Mayrhofer tries to shake him off. "You have no idea."

"I"—and Schubert puts his arm around his friend's shoulders so that he feels it like a support, "I understand you better than you think, Mayrhofer."

At night, lying side by side, they conjure up the two spheres in which they have to live, or exist, or vegetate, in the one sphere drawing deep breaths, boldly playing out their hopes and fantasies, in the other holding their breath, almost suffocating, while obediently subservient to the call of duty.

"That's not the way for you, Franz."

"No, my dear friend Mayrhofer, I have my freedom, so my brother Ignaz tells me. I can live in freedom. But please, dear friend, I didn't really cry out, I'll do as I'm told, but I just want to quietly ask the dark of night, and you in the darkness, what good does my freedom do me."

"Just that you can use it, Franz, that you use it."

That year spring made slow progress in claiming the city, as if it doubted its ability to fight off the powers of winter.

Sufficient opportunities occur for Schubert to make him forget the frost. One of the students, who had taken part in the performance of *Prometheus* at Watteroth's house, appears, uninvited and yet expected, with an invitation: His father, Professor Ignaz Sonnleithner, liked the cantata very much and wants to sing the title role himself.

Schubert had heard of the musical evenings in the Gundelhof. Sonnleithner, who taught commercial law at the university, and was a lawyer popular with the citizens of Vienna, put on soirées every Friday evening with friends and musicians whom he invited to his house. In his heart of hearts, Schubert had been expecting an invitation. He was to play the orchestral part on the piano.

Mayrhofer was annoyed that he could not come. Josef Hüttenbrenner, on the other hand, could crow, he could already tell of the Gundelhof circle, and he would be singing in the little choir.

From then on, Friday evenings are spoken for. Schubert arranges for Mayrhofer to be invited. The renowned and honored Vogl is of course welcome in any musical circle.

Now that Schubert is gaining greater attention, Mayrhofer is concerned about his external appearance, making sure that he does not arrive in dirty clothes, and that he has washed and shaved beforehand.

Sonnleithner cannot understand why no publishing house has accepted his songs. Probably Schubert has not paid enough attention to this.

"Why should I waste my time on these cut-throats, Herr Professor."

So Sonnleithner himself sets about finding a publisher. He succeeds in interesting Diabelli. To be sure, he and a few friends would have to put up some of the costs, fully forty percent.

The new friends do not cause him to forget the old ones. The circle expands, assuming the form of a protective ring. Within it, and only in this arena, can life be lived. It may be in Vienna, or it may be elsewhere. The protective ring goes with him.

"You are a rogue, a real rogue!!!" he writes to Anselm Hüttenbrenner in May 1819. "It will be ten years till you're back in Vienna. First this girl, then that girl catches his eye! The devil take all the girls if you go and get yourself bewitched by any of them. Get married, for goodness sake, and that's the end of the matter. Of course, you could say, like Caesar, that you'd rather be first in Graz than second in Vienna. Whatever it is, I'm hopping mad that you're not here."

Anselm Hüttenbrenner will only act on this cheerfully pressing summons some months later. Duty requires his presence in Graz.

And Mayrhofer's attention seems to be completely claimed by his inexorable master, Prince Metternich. His poetry becomes ever darker. Schubert took one of the most inconsolable poems, as soon as Mayrhofer had written it, and continued it in F minor—"slowly":

Bury me there in the forest, in the forest,
Silently, with no cross or headstone:

For whatever you may build will be covered
With snow, and edged by winter.

Im Wald, im Wald da grabt mich ein,
Ganz stille, ohne Kreuz und Stein:
Denn was ihr türmet, überschneit,
Und überrindet Winterszeit.

Vogl sang the song to Mayrhofer as soon as it was ready, and he sat
with his head in his hands as if he were listening to his own epitaph.

"How can I escape him?" he sighed.

"My dear friend, you are alive."

"I'm not speaking of death, but of the prince. The prince. The
prince!" Schubert threw his arms wide in a theatrical gesture and
skipped round the room, then dropped them to his sides as if they had
grown too heavy for him.

"Come on, we're invited by Senn. I don't want to keep him waiting. We haven't seen each other for ages."

Summer took over in the little room. Schubert got up even earlier
in order to have at least one or two hours in which to work without
struggling for breath or breaking out into a sweat.

More and more they got on each other's nerves. They screamed at
each other, and came to blows until Frau Sanssouci would come storming into the room to calm down the two overwrought men.

Vogl rescued him, and presumably Mayrhofer too. He invited
Schubert to go with him to Steyr, his birthplace, where he spent his
holidays from the opera every year.

"Stay, Schubert."

"It will do us good to separate for a few weeks."

"What shall I do without you?"

"Write poems, Mayrhofer, and when I get back I'll set them to music."

They exchange a kiss in farewell.

Mayrhofer has to go to his office. Schubert waits for Vogl to pick
him up.

"Goodbye, dear fellow."

He breathes a sigh of relief. This summer he does not have to go to the castle, and is not assigned to the bottom table, he is permitted to be the equal of his hosts.

Steyr rises like a living backdrop to the River Enns, projecting its main square like a stage between the bright, handsome rows of houses, and the friends go out walking often enough. "The area around Steyr is beautiful beyond all measure," and they stop to rest on the fringes of the woods, groups of excursionists who blend their many colors like voices in concert, the soft with the loud, the light with the dark, they wander along the banks of the river, and celebrate the daytime and the approach of night in the gardens of inns lit by lanterns.

First he must cope with the turbulent reception. Scarcely had they arrived in Steyr, and had he settled into his room in the house of the mining lawyer Schellmann on the main square, at the side of the stage, than there was one thunderstorm after another. The world threatened to go under, the heavens spat fire. In his fear he fled, seeking the company of other people, playing the battered child to the amusement of all.

"Up till now I have felt very well," he writes on July 13, 1819, to Ferdinand, "only the weather is not favorable. On the twelfth, yesterday, there was a very bad thunderstorm, right over Steyr, which killed a girl and paralyzed two men in the arms. In the house where I am living there are eight girls, almost all of them pretty. You can see how one is kept busy. The daughter of Herr von K[oller], at whose house Vogl and I eat each day, is very pretty, plays the piano nicely, and will be singing various songs of mine."

Eight girls, and another one who sings his songs—in a sentence and a half he creates a charming picture, of himself and his life that summer, which should not be only for his brother. That he could be a much-loving and much-loved cavalier remains, in any case, a matter for conjecture, to be postulated or promptly retracted as fancy takes. He no longer asks after Therese. He permits himself, now and then, a fond memory of Karoline, the child at the castle, like a glance at a hidden medallion.

He does not have to feign lightheartedness. No one makes a lackey of him. At most they expect him to make music with them and to converse with them, if not in harmony with their thinking, then at least in harmony with their moods.

For Vogl's fifty-first birthday, Stadler, his friend from the Konvikt School, writes a cantata that Schubert sets to music, and the celebration in Koller's house pleases and touches them all. Josefine von Koller sings the soprano part, a singer from Steyr takes the bass, and Schubert himself sings tenor.

> You singer, who sings from the heart,
> And directs the word to the heart.

> *Sänger, der vom Herzen singet*
> *Und das Wort zum Herzen bringet.*

Schubert offers his thanks to his famous friend and patron, but not without some cunning. The "singer" is addressed in powerful tones of pathos, in which elements of admiration and a certain distant stance combine as if of themselves.

From Steyr they journey on to Linz and Salzburg. He visits old friends from the Konvikt days, Kenner and Kreil, and especially the Spaun family.

He arrives and he leaves again, replete with images of the landscape. Vogl is borne along on the tide of his euphoria.

Only with Spaun does he have a momentary clash. In Karlsbad the representatives of the European rulers had met and decided, under the influence of Metternich, to introduce the strictest censorship, and to dissolve all student associations forthwith.

Spaun considers the measures ruthless, but necessary.

"You will never be able to convince me, Spaun, least of all with such reasons of state. These are alien to poetry and music."

"You mustn't worry your head about us, Schubert."

"Well, isn't it possible, Spaun, that without my help and your worrying, our halfway friendly world will grow dark and we will be allowed to be nothing but lemures obedient to the state?"

"I beg of you, Schubert. This is not the man I know."

There is utmost tension between them, and they resolve to speak only of everyday matters. About Schubert's experiences in Steyr, and his new works. And Spaun lets him know that he will soon be moving back to Vienna. After the conversation Schubert feels shattered. He could not rely on any of his friends so much as on Spaun. He bade Vogl wait. He wouldn't be long. He had forgotten something in Spaun's house. Spaun immediately understood why Schubert had turned around, and it brought tears to his eyes.

"My friend."

"Don't take my sharp words to heart."

"I would never have done that."

Relieved, he sets off at a run, after Vogl. They still reach the coach for Steyr in good time.

After this, thoughts of Mayrhofer will not leave him alone. He must write to him immediately. "If you are as well as I am, then you must be really healthy," and concludes: "Farewell, now, until the middle of September."

He still has one month left. It is certainly no coincidence that in the piano lessons he gives Josefine von Koller, and which her father and Vogl sometimes attend as guests, he repeatedly comes back to Beethoven and his sonatas, and he remembers with a wave of shame how at the Konvikt, or shortly afterward, he had turned away from Beethoven's music, and had even mocked the master in a letter. Now, in this cheerful place, it is easy for him to renew his admiration, to express it quite casually, and to be certain that he has won his musical independence from Beethoven.

In order that Josefine may have a new composition to practice, but also as a result of this newfound self-confidence, he writes the Sonata in A major, straight out, and sets his audience in transports of amazement and delight when he first plays it to them. The theme of the first movement, allegro moderato, encapsulates the joy of these summer days in the way it gently sings.

A friend and neighbor of his hosts in Steyr, Sylvester Paumgartner, who plays the cello after a fashion, encourages him during a soirée he has given in Schubert's honor to compose a quintet with variations on his marvelous song "The Trout." The spark instantly took fire. He only took a few days to compose it, and caused embarrassment to the patron who gave him this commission—he was not up to playing the cello part.

"Don't keep me waiting," Mayrhofer had written to him.

The prince!

The prince!

Mayrhofer welcomes him, his mood as gray as Vienna in October. He is now the prince's appointed book censor. "I, Schubert, I for whom poetry is a holy cause, I can strike out sentences, make rubbish of words and ideas, I can destroy the life of a book, stifle it, murder it, Schubert, it is I, Johannes Mayrhofer, the poet and the censor. D'you know who you're speaking to, whose arm you've got around your shoulders, who's going with you to the 'Crown'? D'you know if it's the censor or the poet?" He takes a position facing Schubert, a wretched actor, his arms flapping loosely at his sides.

"Don't make a fool of yourself, please, Mayrhofer."

"*I* make a fool of myself?" He raises his voice. Passersby on the street notice him. "I am being made a fool of, Schubert. You know it." He tears at Schubert's jacket. Only when the other friends, Stadler and Senn, join them does he calm down, and is cut down to size, a little man scurrying about, the prince's censor. And the prince is no longer alone. He is joined by "the count"—Count Sedlnitzky, the police chief of Vienna.

Senn speaks of him, and Mayrhofer immediately interrupts.

"If you only knew all the terrible things I know about the count," but he keeps his knowledge to himself.

Since the meeting in Karlsbad, his police have been stalking the students as if they were stray dogs.

"Perhaps that's what we are," Senn thinks.

Schubert has the impression that the tall, powerful man is radiant, that he emits a great strength. He admires Johannes Senn, but nevertheless he avoids him whenever he possibly can. This was the case even at the Konvikt School. Senn was expressly called the "Tyrolean" by his fellow Konvikt students, and not without an element of mockery that was aimed at Senn's stubbornness and arrogant behavior.

When a Konvikt pupil was punished by Director Lang with an unconscionably long period of solitary confinement, a small group grew restive and tried to stand by the wrongdoer with Senn as its eloquent leader. Schubert had kept himself in the background. Not only that, he disliked rebellion, and he feared that taking sides in any way might jeopardize his position at the Konvikt. Although he had urgent need of his scholarship and was a brilliant pupil, Senn had to leave the Konvikt. He left highly pleased with himself. Schubert did not forget him, soon met with him again, and was now freer in his relations with him. Senn had lost none of his liberalism or his quick-tempered sense of justice. He was now studying law. Metternich's policies presented him with a new challenge. But this did not prevent him from being friendly with Spaun, whose decency was beyond dispute, although he took the prince's side.

Senn had founded a student group whose members were mostly from the Tyrol. Schubert avoided the conspiratorial meetings, but still became involved, though unwillingly, in the web of subversion and persecution.

"I must not take note of what Senn says, I really mustn't."

On the way home, after they had taken leave of Senn and Stadler, Mayrhofer held his hands over his ears, and leapt from one side of the narrow street to the other with such violent and furious movements that the impression seemed to come into Schubert's mind unaided that he was dividing, splitting in two. He called out again and again, "What the one hears, the other must keep silent about."

On the first few nights after his return from Steyr, Schubert had lain down beside Mayrhofer, then when the other had fallen asleep, he got up quietly and slipped into his own bed.

On moonlit nights
My heart has learned
Not to dispute fate.

In monderhellten Nächten
Mit dem Geschick zu rechten
Hat diese Brust verlernt.

He sang it to him.

The prince. The prince!

Senn had invited him over to his apartment. "I beg of you, if you possibly can, leave your Mayrhofer behind. Before he mopes and moans and spoils all our fun."

The prince. The prince!

But it is the count who sends out his henchmen.

Senn was alone when Schubert arrived. The other guests, two fellow students, only arrived later.

Senn is undemonstrative when talking. In hesitant phrases, and stopping often in long pauses for breath, he expresses his opinion of Schubert's Goethe songs. The few that he knows appeal to him because the music takes itself as seriously as the poetry. "You are taking liberties with Goethe. . . ."

"I am?" Schubert puts down his wine glass in astonishment.

"It's all right, I'm exaggerating as usual."

Afterward, as he told Mayrhofer later, they talked of Stadler and Kenner. Senn had wanted to know if he was still studying counterpoint with Salieri.

Suddenly there was a furious knocking at the door.

It was a drum-roll. That is how messengers from the count announce their presence. Senn jumps with the shock and freezes, but only for a moment.

Schubert leaps up, holding his glass in his hand as if he were drinking a toast to the men bursting into the room. "I should be singing," flashes through his mind. But he cannot think of anything, not a line or a tune. When they are all four of them standing in the room, three in uniform and one in civilian dress, he is humming "The Trout" to himself. Why that song in particular? It occurs to him that Schubart spent ten years locked in a prison.

The civilian introduces himself as Chief Commissioner of Police

Leopold von Ferstl. They had orders to search the apartment of Johann Senn for subversive papers.

"What do you mean by that?" asks Senn, and with theatrical gestures allocates to the three policemen their areas of search. "You take the desk. You the wardrobe. You the bed. The chief commissioner might perhaps explore the gaps in the floorboards. Who knows what I might have hidden there."

He will be fined for all of that. "If you say so, Commissioner."

Eventually, out of breath and upset, Senn's two fellow students arrive. They had already heard downstairs of the raid.

Like Senn and Schubert before them, they have to show their papers.

"What is the chief commissioner investigating?" they ask with feigned gravity. Senn raises his shoulders in a quizzical shrug. His eyes are dark with rage.

"Perhaps they're looking for one of yesterday's farts," says one.

"Or the imprint of two conspiratorial butts," suggests the other.

"The police don't bother me at all," declares Senn, and invites his friends to be seated at the table, pouring wine for them and for himself. They clink their glasses in a toast, and begin a conversation as if the visit from the police were not taking place.

The commissioner stands in the room and seems to be at loose ends.

The three policemen rummage listlessly through shirts, pillows, and papers. Looking for papers.

"I don't understand it." Schubert is amazed. He manages to talk. "The liberties they can take. Without a by-your-leave—" he looks for an expression that is even halfway polite. Senn completes it with a laugh: "On the trail of a fart."

"And on orders from on high."

The prince. The prince! Mayrhofer's voice screams in his head.

It's enough. The commissioner does not need to issue any instructions to his men. Being excellently trained, they know what they have to do. They seize hold of Senn. He must accompany them to the station, he is under arrest, and the other three gentlemen will please follow them.

"I've been locked up," is the first thing he can think of saying to

Mayrhofer, who has been anxiously waiting for him. "With Senn and two others." He tells his story, can hardly stop, repeating himself and flying into a rage. "These goons, I'm telling you, Mayrhofer."

"You said it, Schubert!"

Leopold von Ferstl reported to Count Sedlnitzky:

"Report . . . on the obstinate and insulting behavior which one Johann Senn, born in Pfunds in the Tyrol, arrested with other members of the student corporations, displayed during an examination and confiscation of his papers carried out according to regulations, in the course of which he permitted himself the following expression, among others, that *he did not have to pay attention to the police, for the government was too stupid to penetrate his secrets.*' At the same time the friends who were found in his company expressed themselves in a similar tone and interfered with the officers in the execution of their duty by railing at them with verbal abuse and insults." Senn was removed from sight by the prince's thugs, forcibly separated from his friends. He sat in detention for fourteen months. Then he was exiled to the Tyrol.

Schubert and he never saw each other again.

Schubert's name disappeared from the files, as he had hoped.

Music, his music, became his cloak of invisibility.

"Don't scream at me, Mayrhofer."

"Who's screaming? Me? You?"

They not only quarrel more at home, but more and more frequently in company as well. Just like a squabbling old couple, thinks Schober, who has returned from Sweden. "If you like, I can show you even more, Schober."

Mayrhofer, a dervish, a shadow-dancer, draws out his umbrella and threatens Schubert with it in blind rage: "I'll impale you, you dwarf, you little wretch, I'll run you through, you little pipsqueak."

"Go on, get lost, you runt, you drip, you lightweight, you wild penpusher."

For two years they have been living side by side, sharing a room, from time to time sleeping in the same bed, quarreling, exchanging views, needing each other.

Mayrhofer knows that he is driving his friend to exhaustion. That he is attacking the fabric of their affection. He cannot expect even his best friend to put up with his wild double life.

"Go, my dear, go."

"The prince. The prince!" he screams.

"His happy, cheerful nature and my introspective personality came into sharper focus, and occasioned us to call each other names as if we were playing out particular roles. It was unfortunately my own that I was playing." Even after many years have passed, after the death of Schubert, Mayrhofer remembers himself as the double, the doppelgänger.

"You're going."

"Are you going?"

"Go."

Who said it aloud?

"Schober has invited me to live with him."

"You're going."

"My dear," said one of them.

And the other one, too.

21

Moment musical no. 7
(Rather slow)

*J*ohannes Senn and Johannes Mayrhofer, the dissenter and the double. I am reading their life stories backward from the end. They almost never cross, but in retrospect I can make them intertwine.

The one, Mayrhofer, remains at his post, more and more torn by the contradiction in which he lives; the other, Senn, is banished and returns—one wonders how penitently—to his post, dons a uniform, and becomes a soldier, an officer in the Imperial Tyrolean Rifle Corps. In 1830 the one, the censor and poet, when he hears of the vain uprising of the Poles against the Russians, throws himself into the Danube and is rescued by a passerby; in 1831 the other, the one-time rebel, goes with his unit to Italy. The one, Mayrhofer, "to illuminate the darkness," begins to study ancient art; the other takes early retirement from the army and works as secretary to an advocate. In 1824 the one, the censor, issues a subscription edition of his poems; in 1838 the other, who has by this time lost the position of secretary as well, is living on odd jobs and deliberately drinking himself to death, publishes his poems "at odds with his circumstances, his surroundings, and the censorship." The one, poet and censor combined, pursued by spirits he no longer needs summon, throws himself from the third floor of a government building in Vienna in 1838, when cholera rages in the city, lives for another two days and nights, then dies. The other, the banned student and poetry-writing officer, succumbs completely to alcohol and retires to die in 1857 in the military hospital in Innsbruck. The one like the other, Mayrhofer and Senn, both with their high hopes dashed, their high standards impaired, reined in by the policies of the prince, they are both captured in their unhappiness by their singing friend, who gradually grows attuned to winter, to a never-ending journey. In the poetry of both companions he discovers the themes set out for him— in a poem by one of them:

> What you are craving will never spring forth
> From the earth, a stranger to ideals,
> Which defiantly opposes its raw power
> To your most beautiful dreams.
> You weary yourself in struggle with its harshness,
> Ever more inflamed with the desire
> To journey to a gentler land
> A persevering companion to the cranes.

> *Nie wird, was du verlangst, entkeimen*
> *Dem Boden, Idealen fremd;*
> *Der trotzig deinen schönsten Träumen*
> *Die rohe Kraft entgegenstemmt.*
> *Du ringst dich matt mit seiner Härte,*
> *Vom Wunsche heftiger entbrannt:*
> *Mit Kranichen ein strebender Gefährte*
> *Zu wandern in ein milder Land.*

And in a poem by the other one:

> It lamented, it sang,
> Fearful of extinction,
> Joyful at its transfiguration,
> Until life fled away.
> That is the meaning of the swan's song.

> *Es klagt, es sang*
> *Vernichtungsbang,*
> *Verklärungsfroh,*
> *Bis das Leben floh.*
> *Das bedeutet des Schwanen Gesang!*

22

Life in Vienna

I am looking at the topography of the city as he knew it. I outline streets, arrange blocks of houses, hatch squares, looking for names and making an occasional mess of it. There are houses that become important in his daily life, now a part of my recollection, apartments that open their doors to take him in. Vienna the great city, with its imperial mien, becomes a landscape where the Danube swallows up streets and quays as if they were tributary rivers and streams, and where the rows of houses darken one's path like forests.

The pattern of life becomes the town plan. Narrow, sparsely furnished rooms, little apartments in which he is almost never alone, festive salons in which he appears of an evening, usually as the center of attention, loved, honored, and teased; courtyards and gardens, still warm from the summer days, still light in the early evening, where people sing, eat and drink, talk and argue.

This world is ordered and administered by the middle class, not by the nobility. It is dominated by comfort and by fear, by solidity and by the political police (by a repeatedly active imagination which demonically expands the vision of the world), and by Metternich in 1821, appointed by the Emperor Franz to be Court and State Chancellor, and whose insect-like being can now roam quite freely: "I feel that I am at the center of a web like my friends the spiders whom I love, since I have so often admired them," and here the great controller of

Europe portrays himself exactly and yet not without some metaphorical sense, and he in no way contradicts himself when he acknowledges, with individual troublemakers and dissidents in view, "Our people does not understand why it should approve political agitation when it may enjoy in peace that which has been gained by the agitation of others. Personal freedom is complete, equality of social classes before the law is perfected, all bear the same burdens. There are titles, but no privileges."

(*Ritardando.* I copy down Metternich's principles, and I cannot immediately succeed in applying them to Schubert. The import of these sentences sails over his head and reaches me directly. The prince might have spoken them today. The agitations, as he calls the revolutions and uprisings, are over. The things that they were striving for have benefited the people, at least in Europe. Now there is no further need for radical change, but on the contrary, an urgent need for calm and order. Anything disturbing is calmed down and pacified. The storms must make way for a clear sky. The arts, whether they be music, poetry, painting, or theater, move away from world-shaking themes and content themselves with the complacent ego, with feelings of happiness and comfort, images become more pleasant and ideas conventional—and here the spider watchers, the self-righteous and the self-satisfied, fail to observe the double bottom, the hollow, crumbling walls. Repressed fears begin to take concrete form, dark elements encroach upon the cool of comfort, and demons gnaw at the sated, pacified ego.)

There is Schubert again, he has left Mayrhofer, but he has not moved in immediately with Schober, as he threatened he would to make his friend jealous. He finds a room just a few doors down from Mayrhofer's quarters, at Wipplingerstraße 15. It is not known who rented it to him, but Moritz von Schwind made an ink sketch of how the room looked, or at least one corner of it, so that in one's imagination one can fill in the details.

There is a piano at any rate, a small grand, on top of which are piled sheets of manuscript and especially books, which look from their covers to be anthologies, collections of poetry. Under the piano stands a wooden chest that also contains books, probably the rest of the "library," since their owner, constantly on the move from one lodging to another, never gets around to unpacking properly. A chair and a piano—he does not need much more. Schwind indicates that the room will have been very sparsely furnished. Table, bed, cupboard, two or three more chairs. In winter the room is icy cold, and hot in summer.

For the first time he is living alone. He enjoys this as long as he is working. Afterward, the room becomes his prison. Although he does not admit it, he misses Mayrhofer.

In the afternoons he quite often intercepts him. He waits by the window, and as soon as Mayrhofer appears, always dressed in black and surrounded by a dark aura, he calls down to him. Sometimes his friend declines to be his companion into the night. "You have enough good friends, Schubert, what do you want with a wet blanket like me."

It is true. Schubert's circle of admirers is growing and becoming more colorful. Besides the old intimate friends like Vogl, Spaun, Schober, and Mayrhofer there are the young painter Moritz von Schwind, the dramatist Eduard von Bauernfeld, Franz Grillparzer, the painter Leopold Kupelwieser, and the Fröhlich sisters Anna, Barbara, Josefine, and Katharina.

They all get involved and have a part to play in the course of his story, as do Therese Grob or Karoline Esterházy, and the Konvikt friends Kenner and Randhartinger, as do Ruzicka or Salieri, and Hummel or Beethoven.

I let them come onto the stage, and I forget several of them again. I am sure that I confuse them from time to time, as he did.

Often enough he is afraid of them as individuals, and likes them better in larger gatherings, as voices and as colors.

This network of friends, acquaintances, and fleeting contacts nevertheless brings him in enough money so that in 1821 he can live modestly from it. He is known in the city, his name is quoted by the critics, he is often invited out. His first songs are published by Cappi & Diabelli. Vogl kept his promise. His singspiel, *The Twin Brothers*, is performed at the Court Opera House. In the *Allgemeine Musikalische Zeitung* he can read the first extensive criticism of one of his works:

"Herr Schubert . . . has hitherto been known to us through a few meritorious romances." (It is strange, this use of the word "meritorious": The artist as a member of a society that is served by the arts, and that regards it as a meritorious service if something serves as entertainment, a handful of "romances" for instance.)

"There was mention of his opera, which he modestly presents under the title of 'farce,' as early as the end of 1818, but we have only seen it now, despite the exercise of powerful influence." (A reference tinged with irony to the influence and persistent efforts on the part of Vogl and probably others as well, and proof of the growing attention that Schubert's compositions were attracting, and not least of the noise that his friends were making in promoting them.)

"It is testimony to the fact that its composer is a man of talents, full of power and creativity, a prime advantage, since everything else may be *acquired;* however, it demonstrates at the same time that Herr Schubert has more skill at tragedy than comedy, and therefore we would advise him strongly to choose the former genre, at least for the time being." (In any case, he was only able to note this advice from the critic, who though he may have been full of his own importance still listened intelligently, three days after the first performance. He did not attend the premiere. He had resisted going, for he couldn't take it. He said he wasn't prepared for all the things in store for him. He would disgrace his good helpers. Which all goes to show that his friends had Schubert back in their midst, trying to hide out of sight in their protective ring, a Schubert who needs them all but wants to be quite independent. Perhaps he had a premonition of how the premiere would end.)

The critic has preserved this for posterity too. "The ending gave rise to a dispute between the factions, in that Herr Schubert's friends wanted him to appear, but many opponents let their disapproval show. The majority of the audience remained calm during this altercation, which had in fact nothing to do with art, since the composer deserved neither one nor the other, but merely encouragement. Herr Vogl, to whose care and nurture we are largely indebted for the young musician, appeared, announced that Herr Schubert was not present, and thanked everyone on his behalf."

Schubert waited in an inn near the Kärntnertor. He was entertained by friends who had not gone to the premiere, but had stayed behind in order to look after him. His silent good humor made all their words seem trivial. He sank into a state of numbness, which he prized, a sort of absent awareness: everything, people and objects, draws in on him, becomes excessively tangible, yet at the same time so artificial, so "imagined," that they seem like a memory. After the performance the mob comes bursting excitedly into the room. "Victory, Schubert. It's a conquest! People clapped like mad."

The information and the answers reach him as if delayed, as if spoken in another language.

Who brought him the first reactions of the critics three days later? He will have been eager to read them. He has waited long for moments like this. Probably it was Vogl.

He waited at home. "You will bring me the paper?" He is impatient, unable to sit still or concentrate. Now he is missing Mayrhofer's support. To distract his mind, he flicks through the score of *The Twin Brothers*. Every bar he reads, repeating it to himself, every aria, every duet, suddenly acquires a veneer of the dilettante. It becomes clear to him that the antipathy that he often felt for the text even when he was at work on it has laid itself like a varnish on the music.

Without stepping to the open window, he listens to the voices that come up to him from the street. He runs down the stairs, out in front of the house, and back again into the entry-way. It is hot and sweat runs down his neck.

Why is he so upset about a work that he has long left behind him, with which he is no longer occupied?

At one of his Friday evening concerts, Sonnleithner had introduced him to Hermann Neefe, the stage designer at the Theater an der Wien, and Neefe had encouraged Schubert, not with a definite offer but with the clear intention of making one, to write an opera or a singspiel for his house. If Schubert was interested, Neefe happened to have a libretto already in hand, a piece full of decorative and mechanical effects with the title *Die Zauberharfe* (*The Magic Harp*). If he might find this of interest, then they could meet the very next day, and he let himself be interested, but not because he valued the libretto, or because the material said anything special to him, but for another, miserable reason, which he would only admit to between wine and sleep: that inspiration had abandoned him, poems almost never stimulated him any more, and he was having no success at writing the sonatas and the symphonies that he was planning and had already noted down in short bursts.

At this point, when a small shaft of fame had finally reached him, when his friends were taking care of his day-to-day support, and when he could make the city his own, as his dwelling-place, he was actually wandering lost through a desert region, and he heard the calls and acclamation of his friends as from a distance.

Vogl is not alone. Schober comes with him. Schubert sees them as he hides in the doorway. Now his curiosity is an embarrassment for him. Schober has seen him and calls out. Vogl waves the newspaper.

"I'll read it upstairs in my room." That they understand, but not his desire to be left alone.

"I beg of you."

But he is not being written about in any derogatory fashion, rather with praise. They cannot understand that every sentence, which applies to him but also is intended for the public, hurts and displeases him, and that as he reads, even when he is named in the same breath as Mozart and Beethoven, as Schober and Vogl point out, it still makes him feel naked and besmirched.

"These are just intermezzos, bagatelles, practice pieces—nothing more. And they write half a novel on the subject!"

Schober and Vogl are shocked at the vehemence with which Schubert furiously casts aside the singspiel on which he had staked his name.

Now the old songs from an earlier time are resurrected and make the rounds. He reworks them, playing and singing them, with the greatest enthusiasm.

He allows himself to drift more and more in this fashion, and hopes that the barren period will eventually come to an end, but should this not happen, so he comforts himself, then he could pass the years in entertaining larger and smaller social gatherings with his songs and piano pieces.

The damning reviews of *The Magic Harp*, which was performed six months after *The Twin Brothers*, are indeed painful to him, although he had prepared himself for them.

He deceives his friends. Perhaps he is a touch more exuberant than he used to be, and is more speedily persuaded to play waltzes after his songs, and to improvise for dancing.

"Hello, Mayrhofer."

"Good evening, Schwind."

"Hello, Schober."

He runs around beside them and behind them. If he is asked to play the piano, he never hesitates. He takes cover behind the instrument, and need not take part in conversations that annoy him, nor dance. They come and see him at the piano, inquire after his welfare, bring him a glass of wine, and pay him compliments, and this Moritz von Schwind, who looks like an impish fairy from *A Midsummer Night's Dream* with his sixteen years, manages to do in a particularly elaborate way.

After a wild and confused conversation that lasted the whole night through in the Seiterhof tavern, where, as Spaun afterward summed up peevishly, they discussed God and the world, Schubert ran out ahead of his friends onto the street, wandering through the sleeping city, disturbed as it was with few noises, but those all the louder, and wrote straight out a poem that speaks of the "Spirit of the World," but also of his situation:

"Leave them to me in their folly,"
Thus speaks the Spirit of the World,
"It is that which preserves them
For me in their tossing boat.

"Let them run, chasing after
A distant goal, let them believe
Many things, prove many things,
In their gloomy chase.

"None of it is true,
Yet this is no loss;
Their world is but human,
I, as a God, can understand it."

Laßt sie mir in ihrem Wahn,
Spricht der Geist der Welt.
Er ists, der im schwanken Kahn
So sie mir erhält.

Laßt sie rennen, jagen nur
Hin nach einem fernen Ziel,
Glauben viel, beweisen viel
Auf der dunkeln Spur.

Nichts ist wahr von allen dem,
Doch ists kein Verlust;
Menschlich ist ihr Weltsystem,
Göttlich, bin ich's mir bewußt.

On November 21, 1820, Therese Grob was married. It may be that Schubert learned this from one of his brothers, although at this time they did not often see each other. The definitive break with the house in Roßau is still in place, and affects them all.

"Therese was married yesterday, Franz."

"I expected it."

He does not let anyone see how much this piece of news, which he had been expecting, shatters him.

I can visualize him with Ignaz on the Graben. The first snow has fallen. The wheels of the horse-drawn cabs throw up dirt on the side of the street. They pick their way like stilt walkers side by side, the little one and the hunchback.

"I expected it." He pauses for a moment, pushing his glasses up his nose.

Ignaz is two paces ahead of him. Without turning around to look at his brother he asks, "Should I send your greetings to her and to her good husband? You do know him."

"I beg you to do that."

In their embarrassment their conversation is stilted.

"Perhaps I'll hear Therese sing again some time."

Perhaps he will. But she has not sung in the Lichtental Church for a long time.

"It doesn't really matter."

Ignaz has fallen back into step with his brother. They turn the corner into the Wipplingerstraße. The hunchback shivers as he pulls his coat closer over his chest.

"Are you coming up?"

"I have to get to school."

"Yes, yes, you have to get to school."

His eyes follow his brother, and he is taken aback at how much this sight touches him. It is as if some part of him had gotten out and run away. "Goodbye, Ignaz," he says to himself. Therese, well . . . He takes some pleasure from putting his melancholy at this long-accepted loss into stylized form. A poem by Heinrich Hüttenbrenner, a brother of Anselm, provides by chance the background stimulus: He sings to himself the song of a youth who watches "grieving, from a hill-top" as his little Rose is carried to her grave. As the night falls it gives him a heavenly promise:

> And as the stars came out,
> And the moon sailed into view,
> He could read in the starry sky
> The great message of hope.

> *Und wie die Sterne kamen,*
> *Der Mond heraufgeschifft,*
> *Da las er in den Sternen*
> *Der Hoffnung hohe Schrift.*

The melody that he finds to accompany this is quite simple, as if he had drawn it from his memories of childhood.

It is one of the few songs that he writes during the years 1820 and 1821. He attempts to compose symphonies and quartets, but never gets beyond sketches. The pauses between these efforts, often dogged work, are filled with busy socializing. The old songs are a comfort to him. They are sung, and not only in Vienna now.

An article in the *Dresdener Abendzeitung* of April 26, 1821, reflects the enthusiasm of his supporters. "A few songs, set to music by the talented young composer *Schubert,* were the greatest sensation here. In particular, the 'Erl-King' was very well received, performed by *Vogl* with his well-known mastery, and this had to be repeated. This magnificent composition is bound to move listeners. It has now been published here in an engraved edition by *Cappi & Diabelli,* and I am convinced that every reader who acquires a copy of this masterwork will be grateful to me for drawing it to his attention."

Schubert collects such triumphs as this, set down in black and white, then forgets about them again, and Ferdinand, who looks in regularly, takes them to show to their father in an attempt to allay his terrible fears. On the other hand, if his father had even the slightest inkling of the minor catastrophes and general mess that are a part of his son's everyday life, he would feel his fears were confirmed.

To be sure, Schubert is often invited out, and most of his very well-to-do friends take care of his bodily needs, but they only gradually come to realize the other unpleasant incidents. How the landlord threatens to evict him because he is months in arrears, how the tailor, who is well disposed toward him, gradually grows impatient when payment for the suit is not forthcoming despite all his gentle reminders.

"I am so sorry, how could I have forgotten."

"I beg of you, please just be patient until tomorrow."

"Please, don't hold it against me."

He forgets it, represses it.

How can he be remembering such trifles when he is obsessed with doubts, when he is composing an oratorio on the subject of poor Lazarus, and in the evenings is concerned with appearing to all his friends, male and female, as the person whom they expect to see, the citizen as Orpheus.

The bookseller Josef Huber, whom Schubert avoided walking next to when they went out, as he was more than two heads taller than he, had recently become, along with the painter Leopold von Kupelwieser, one of his most emphatic patrons, and was soon also to be his landlord. In a letter Huber describes the beginning of the institution that united them all, binding them together, the Schubert evening, the Schubertiad. These were evenings primarily devoted to himself and to his art, with the company surrounding him as their musical focus, and stimulated in this way, they celebrated their good mood and constant high spirits until late in the night or the early morning hours. Such festivities were on many an occasion followed by a dreadful hangover.

Huber wrote to his fiancée, who for her part, such coincidences being quite the rule in the circle of Schubert's friends, was a friend of Franz von Schober's sister Sophie:

> I had a very pleasant evening last Friday. As Fräulein Schober was in St. Pölten, Franz had invited Schubert for the evening, and fourteen of his good friends. A whole lot of magnificent songs were played and sung by Schubert himself, and this lasted until after 10 P.M. Then we drank punch that was donated by one of the party, and as it was very good and available in large quantity, the company, which was already well-disposed to enjoy itself, became even merrier, and so it was 3 A.M. before we parted. . . . For such an occasion, I would gladly leave everything that people call "entertainment" behind.

The letter is placed as a motto at the beginning of a folding sequence of pictures that, when spread out, contains scenes similar to each other, although no two are exactly alike. Thus there is no repetition of the fact that only men are present, or that pleasure in the musical performance degenerates into a drinking session, so that Schubert has to report to his brother Ferdinand that he is unfit to work "as I was out of sorts today after yesterday's overindulgence."

The women, particularly the Fröhlich sisters, will see to it that a little more time is devoted to music, and that guests take their leave at an earlier hour, which does not prevent the men from celebrating the later hours of the night in a nearby inn.

The hosts of the Schubertiads change, although for a time there is a regular weekly arrangement for Friday at Schober's, and on two further weekdays guests gather to read together. The names of the hosts are, and this is far from being an exhaustive list, Witteczek, Enderes, Spaun, Fröhlich, Sonnleithner, Schober, Watteroth, Bruchmann, and Geymüller.

Anyone invited to these evenings is the envy of those who have musical interests and are socially active. Those who are part of the inner circle become increasingly addicted. A young woman complains to the Schubert intimate Leopold Kupelwieser: "While you were away there was only one Schubertiad at Bruchmann's, but there were many other parties in which your friends did not take part."

He liked these voices, girls' voices, women's voices. He preferred them from a distance and heard in retrospect—or as part of a chorus.

Grillparzer observed Katharina Fröhlich, his eternally betrothed, as she was listening to Schubert playing, from her seat beside the piano. It is as if the spirit of Schubert's music infects him, he woos her, then draws back, he sings, then is silent.

> She sat there quietly, the loveliest of them all,
> Listening, with neither criticism nor praise,
> The dark shawl had fallen from her breast,
> Which rose and fell, its only covering her dress;
> Her head inclined, her body bending forward
> As if drawn by the fleeting tones . . .
>
> Then I was roused: now she should hear
> What had long troubled me, now I would tell her;
> But she looked away, lest the musician be disturbed,
> Placed her finger silently to her lips, a command,
> And again I see her bending forward to listen,
> And again I must sit and be silent.

> *Still saß sie da, die Lieblichste von allen,*
> *Aufhorchend, ohne Tadel, ohne Lob;*
> *Das dunkle Tuch war von der Brust gefallen,*
> *Die, nur vom Kleid bedeckt, sich atmend hob;*
> *Das Haupt gesenkt, den Leib nach vorn gebogen,*
> *Wie von den flieh'nden Tönen nachgezogen . . .*

Da trieb's mich auf: nun soll sie's hören,
Was mich schon längst bewegt, nun werd' ihr's kund;
Doch sie blickt her, den Künstler nicht zu stören,
Befiehlt ihr Finger, schwicht'gend an dem Mund;
Und wieder seh' ich horchend sie sich neigen,
Und wieder muß ich sitzen, wieder schweigen.

Schubert often notices while he is playing that some of the guests, including his friends, are definitely not present only on his account. They conduct their business, they talk politics. And as it all centers on the diminutive figure of Schubert, they do not attract the attention of Metternich's spies.

Maybe it was on one of these evenings at Schober's house that he suddenly jumped up and left the piano and the party. And Schwind who had run out after him discovers only after some quick explorative exchanges what is troubling Schubert and has driven him away.

"I can put up with their not always listening. They are discreet about that."

Schwind contradicts him: "I got annoyed with Witteczek and the newcomers. They didn't stop whispering the whole way through."

Schubert laughs. "Of course Witteczek already knew what I was playing."

"Then he didn't have to come. He could have gone somewhere else."

Only now does Schubert remember that he has forgotten his hat and coat.

"I've left my coat up there, Schwind. Could you bring it down for me, and my hat." Schwind pulls him timidly by the arm. He hardly dares to touch Schubert. He had never dared before. "Come with me. You're punishing those of us who meet because of you, on account of a few who love you too, Schubert."

He quickly lets himself be persuaded. On the stairs he mumbles so that Schwind has to strain to understand him. "D'you know, Schwind, in actual fact they use me as a musical clown."

Upstairs in the apartment they are all waiting in silence, still upset. Schwind is amazed how humorously Schubert covers up the embarrassment of the others.

They had wondered about his abrupt departure or even been horrified at it.

Of course, of course. He had only been troubled momentarily, a sudden idea that for various unfortunate reasons had not worked out, but he would have liked it to. "I beg of you, do not think badly of me, an inspiration that was mere illusion."

That's all. He sits down at the piano and plays one of those German dances that set the ladies' feet tapping. "Now let's have some dancing."

Schober tears him away, takes him home. From now on he will assume the role of the trusted friend who tries in his own way to keep Schubert in good shape and in good spirits. Schober becomes his animator, in a good as well as bad sense.

Although he writes poems and libretti for Schubert, although he deals with his friend's demons in a far from oblivious fashion, yet he comes across like an extra in *The Tales of Hoffmann*.

Have I already given a portrait of him?

I like him, this Schober, I prefer him to all the cultivated solid citizens—Schubert's Schobert. He is a year younger than Schubert. He was born in Malmö in Sweden, but after the early death of his father, a high German official, he returned with his mother and sister to Vienna which was his mother's birthplace. He attended the abbey school in Kremsmünster, and was studying law in a fairly relaxed fashion, preferring to write poetry, to paint, and to appear on the stage.

"Schober is our superior in all matters of intellect, and indeed in debate! Yet much about him is affected, and his best abilities are in danger of being extinguished in idleness."

He was not short of money. Schubert was subsidized by him as a matter of course, without reproach. He was successful with women, and without doubt he was a boaster.

Leopold Kupelwieser made a pencil sketch of him, and even though he envied Schober his close relationship with Schubert, he could not help but fall under the somewhat oily charm of this man. He made an impression, presented a glittering appearance as did many of these gentlemen of the Restoration period in the salons, at conferences and at balls, a type who stood out in contrast—the well-turned man of the world. He looked like this: Thick dark curls of hair over an alabaster brow, quite incapable of a wrinkle, powerful eyebrows above warm and wooing eyes—always a little moist, the eyes—a strong classical line to the nose, and beneath it a carefully trimmed moustache that hid the boyish upper lip and emphasized the sensual lower one. The chin, in Schober's case, is powerful, and very suited to resting on the high collar.

Schubert travels with him to Atzenbrugg, St. Pölten, and Oxenburg, spending the summer and autumn with friends.

In June he had made two attempts at writing a symphony, without enthusiasm and beset with doubts. He just could not hear it in his head.

"Am I a summer man?" he asked Schober, in high spirits.

"In summer, without doubt, Schubert."

"And in winter, Schober?"

"I cannot answer to you for the winter, Schubert."

"I just wish that you had been there," Schober writes on November 4, 1821, to Spaun, after their return to Vienna, "and could have heard the wonderful melodies as they were created. It is wonderful how richly and luxuriantly he poured out his ideas again." Schubert had composed dances, the *Atzenbrugg German Dances*.

"Our room in St. Pölten was particularly attractive, the two double beds, a sofa placed near the warm stove, and a fortepiano all gave it an uncommonly comfortable and cozy atmosphere. . . . We had a few Schubertiads. . . ." Scarcely had they returned to Vienna than Schober took him by surprise.

"We shall drive around to your place, pick up your stuff, and have you move in with us. Mama and Sophie wish your presence and so do I. No argument, I won't hear a word against it, Schubert."

He does not argue.

23

A Dream

One Sunday he caught a glimpse of Karoline Esterházy in the distance. She was sitting in a landau with an older lady whom he did not know, and apparently discussing something funny, for she kept stifling her bursts of laughter with her hands, then throwing her head back. This was the picture he kept of her in his inner eye. He walked on without turning around, seeing the breathless, merry young lady, a child no longer and yet still a child, and he had not forgotten his love for her. Now she returned triumphantly. By chance it so happened, just as he wished, that during this month of June, which soured him on the city that he and Schober would soon be leaving, he received an invitation from Count Esterházy to give a concert at which Schönstein would be singing. This gave him particular pleasure. When he greets Karoline in the Esterházy house she scarcely notices him, so he thinks, and she is even sparing with her applause, giggling and gabbing with a young man whom he does not know but would like to meet. And Schubert concentrates his attention entirely on Schönstein, for whom he has just recently transposed "Rastlose Liebe" ("Restless Love"):

How shall I flee?
Shall I go to the forest?
All is in vain!
Crown of life,
Happiness without peace,
Love, that is you.

Wie soll ich fliehen?
Wälderwärts ziehen?
Alles vergebens!
Krone des Lebens,
Glück ohne Ruh,
Liebe, bist du.

After that he composed the two German dances at the head of which he had written in beautiful handwriting before leaving home: "For Countess Caroline."

He had wanted to present her with the manuscripts immediately after the concert, but now, back home again after a brusque farewell to the Esterházys, he picks up his pen and crosses out the dedication with a stroke that makes the ink spurt.

Onward, ever onward!
No peace, no repose!

Immer zu! Immer zu!
Ohne Rast und Ruh!

Ferdinand invites him to the "Red Cross." He would like to discuss with him the program of the "Friends of Music," since they are thinking of including his songs, and so he strolls back after a long absence to the Himmelpfortgrund, hearing forgotten snatches of speech that wake in his memory, breathing an atmosphere that he liked as a boy. After they had speedily agreed on the program, he asked Ferdinand about Therese's wedding, whether they sang afterward among the circle of friends and relatives, and Ferdinand relates reluctantly yes, they had sung two songs, "Gretchen" and "Nähe des Geliebten" ("Nearness of the Beloved"), but they had not talked about him, which he would understand, or which he says he understands, but he interrupts Ferdinand in the middle of a sentence, makes his farewells, and hastily leaves the inn—"Onward, ever onward! No peace, no repose!"

He turns up early at Schober's house for an evening of readings, and deceives his friends that he is paying careful attention to their rhetoric, he declines to read himself, he hopes they will understand, but he is too exhausted today from his work. But he has not really done a stroke. He drinks too much, accepts another glass, and at some point after most of the company has gone home, Schober and Schwind drag him back to his apartment, pull off his coat and boots, put him to bed, and leave him alone with the wish that he have sweet dreams, a wish that echoes on in his sleep, for everything that he had done to himself, that love had caused him, everything that he had desired but only dared in his songs, all the childhood images that preceded his love and which cushioned the subsequent wounds, these erupt as a dream in his sleep. This is the dream that he writes out the following morning, without looking up, as if the sleeper were dictating to the man who has just awakened:

3 July 1822

My Dream

I was a brother among many brothers and sisters. Our father and our mother were good people. I loved them all dearly.—On one occasion Father took us to a banquet. There my brothers were very merry. I, however, was sad. Then my father came up to me and commanded me to enjoy the excellent dishes. I, however, could not do this, whereupon my father angrily banned me from his sight. I turned my steps, and with my heart full of love for those who scorned it, I journeyed to a distant place. For many years I felt torn asunder by the greatest pain and the greatest love. Then I received news of my mother's death. I hurried to see her, and my father, softened by grief, did not forbid me to enter. There I saw her body. Tears flowed from my eyes. I saw her lying there, like the dear days of old, in which we were supposed to live in accordance with her wishes, as she once did.

And we followed her body, grieving, and her coffin was lowered into the grave.—From this time onward I again remained at home. Then my father took me once more to his favorite garden. He asked me whether I liked it. But the garden was repellent to me, and I did not dare reply. Then he asked me for a second time, in agitation: did I like the garden? Trembling, I said no. Then my father struck me and I escaped. And for the second time I turned my steps and with my heart full of love for those who scorned it, I again journeyed to a distant place. For many long years I now sang songs. If I wanted to sing of love, it turned to pain. And again, if I wanted to sing of pain, it turned to love.

And so love and pain tore me asunder.

And one day I heard tell of a pious maiden who had just died. And a circle formed around her grave in which many men, both young and old, walked as if in eternal bliss. They spoke softly in order not to wake the maiden.

Heavenly thoughts appeared to shower constantly from the maiden's grave over the youths, like bright sparks, creating a gentle rustling sound. Then I felt a great longing to walk there with them. Yet only a miracle would lead to that circle, so people said. But I approached the grave with slow steps, my eyes lowered, with reverence in my heart and firm in my belief, and before I knew it, I was part of the circle, from which issued a most wonderful sound. And I felt eternal bliss compressed into one moment. I saw my father also, reconciled and full of love. He enclosed me in his arms and wept. And so, even more, did I.

24

The Picture at the Window

*T*he time with Schober begins in a mood of elation. The Schobers lived on the second floor of the Göttweigerhof in the Spiegelgasse. Schubert already knew the apartment from visits there, but Franz von Schober had arranged for the bedroom that they would be sharing to be newly decorated and comfortably furnished especially for him. Schober preferred to have furniture hand-made according to his own design, including the beds and a fine tall mirror wardrobe.

Now, as he made himself comfortable, putting his clothes in the wardrobe and the drawers, placing his manuscript paper on the little table by the window, and as Schober conducted him through the other rooms, where he could pay his respects to Madame von Schober and to Sophie, now it really dawned on him how every decorative item, from the curtains to the wallpaper and the furniture, was chosen to catch and reflect the light, whether flooding in through the window or the abundant illumination of the evening. This pleased him just as much as the cheerfully regulated life of the little family. There were fixed hours at which the midday and evening meals were served, and it was also the rule that, time permitting, they would meet for half an hour in the afternoon in Madame Schober's salon. The morning could be spent by each as they wished. Frau von Schober had the help of a cook and two maidservants. Guests were expected almost every evening. Schubert found in the salon a decent piano, which he had often played on before.

Here, he hoped, he would be stimulated and able to work without distraction, cared for by a friend and surrounded by conveniences. The Schubertiads were maintained. He continued to concentrate on the composition of the opera *Alfonso and Estrella.* Schober had a few months previously, in September 1821, ceremoniously presented him with the libretto he had requested: "Now all that is missing is your music, Schubert, and the public will lie at your feet." As always, he put on an exaggerated show, putting himself and his friend in a mood he enjoyed like a mild intoxication. "And then, Schubert, the two of us, Schubert and Schobert, will show Mozart a thing or two." That was too much for Schubert. "Leave Mozart out of it, Schober. His name is sacred to me." Whereupon Schober executed a deep bow, with his back turned: "I most humbly ask for forgiveness, Maestro Mozart, but I did mean it the way I meant it, even if Schubert doesn't take it the way I mean it, so we couldn't both mean it as we really would have wanted to mean it if we are permitted to mean anything."

"Cut it out, Schober."

In the city they were even speaking of songs that were not yet to be heard, or which he might even not have composed so far. In the *Wiener Allgemeine Musikalische Zeitung* a critic was spreading rumors: "We are aware of several more songs available in manuscript by the same composer, which promise to offer much pleasant enjoyment in our musical circles when they are introduced to the public."

"Help me, Schober, it's your libretto." Their chairs side by side, they sit at the table which is really too small for them to work at, like two schoolboys, older Konvikt students. "This sentence just doesn't ring: 'When I behold you, my beloved, then my pain swiftly departs.' That needs to be more ambiguous. Alfonso feels his pain, but doesn't believe in it. And not so fast. *Andante.*" He hums, listening to his inner voice. Schober looks at him sideways and pulls his chair a shade closer. "What should my Alfonso say then, Schubert?"

"Listen, my Schober. Couldn't it go something like this," and he sings:

When I behold you, my beloved,
Then I no longer believe in pain.

Wenn ich dich Holde sehe,
So glaub ich keinem Schmerz.

Schubert has the work completed in February. Both he and Schober
hope for an early performance date. I know better. It is not until 1854
that *Alfonso and Estrella* appears on stage, and then it is in Weimar,
conducted by Franz Liszt, no less.

Josef von Spaun asks Schober, in a letter from Linz, not without
some amicable envy, what the triumvirate of poet, musician, and artist
has created? Here he was referring to the current core of the
Schubertiads, Schober, Schubert, and Kupelwieser.

"Persuade him to send me a few new songs sometime. Where were
the Schubertiads held this winter, how are things at 'The Crown,' to
whose people I send my greetings, and does the clock play Schubert's
song yet?"

"Yes, it does," Schober presumably answered. It is one of their inn
stories.

They had had a heated discussion in the "Hungarian Crown," not
directly about music and poetry, but about female singers and women.
On this subject no one could outdo the most varied reminiscences of
Schober. After Mayrhofer had departed, Kupelwieser was drunk, and
Schubert exhausted, the innkeeper asked if he might tune the pipes of
his newly acquired mechanical clock to a song by the honored Herr
Schubert. This roused the attention of them all. They got caught up in
a debate as to which song would be most suitable, tried whistling, humming, or warbling one and then another, and only fell silent when the
innkeeper, without paying any attention to the state of the discussion,
called out: "I have decided on 'Heidenröslein' ('Meadow-Rose')."

They listened to his loud interjection with mouths open, eyes closed,
heads on the table or thrown back, bathed in sweat and out of breath.

"Why not?"

"Yes."

"And you, Schubert, what d'you think?"

"Were you asking me?"

They clink glasses with him and fail to notice that he has remained sober.

He asks Schober to write to Spaun and tell him also that he has dedicated his Variations on a French Song to Beethoven. With his permission, of course. He had wanted to take it to him at his house but had not found him at home. Herr Schindler had assured him that he would give the master the music immediately.

The Schobers are planning to move for the summer to Atzenbrugg. The anticipated pleasure of Schubertiads in the open air, and evening concerts out of doors, always refreshes their spirits. The inspiration for songs has come back. When he picks Mayrhofer up one evening, he finds on his desk, which not so long ago was his composition table, a newly written poem. He reads it, at first to himself, then out loud, causing Mayrhofer some embarrassment, then he asks for a piece of manuscript paper and only has to write it out. Mayrhofer watches over his shoulder and bursts into tears.

> In the cold, raw north
> I heard tell
> Of a city, the city in the sun.

> *Im kalten, rauhen Norden*
> *Ist Kunde mir geworden*
> *Von einer Stadt, der Sonnenstadt.*

Schubert is in a hurry, they might be late at Sonnleithner's. Vogl has recently been showing signs of impatience. There is a Schubertiad waiting for them as on many other evenings this year. He knows the houses and the gardens well. He knows the peculiar foibles of the pianos, and could name in his sleep each and every participant by their voice, from soprano to bass.

The longer he is living with Schober, the more sensitive he becomes to any nuances in conversation, to innuendos and gestures. Gradually he notices how the boundaries blur between lightness and lightmindedness. Even Madame Schober takes pleasure in ambiguity. If court is paid her at social gatherings, then she slyly plays along with it. Sophie takes care of the subsequent comments. The order that so impressed him when he moved in proves to be a useful but fragile masquerade.

The conversation he hears daily revels in hidden lewd innuendos. If Madame Schober pokes fun at Ignaz for constantly wheedling candy lumps from Sophie, then everybody laughs and draws his own conclusions, and looks at her admirer, the geometrist Ignaz Zechenter, with Madame Schober's eyes. At such moments Schubert sometimes has the feeling that he is the only person sitting in his clothes, surrounded by nudes, and that he is therefore behaving most unsuitably. As soon as Schober starts talking about women he just listens and does not utter a word, and Schober does not expect him to. Schober is content if his friend smiles. He speaks of bodies and faces, of ugly mugs and buttocks, and perhaps Schubert is pursued in his sleep by such words, which put themselves together as in a game into curvaceous bodies, but as soon as he touches them they fall apart. Then he wakes up, hot with desire. At this time Schubert is involved with two society ladies, or rather, they are involved with him. He maintains that he prefers to flirt with two, then one is always distracting him away from the other.

"Come to the girlies with me, Schubert."

He could sing the praises of the prostitutes in the alleyways down by the Danube. They were sweet, ready for anything, even the craziest requests. "Come on."

He gave in once, late at night, after a Schubertiad at Mayrhofer's. He set off at Schober's side without looking where they were going. Wine and exhaustion had made him dizzy. He was reeling a bit. Schober took him by the arm. Lamps were flickering in the doorways and noises were coming from the houses.

Schober hesitated briefly in front of one entry-way and seemed to be considering, then pulled him further along. "We'll pay a visit in here, there's someone I know here who might suit you, Schubert, and you'll be able to forget her again without any trouble."

Schober towed him in his wake.

A powdered mask of a face with two big watery blue eyes hovered over a fire in the open doorway and gazed at them.

"No, Schober." He tore himself away, tumbling backward, and saw Schober standing in a glowing orifice, and turning around toward him, very slowly. "What's up?"

The question brought him to his senses. With one bound he was awake. He ran off without replying.

"You seemed to me," he told Schober later, trying to avoid the mocking of his friend, "you seemed to me like a disgusting combination of Don Giovanni and the *Commendatore*, and the flames of hell were already licking at your feet."

That's a fantastic interpretation, sneers Schober, and pointedly wants to know who on earth he thinks he is, turning away at the gates of hell.

Schubert takes off his glasses, looks across at Schober, his eyes twinkling, and gives him this astonishing answer: "Who did I think I was? Why, Leporello having a nightmare that he has to be Don Giovanni, and deciding right at the last moment to remain Leporello."

"Kupelwieser tells me that Marie,"—they are at lunch, sitting at the round table, and Schober raises his fork to his eye and peers through the prongs—"that Marie is no longer getting along with her husband, that Ottenwalt." Sophie contradicts him, she knows differently. Even Schubert finds it unthinkable. But it is clear to them that Schober wants to spoil a story that was spoiled for him. Six years previously he had courted Marie, the sister of Josef von Spaun. Successfully. The young woman loved him, and they planned to be married. Quite mercilessly the Spaun family called her home. For one thing, Schober was a dreadful freethinker, for another, he was a rake with the worst of reputations, and for a third, he was a devious character. She simply disap-

173

peared, jilting him without a word of explanation or farewell. He had been serious about her. Schubert knew that and at the time he had blamed Spaun for this harsh decision.

Now Schober parades his wound and takes comfort as and where he can find it. "Go and get a girlie, Schubert."

"Leave me in peace, Schobert."

But the image of the glowing doorway and the hovering chalk-white face will not leave him in peace.

He searches for it, wandering during the daytime through the alleyways by the Danube, avoiding the magical simplifications of the night, pretending to be going about his business, but collecting visual impressions.

He cannot find the doorway. Or rather, he finds several that are alike and remain closed.

But in an uncurtained window he sees the reflection of a girl, a woman, not clearly but like Ophelia swimming in the glass, her hair loose, a pale indistinct face, and a long neck. The reflected figure seems untouchable and enticing. She can't be real, he says to himself as he looks back, and the window no longer reflects anything.

He does not give up. Again and again he steals out of the Schobers' apartment, feigning some important appointment if he meets Sophie or Schober on the way, and strolls in an ever more relaxed fashion through the red-light district, recognized by someone here, someone there. The women nod to him but do not try to proposition him, as if they knew that he is chasing a mirage.

It pursues him, even when he moves with the caravan of friends to the summer atmosphere of Atzenbrugg, and is again swept up, as in the previous year, in a long round of festivities, nocturnal revels, charades, and Schubertiads.

Schober's uncle, Josef Derffel, is the steward of the mansion attached to the Klosterneuburg monastery, a spot that positively attracts the sun, dominated by the ochre-washed mansion with its two wings that, as soon as the courtyard and garden are alive with people, recedes and becomes a beautiful backdrop, leaving the considerably smaller pavilion in the park as the stage.

It is there, on the very first afternoon, in the cool of the rotunda bathed in light, that he plays Schober's song that he had set to music exactly five years before, an anniversary that he does not immediately reveal:

> Beloved art, in how many bleak hours
> When I was tangled in the fury of life's round
> Have you kindled my heart to the warmth of love,
> Have you borne me away to a better world.

> *Du holde Kunst, in wieviel grauen Stunden,*
> *Wo mich des Lebens wilder Kreis umstrickt,*
> *Hast du mein Herz zu warmer Lieb entzünden,*
> *Hast mich in eine bessre Welt entrückt.*

While he is singing he observes Schober, and wishes that he could read his present thoughts.

His friends perform a charade for him on the Fall of Man, and Schober, as if he wanted to provide him secretly with an answer, performs the serpent.

Everything taking place round him closes in on him. It seems to him as if he is being touched by the aura of objects, of people and words, and this excessive proximity creates an atmosphere in which he misses nothing, he seems to actually feel thoughts and feelings, the bad temper of Madame Schober as well as the happiness of Kupelwieser, who pursues Johanna Lutz, his darling, with his eyes.

While out walking late one day, just the two of them, Schober, no longer sober, starts fantasizing, describing women here and there, confusing faces and bodies. "Just watch Johanna, when she's flirting with Poldi. It's enough to drive you mad. But I've got hold of Marie from the kitchen for these few weeks," and he describes her for him, her calves, her firm belly, her breasts "like two surging waves, I'm telling you, they come at you like two waves."

"Cut it out, Schober."

Every word leaps about, forming an image in his imagination. He can't love like that.

On an excursion to Kremsmünster he discovers lying on a table the poetry of Platen. He leafs through the volume, finding the poem that speaks for him. The song comes to him in syncopated rhythm. Out of the allegro of the words comes a moderato:

> My heart is broken, you do not love me!
> You gave me to know, you do not love me!
> Although I came to you, imploring and wooing,
> Fervent with love, you do not love me!
> You spoke it aloud, you said it in words,
> All too explicit words, you do not love me!

> *Mein Herz ist zerrissen, du liebst mich nicht!*
> *Du ließest mich's wissen, du liebst mich nicht!*
> *Wiewohl ich dir flehend und werbend erschien,*
> *Und liebebeflissen, du liebst mich nicht!*
> *Du hast es gesprochen, mit Worten gesagt,*
> *Mit allzu gewissen, du liebst mich nicht!*

He cannot know that this lament from the poet is for a boy. That would have made no difference to him.

Gradually summer passes him by. When he walks along the single-story front of the mansion he catches himself looking in through the open windows to see if by any chance the sought-for image is to be found. At the last of the Atzenbrugg Schubertiads he confounds the circle with the Platen song. Kupelwieser inquires almost rudely to what mood he had succumbed this time.

He looks up mischievously from the piano and plays a German dance, in no way an answer. Schober finds him increasingly unpredictable.

The autumn mist creeps up from the Danube, taking captive the gray and dirty outskirts of the city.

How can he find her again?

Whispers follow him, a bevy of calls.

Then suddenly she appears. Not as a reflection. She is standing in a doorway. The light falls on her from such an angle that he sees only her head and neck, as at the window.

He wants to pass by, taking the image with him as before. The sight of her stops him in his tracks. He stands and stares. He sees the whole of her and is no longer sure if it is the girl from the window.

She calls out. He understands what she is calling to him, and yet does not want to hear it. Step by step he approaches. Her laughter goes with him.

"Come on." She takes his hand, pulling him behind her, up a flight of stairs, past an honor guard of half-naked women, of heavy breathing and curiosity.

"You've caught yourself a cute little dwarf there." He stumbles. A helping hand grasps him under the shoulder and heaves him onto the landing.

"I mustn't lose my glasses," he thinks to himself. The sentence sticks, pleading, in his mind. Just don't lose the glasses.

Then she asks him to take his glasses off. She has led him into a little bedroom that gets scarcely any light from the alleyway.

"I'll be as blind as a bat."

"What d'you need to see for."

He raises his hands protectively toward his glasses, but she carefully pushes them aside, taking them off for him as she says, "I'll take care of them. I'll put them here on the nighttable." He hears her, feels her.

She draws him to her, pressing his head to her breasts, pulling him down on her. He breathes in unison with her. Without his noticing, she has taken off his jacket. She slips his trousers down.

He breathes with her, or she with him. She arouses him, massaging him.

He seeks her mouth, but she pushes his face onto the pillow.

All thoughts disappear, he forgets himself, he hears his breathing quickening. She is hot. He feels her like an open wound. "Come," she says.

But it isn't her, he thinks, it can't be her. Again she helps him to get dressed, and she hands him his glasses.

"What's your name?" he asks.

She laughs. "Go on with you," she says, "Don't waste my time."

It can't be her, he says to himself.

On the stairs the honor guard of bodies is waiting for him. She takes him to the door. He stumbles over the threshold. As he looks back the door is closed.

He hurries into the city. For a moment he plays with the idea of going to Roßau, to the school, to his father, but he would have had too much explaining to do.

Schober does not ask where he has been, but drops hints of his suspicions.

For a few days he struggles with the desire to repeat the visit until his memory blackens in a strange way and the image at the window disappears. He is just left with an inexplicable fear that he left something behind with the girl.

On October 30, 1822, he plucks up his courage and begins a symphony. His previous one, in C major, had been completed four years ago, and he had been at first happy then finally displeased with the result.

He is almost certain on this particular night that he has been infected. He forces the light and the reflected image into a wide and leisurely movement, in true classical form and in the prescribed order, but with the second theme, where he is trying to break away from his memory, he stumbles, consciously. The general pause bears the pain. Will the audience notice it? After the second movement there is nothing more to come. But he wants to develop the time sequence he has established, three-four, three-eight, three-four.

"I'm ill," he could have confessed to Schober, "I've been infected."

He learns from Vogl, who is leaving the Court Opera, that *Alfonso and Estrella* will not be performed.

He could have inquired from Schober if he should visit a doctor. He forgets.

Because it has to be that way, "his" song comes back to him at this station on his Way of the Cross.

At a Schubertiad he makes the acquaintance of one of Hummel's pupils who, so he learns, is an excellent pianist, and can afford to do as he likes. The Honorable Liebenberg de Zsittin owns lucrative estates.

The man goes on and on. At first Schubert scarcely listens to him, until Liebenberg begins to illustrate by singing or speaking the rhythm.

> The sun seems so cold to me here
> The flowers faded, life seems old,
> And their message seems a hollow sound
> I am a stranger everywhere.

> *Die Sonne dünkt mich hier so kalt,*
> *Die Blüte welk, das Leben alt,*
> *Und, was sie reden, leerer Schall—*
> *Ich bin ein Fremdling überall.*

How did he happen on just this song?

He had heard Schönstein singing the "Wanderer," and Jäger too. Liebenberg looks around, casting an eye over the company, and points to Vogl: "Couldn't the esteemed Herr Vogl sing the 'Wanderer' now?"

"I will ask him." But before Schubert moves away, Liebenberg, a knowing spirit by the wayside, gives him the commission he has been waiting for: " 'The sun seems so cold to me here'—if you were to write piano variations on this part of the song, you could count on a reward, Herr Schubert."

He worked on the commission, which he had basically assigned himself, for half of November. Liebenberg could not know that he had not only given impetus to a fantasia, which much later acquired the title *Wanderer Fantasy,* but that he had helped Schubert to cross the divide. Now he no longer needed to search and experiment, he was on his way.

"I have to go home for a while, to Roßau." Schober's reaction to Schubert's decision was one of panic. "What have I done to you? Why are you escaping from me? How can you hurt me like this? How shall I explain this separation to my mother, Sophie, and the friends? Schubert, I beg of you."

Meanwhile, his parents and brothers know nothing about it. He will simply turn up, a guest who hopes he is welcome.

"Nothing surprises me," states his father when he greets him, and he notes that he looks worn out and tired.

His second mother folds him in her arms. He can move into the bedroom behind the second schoolroom. Nobody will disturb him there.

They organize his day in an unusually restrained and helpful manner.

He sees *Fidelio* with Ferdinand at the Kärntnertor Theater.

Schober visits him before New Year's Eve 1822 and persuades him to celebrate the incoming year with a Schubertiad. "You can't leave us in the lurch, Schubert."

"And I don't want to, Schober."

In a long poem Schober will expressly pay tribute to his friend and have one of the passing canonical hours say to him:

> I have given the singer melodies to sing,
> you are still moved by their sound,
> and the power of the philosopher has led you
> to the spirit and the inner life of things.

> *Dem Sänger hab' ich Weisen eingegeben,*
> *noch seid ihr ja von ihrem Klang gerührt,*
> *und in der Dinge Geist und inn'res Leben*
> *hat euch die Kraft des Denkers eingeführt.*

At midnight the merry company forms a procession, Schober presses lighted torches and lanterns into their hands. They rush down to the street to welcome in the New Year with plenty of noise.

First Kupelwieser is at his side, then Sophie.

The city is aflame, the towers of the cathedral stand out dark against the changing lights of the sky where the stars float as if they had lost their way.

He is in pain. For a few days now the large pustules on his penis and his testicles have been discharging. There are round sores coming up on the palms of his hands as if coins had left their imprint.

"I'm ill," he admits to Schober as he takes his leave.

"Me too, my Schubert, I'm drunk."

He escapes, to Roßau, and every step is made with pain.

Probably Schubert was too late in entrusting himself to the care of a doctor, August von Schaeffer. He knows him through the Spaun family, who had recommended him as their family doctor. He had met him at several Schubertiads. During the consultation he holds his breath in pain and shame.

Schaeffer does not ask where he might have got the illness from.

"Treatment will be prolonged. I'll have to cause you pain, my dear Schubert."

He asks him to remove his trousers. The doctor scoops some salve from a mortar, spreads it on a piece of linen, and bandages the sore places. He can remove the dressing at any time and replace it. The salve contains a mixture of ground lignum vitae and mercury. He informs Schubert of the trials and tribulations that he may expect. At first the swellings will increase and the sores break, a kind of gangrene may appear, his mouth will become dry and may be sore, there will be painful swellings on his neck and under his armpits, and his hair will fall out.

"Thank you, Doctor."

"I'm here for you, Herr Schubert."

He lets nothing be known during the creeping course of 1823. All the doctor's prophecies come true. Nevertheless, he has sufficient strength to travel to and fro between Roßau and the Schobers' house in the Göttweigerhof, and in the autumn to go on trips. The Linz Music Association has elected Vogl and him to be honorary members.

In May Sophie von Schober marries her geometrist. "My health still does not allow me to leave the house," he writes to an acquaintance.

(*Ritardando*. The few scraps of information and communication about his illness are spread over the whole of the year. It is never named. There is only one written reference to his losing his hair and wearing a wig. I shall retell what has been suppressed. He laid a trail, and he is ready to set out. The Wanderer is in earnest. On April 10, 1823, he terminates the unsatisfactory relationship with his publisher Cappi & Diabelli: "In conclusion I must further request that you kindly return to me all my manuscripts, both the works that have been

engraved and those that have not." At about the same time he withdrew from a commission, and brought to a close his service to art as
sociable entertainment, which his audience had up till then regarded as
a matter of course. He answered his patron Sonnleithner's question
whether he would compose a quartet for four male voices for a forthcoming Schubertiad: "People have had enough of them. I might be successful in devising a new form, but one cannot be sure of that. As,
however, my future fate is of some concern to me, you who, I flatter
myself, have some share in it, will have to admit that I must be sure to
move forward and am in no way able to entertain your most flattering
invitation.")

In the autumn it becomes too much for Schober. He gives up, and
flees. "D'you know, Schubert, I'm beginning to be afraid of you?"
Schubert had shortly before this moved back to the Schobers' in the
hope that his illness was in remission. But it was soon apparent that the
sores continued to break out, and his last hair fell out under the wig.
"Tell me if I become a burden to you."
"Certainly not." Schober dismisses the idea energetically. "You've
changed, Schubert. So have I." In this way he prepares Schubert and
himself for something that it is difficult for him to put into words. In
passing, quietly and quickly, he blurts it out: "I'm leaving Vienna, dear
friend. I am offered an engagement at the theater in Breslau. For two
years." He cannot go on. Schubert huddles back into the corner, looking at him as if he were a ghost, and he begins to giggle, a tremendous
crescendo, and can hardly stop. At that Schober, baffled and annoyed,
throws open the door and says that when he has calmed down he can
come to him and they will talk about their future plans and intentions.
They did this, but not without getting drunk. It took Schober two
attempts before Schubert understood that he had already arranged
lodging for him. He could, if he had no better plan, move in with Pepi
Huber, "Big Huber," at the Stubenhof Bastion. He would himself issue
an invitation.
"Come back soon, Schober."

"I promise I will. I just need some space."

"Take it, Schober, and write and tell me how you're getting on."

"Goodbye, dear friend."

"Goodbye, my dear."

As a parting gift, and a talisman, he gives Schober a poem that he has written at Roßau during the summer when he had no hope of recovering his health:

Out of deep longing, my holy fear
Would transport me to a better world;
Would fill this dark space
With the almighty dream of love.

Great Father, give now to your son
As his reward for deep suffering,
Finally as a redemptive meal
The eternal radiance of your love.

See, lying destroyed in the dust
Prey to untold misery,
Is the tortured course of my life,
Close to eternal destruction.

Kill it, and kill me with it,
Plunge it all into the waters of Lethe,
And allow, Great Lord, a pure and stronger
Being then to arise from it.

Tiefer Sehnsucht heil'ges Bangen
Will in schön're Welten langen;
Möchte füllen dunklen Raum
Mit allmächt'gem Liebestraum.

Großer Vater! reich' dem Sohne,
Tiefer Schmerzen nun zum Lohne,
Endlich als Erlösungsmahl
Deiner Liebe ew'gen Strahl.

Sieh, vernichtet liegt im Staube,
Unerhörtem Gram zum Raube,
Meines Lebens Martergang
Nahend ew'gem Untergang.

Tödt' es und mich selber tödte,
Stürz' nun Alles in die Lethe,
Und ein reines kräft'ges Sein
Lass', o Großer, dann gedeih'n.

On Christmas Eve 1823 Schwind writes to Schober in Breslau: "Schubert is better. It will not be long until he can appear showing his own hair, which had to be cut as a result of his rash. He is wearing a very comfortable wig. . . . "

Schubert has now been living for two months with "Big Huber," who although he has no piano, does not distract him when he is composing at his table or by the window, and "playing" the first songs of his now never-ending journey.

To wander is the miller's joy,
To wander!
He must be a bad miller,
Who never thought of wandering,
Of wandering.

Das Wandern ist des Müllers Lust,
Das Wandern!
Das muß ein schlechter Müller sein,
Dem niemals fiel das Wandern ein,
Das Wandern.

25

Moment musical no. 8
(*Fast*)

*N*ow, in the year of his illness, he appears before him again—the censor. A figure at the edge of the stage, gray, inconspicuous, and powerful.

Nothing can strike him as odd any longer, while Kupelwieser, who had written the libretto for his opera *Fierabras*, has to wait for the gracious acceptance and the censor's recommended changes, and in this case there are two signatures, that of the chief police commissioner for the Kärntner Quarter, Philipp Letocha, and of the court secretary for police and censorship, Alois Zettler, who grants the manuscript a certificate of *omissis deletis*, which means that this piece may be performed so long as the incriminating parts are removed or changed: Roland may not be a "Spanish general," and there may be no such place as Franconia or France in the opera.

It had all begun much earlier, however, in 1821, with a dedication of the "Erl-King" to the Chief of the Kärntnertor Theater, Count Moritz von Dietrichstein, who first had to acknowledge his acceptance in writing so that the censor could approve the dedication;

and so it continued, with Count Esterházy, to whom he also wanted to dedicate five songs, and whose acknowledgment came too late for the censor;

and so it continues, after *Fierabras*, with the prohibition of a whole libretto, that of the *The Count of Gleichen* by Eduard von Bauernfeld, in which—and this enraged the bigoted censor to the utmost—there was a case of bigamy;

and so it continues with an official sanction, *excudatur*, issued on February 26, 1827, by the censor in Vienna for three songs to poems by Johann Friedrich Rochlitz, "Alinde," "An die Laute" ("To the Lute"), and "Zur guten Nacht" ("For Good-Night");

and so it continues with someone who appears by name, who is given something to read that he cannot yet hear, Censor Schodl, who appropriately enough first sprang into action when he issued the *excudatur* for the trio "Die Advokaten" ("The Advocates") on May 12, 1827, and for the quartet for male voices "Wein und Liebe" ("Wine and Love") on June 2, 1827, and who finally, on October 24, issues his *excudatur* for a bundle of songs that were written so fast and illegibly by the composer that he does not read them through to the end, sparing both himself and the composer some trouble—but what can a censor expect from a title like *Die Winterreise* (*The Winter Journey*)?

And so it continues, with a better outcome, for a poem by Grillparzer, who cheered Beethoven at one point by writing in his conversation book about the censor: "If they only knew what was in your mind when you were writing your music":

> Art of Music, I praise you above all others,
> The highest prize falls to you,
> Of the three sister arts,
> You are the freest, uniquely free . . .

> *Tonkunst, dich preis' ich vor allen,*
> *Höchstes Los ist dir gefallen,*
> *Aus der Schwesterkünste drei*
> *Du die frei'ste, einzig frei . . .*

26

Die schöne Müllerin

he subtitle "To Be Read in Winter" appears over the poems of *Die schöne Müllerin* (*The Lovely Maid of the Mill*). It was the hope and wish of their poet that his songs would be played and sung, and in the Berlin Salon of the much lionized Luise Hensel this did indeed take place.

> I invite you, beautiful ladies, clever gentlemen
> And you who like to see and hear something good
> To a brand new game
> In a completely brand new style . . . .
>
> But if you ask about the players of the game,
> Then, alas, O Muses, I can only present
> One of them in proper fashion,
> And that is a young, blond miller's lad.
>
> For even if the brook speaks the last word,
> A brook is nevertheless not a person
> Therefore take the monodrama as it stands today:
> He who gives more than he has, is called a thief.

> *Ich lad' euch, schöne Damen, kluge Herrn,*
> *Und die ihr hört und schaut was Gutes gern,*
> *Zu einem funkelnagelneuen Spiel*
> *Im allerfunkelnagelneusten Stil. . . .*

Doch wenn ihr nach des Spiels Personen fragt,
So kann ich euch, den Musen sei's geklagt,
Nur eine präsentieren recht und echt,
Das ist ein junger, blonder Müllersknecht.

Denn ob der Bach zuletzt ein Wort auch spricht,
So wird ein Bach deshalb Person noch nicht.
Drum nehmt nur heut' das Monodram vorlieb:
Wer mehr gibt, als er hat, der heißt ein Dieb.

The little volume in which Schubert found the songs had appeared three years earlier: *Poems from the Posthumous Papers of a Traveling Horn-Player.* The scenic epilogue set him going, he only needed to expand its scope in song. Wilhelm Müller, none of whose works he had come across before, presented him in this cycle of poems with a different concept of freedom. Even metaphors could be cunning or stubborn here: green, the hunter's green! From this point on no one could stand in his way nor impede him. From the first bar of the first song he broke free, once and for all.

It must have been in the autumn of 1823 that Schubert first opened this book. Where did he find it? Who did he get it from? Perhaps from Huber, who was a great reader? I suggest that it was one of the Fröhlich sisters, Josefine or Katharina. He has returned from Linz and is living again in Roßau, or he has already moved in with Huber. Illness is tormenting him. Schober has left Vienna. Then he and Mayrhofer receive an invitation from the Fröhlichs. He finds this sort of small reception very pleasant, not a Schubertiad, but there will certainly be music, Josefine will sing, and he can play the piano as he likes. At the end of the evening Katharina puts a little book in his hands. She found the poems very touching, and she imagines that they would appeal to him as well.

He says: "I've heard of him. He's known as the Greek Müller, because he is so enthusiastic about the Greeks—their struggle for freedom."

He never said anything on the subject.

Just as little as Müller, who would have been able to hear the musical version of *The Lovely Maid of the Mill.*

They pass each other by without contact, and all of a sudden they belong together. Brothers. Doppelgänger. Even though they know as good as nothing about each other, never exchange letters, and have no friends in common, yet the musician fulfills the wish of the poet. The latter wrote in his diary in December 1822:

I can neither play nor sing, and yet, when I write poetry I am both singing and playing. If I could create the melodies, then my songs would please better than they do now. But let us hope that there is a like-minded soul who will hear the tunes in my words and return them to me.

"Thank you, Demoiselle Fröhlich."

"Will I be hearing from you, dear Schubert?"

"Most certainly."

He is receiving medical treatment again, this time from two doctors, Schaeffer and Bernhardt. The pains are wandering, and his whole body is prey to them. "Schubert is not entirely well. He has pains in his left arm, so that he cannot even play the piano. But in general he is in good spirits." That is Moritz von Schwind's voice. He mentions the affliction, and is immediately reassuring.

"To Be Read in Winter," to be sung in winter.

Let's go right back, to an image presented in deep perspective in the memory, where the examination candidate stands, washed and brushed by his mother, as a miller's child in a white suit. The picture at the window is not missing either, but now it appears as a shadow on the water, on the brook, like a crack in the glass. And in magical fashion the doppelgänger appears again, this time not as a person but as an inconstant part of nature, an elemental spirit—it is the brook that from the first song onward determines the tempo, the rhythm that carries the Wanderer onward, and finally bears him away.

Moritz von Schwind is the closest to him during these weeks. Schwind's propensity for seeing in images, for making excerpts from a larger view, and for enlarging the inconspicuous, all help Schubert while he is still beginning, still reading the twenty-three poems and listening to how they will sound.

In his letters to Schober and other friends, Schwind tells of several Schuberts. The one whom he knows to be "expressing himself" in a song cycle has scarcely anything to do with the one who complains that his wig constantly slips, or about the pains in his limbs, or with the one who, coming back drunk from the inn, in a terrible rage attacks Mayrhofer, in the street, who is equally drunk, and calls Schubert a fat little blackamoor.

"You hell-hound, you dirty skeleton, you quibbler by the grace of Metternich, you"—punching with both fists, he falls on Mayrhofer, who is surprised by the attack and belatedly tries to pull out his ever-present weapon, his umbrella, which Schubert, much practiced in such skirmishes, prevents by kicking the umbrella from Mayrhofer's hand with a fast piece of footwork.

Schwind does not get involved, he looks on. A day or so later he gives Schubert an account of the fight.

"You're making it up, Schwind. I'd like to have your imagination."

"It's true. It was just like that. You kicked Mayrhofer's umbrella out of his hand with such force that it was launched like an arrow. Mayrhofer looked first at his hand, then at you, the blackamoor, as he kept shouting, 'you fat drunken little moor,' that's what he kept yelling and trying to hit you, but with one bound you got away from his arm, which he was using like a flail, and went searching in the darkness along the muddy street for the umbrella."

Schubert takes off his glasses as if in this way he could no longer see what Schwind was retelling with growing pleasure.

"There you were, crawling round on all fours! 'Where's the blasted umbrella?' you shouted. Again and again. I thought to myself, Schubert could sing that too. 'Where on earth is the blasted umbrella?' That's what Mayrhofer asked too. He slipped past you like a shadow. But you got him by the foot and hung on, so he fell over backwards, and cursed and screamed worse than ever, and then you both suddenly grabbed at the umbrella, tore at it, on your knees, crouching, standing up, crouching again, until you started to laugh and Mayrhofer to howl and you both fell into each other's arms. It's true, I swear it is, Schubert. I brought you home. Huber brushed the mud from your overcoat."

Is that the Wanderer?

He does not doubt even for one bar where the path will lead the miller's lad on his way out from a picture-book. He composes the ending as he goes along.

The brook, which in the opinion of the poet cannot "be a person," becomes his companion along the way. And his tutor.

> We have learned it from the water,
> The water!
> It takes no rest by day nor by night,
> It is always intent on wandering,
> The water.

> *Vom Wasser haben wir's gelernt,*
> *Vom Wasser!*
> *Das hat nicht Rast bei Tag und Nacht,*
> *Ist stets auf Wanderschaft bedacht,*
> *Das Wasser.*

The Wanderer is still pausing, letting his thoughts run ahead. Until in the second song "Wohin?" ("Whither?") his wandering becomes serious, with striding quavers, and his elemental companion becomes visible:

> Downward and ever further,
> Always following the brook.

> *Hinunter und immer weiter*
> *Und immer dem Bache nach.*

The brook becomes his partner in conversation. It leads the Wanderer onward to the maid of the mill, and is supposed to provide him with an answer to the anxious question:

> Tell me, little brook, does she love me?

> *Sag', Bächlein, liebt sie mich?*

When the miller's lad believes his love to be fulfilled, then it is supposed to stop its rushing. When the green huntsman appears as his rival, it is supposed to pursue him wildly. It must scold the fickle maid of the mill. But for the space of several poems it dries up, providing no aid, no company, at the point where the "white" miller's lad becomes "green" from pure jealousy, and finds the color green at one time to be "good" and another "evil."

> My darling is so fond of green.
>
> *Mein Schatz hat's Grün so gern.*

comes first, and in the following song:

> If only it were not so green, so green.
>
> *Wenn's nur so grün, so grün nicht wär.*

(Here Wilhelm Müller, who had violent altercations with the press censor, was presumably alluding to the color of official uniform coats.)

The penultimate poem now really develops into a dialogue between the miller and the stream. The natural element consoles the inconsolable:

> And when love
> Struggles free from sorrow,
> A new little star
> Twinkles in the sky.

> *Und wenn sich die Liebe*
> *Dem Schmerz entringt,*
> *Ein Sternlein, ein neues*
> *Am Himmel erblinkt.*

The beat changes. The walking pace no longer contains the melody, the conversation is carried in the rhythm of a stumbling sarabande, the last step is already being prepared. The brook welcomes the Wanderer, fallen from love, and sings him the cradle song of death:

Here is constancy,
You shall lie with me,
Until the sea shall drink up the streams.

Die Treu' ist hier,
Sollst liegen bei mir,
Bis das Meer will trinken die Bächlein aus.

As so often in Schubert's music, grief, exhaustion, and absorption appear not in the minor, but in the major key.

"To be read in winter," to be sung in winter.

I do not know who was the first to sing these songs, trying them out, whether it was Vogl, Jäger, or Tietze. Schönstein, to whom Schubert dedicated the cycle, sang them later, in the summer, and Schubert transposed three of the songs for "high baritone." But I can imagine that the first singer, like many of his successors, did not understand how imbued with death is this Wanderer, who for just one moment, as jubilant as a lark, banked on the immortal nature of his love.

There, I catch another glimpse of the miller's child dressed in white at the beginning of a long street with tall houses on either side, and somewhere along the way a window opens in which there swims a beautiful but fleeting image.

On January 31, 1824, he celebrates his twenty-seventh birthday surrounded by his male and female friends. Recently he has always been accompanied by his "second doctor," Dr. Bernhardt.

They do not talk of the *Lovely Maid*. Is he still keeping the memory of her to himself, is it difficult for him to detach himself from the songs?

They do not just drink, they carouse wildly and without feeling the need to converse with each other. They wish him a happy birthday, hug him, the women kiss him again and again. Bernhardt lifts off his wig like a lid from a pot. Someone pukes out of the window, then has a quarrel with a passerby on whom some of the blessing fell. ". . . And though we were all very drunk, I still wished that you . . . had been there. When I was quite under the influence I could see them all as they really are. Each more or less idiotic, and Schubert asleep," Schwind writes to Schober, and again a few days later: "Schubert is now fasting for two weeks, and remaining at home. He looks much better and is very cheerful." Schwind, to be sure, conveys his impression; he would like to see Schubert cheerful. He does not want to acknowledge the volatility, the fast and frightening alternation of moods. Schubert, on the other hand, is misleading his younger friend. He keeps more and more to himself, talks to himself, and starts to keep a diary again: "No one who understands the pain of another, and no one who understands their joy! We always think that we are coming together, but we are only walking side by side. Oh, what torment for anyone who can see that this is so."

In the spring he can lay his wig aside. His head is showing a "dear little crop of curls," as Schwind describes it. The moor's curls soon grow back strongly.

But the pains in his arms do not go away, and indeed they are sometimes so bad that he cannot play the piano for days on end.

The great work is finally announced in the *Wiener Zeitung* on February 17, 1824: "From Sauer and Leidesdorf, Kärntnerstraße No. 941, there is newly published: *The Lovely Maid of the Mill.* A Cycle of Songs to Texts by W. Müller. For Solo Voice with Piano Accompaniment by Franz Schubert." The course of treatment prescribed by Bernhardt is helping him to recover. It obliges him to drink more tea than wine, and to eat sparingly, with a vegetarian diet.

He is going out more again now, and letting himself be feted.

The Quartet in A Minor is performed for the first time in the hall of the Philharmonic Society; "as a whole it is very gentle, and written so that a melody lingers as from a song, pure feeling, and perfectly expressed."

He misses Schober greatly, his foolhardiness and his lightmindedness. He could confide in him without immediately afterward having to mull over God and the world. He need not dispel his dark moods since Schober shared them intuitively.

How successful he was in confounding the people around him is shown by two letters to a single person, a voice and its counterpart. Leopold von Kupelwieser had been living for a time in Rome, following the latest fashion in painting, and was not sparing in his own enthusiastic descriptions of the company at the Café Greco. His fiancée, Johanna Lutz, sends him regular reports on social events in Vienna, and what the friends are doing: "Schwind is complaining that there is a new atmosphere in their circle since you and Schober are no longer present. There are new people there, nice lads, but a bit uncouth. . . . Schubert was there too, and he was very sweet. He was quite jolly, which made me glad."

It must have made Kupelwieser glad, too, as he was worried about Schubert's situation, yet only a little later Schubert corrected the kind illusion with an unequaled outburst. Never before and never again did he lay himself so bare. The *Pittore tedesco* Leopoldo Kupelwieser in Rome heard it undisguised:

Dear Kupelwieser, I have wanted to write to you for a long time. . . . You are so good and upright that you will be sure to forgive me many things which others would take amiss from me. In a word, I feel that I am the most unhappy, most miserable man on the face of the earth. Imagine a man whose health will never be right again and who in his despair at the situation makes it worse rather than better, imagine a man, as I say, whose brightest hopes have been reduced to nothing, to whom the joy of love and friendship can offer nothing but the deepest pain, whose enthusiasm (at least of a stimulating kind) for beauty threatens to vanish, and ask yourself, is that not a miserable, unhappy man? "My peace is gone, my heart is heavy. Never, ever again, shall I find peace." [Meine Ruh ist hin, mein Herz ist schwer, ich finde sie nimmer und nimmermehr.] That is indeed what I can sing every day now, since every night when I go to sleep I hope that I shall not wake, and every morning bears witness to the sorrow of the previous day. So I spend my days, without joy, without friends, unless Schwind should come to visit me sometimes and bring me a gleam of those sweet days long gone.—Our circle (our reading circle) has, as you probably already know, has dealt itself a death-blow because of the increase of the coarse beer-drinking and sausage-eating element, and its dissolution will take place in two days' time; but I have hardly visited it since your departure.

He is nowhere near the end of his creative art. He knows that. But the absence of old friends bothers him in just the same way as his physical condition. The "coarse tone" that annoys him, and which he fights against, is after all not so alien to him, it is just that it is not the close friends who set it, and obviously an increasing number of uneducated and ill-mannered people have pushed their way into the reading circle, which was really founded in order to read beautiful literature together, to discuss it, and now and again to make music together.

Against all the misfortune, which after all he exaggerates, stands the fact that all his composing is successful. The *Lovely Maid* songs are followed by the great octet, which Count Ferdinand Troyer had commissioned, and which was performed in April 1824 at his house. Schuppanzigh, who was without doubt one of the most famous violinists of the period, played the first-violin part on this occasion.

Why, Schubert asks himself, should he remain in the city when his friends have left it? He feels better, and is not so irritated by the wandering pains. A messenger should come and present him with a journey.

It is immaterial whether he suggested the journey, or whether he received the invitation without any action on his own part. Karl von Schönstein, the nobleman singer, invites him, on behalf of Count Esterházy, to spend the summer at Zseliz and to improve the piano playing of the two countesses.

On May 25 he takes the mail-coach. Everything repeats itself, and yet it is not the same.

It is a different man who sets off on this journey from the expectant youngster of six years ago. He has had a long battle with illness, he has shut himself off, shut himself away, putting on an act for his friends which he often finds painful.

Now he not only starts on his journey, he breaks free. He now endures both, this Wanderer, the "good" and the "evil" green.

What Johanna Lutz sees, and immediately passes on to Leopold von Kupelwieser, is to be interpreted as a sign of departure: "Schubert did receive your letter. He must, however, be away now, since the windows of his apartment, which always used to be closed, are now wide open."

He climbed aboard the coach with a swing to his step, and without plans. Many a landscape picture flashes past—this group of trees by the Danube, that lonely staging post by the river, this forest skipping over the brow of the hill—as if he had preserved them in his memory as in a gallery. But the nearer the mail-coach comes to Gran, where he will be picked up by one of the Count's carriages, the more uncertain he becomes. He is also journeying back into an area of his life that he explored when he was uninhibited and impressionable, where he had tried his hand at love, and had only with difficulty overcome his first disappointment.

Schönstein had let him know that this time he would be allowed to occupy a room in the castle, not in the servant quarters. His reputation had therefore raised his rank. Perhaps when he received the news he was relieved because Pepi would not be able to visit him there. Josefine's image only comes to life again for him in the last few hours before he arrives. He had lost it, but not Karoline's. He had been able to refresh that one in his mind through their encounters, though few and far between, in Vienna.

Schönstein will come on to Zseliz later, which is a matter of regret for Schubert since his singer could also be a sensitive intermediary.

Once again the weather is warm when the carriage rolls up to the castle. The two horses trot along. They want to get to the pasture. It has been raining and the earth is steaming.

> Then tears flowed from my eyes,
> And the mirror became blurred,
> She said: "It will soon rain,
> Farewell, I am going home."

Da gingen die Augen mir über,
Da ward es im Spiegel so kraus.
Sie sprach: es kommt ein Regen,
Ade, ich geh nach Haus.

He hears the Wanderer singing and glimpses a different scene. The count steps out of the door with Karoline onto the bright stone steps. Karoline waves and speaks lightheartedly to her father. She is wearing a white dress with green ribbons.

He will see them all again, in the courtyard and in the park, as if they had been called to the stage, one after the other, except for the old musician Fröhlich, who has died in the meantime.

Josefine crosses his path on the very first evening, and gracefully dispels his shyness by blowing him a kiss, as if she were the one keeping her distance.

"Hello, Herr Schubert."

"I'm honored, Herr Schubert."

His fame has spread as far as Zseliz. His pieces are frequently played at the castle, and Countess Marie sings his songs.

He is invited to sit at table with the count's family, and no longer eats "over there" with the lackeys. He despises himself for the pride that he feels for a moment over this. At table his place is between the "little brother" Albert, who is now eleven years old, and Karoline. He is so overwhelmed in the first few days by the fact that she is so close to him, that he could brush against her hand or her arm, that he behaves in a clumsy fashion, knocking over his glass and dropping his fork. She observes this with childlike pleasure.

He settles into his room, which is on the first floor, off a long corridor facing the courtyard. It is not particularly large, but the countess has installed a desk for him by the window so that when he is in the mood and has a sheet of manuscript paper in front of him, he can let his thoughts wander, hearing all the sounds in the courtyard, the conversations and shouts, often in the Hungarian language, the commotion in the stable, the barking of the dogs, the giggling and the warbling of women's voices, the rustling of the wind in the trees.

Dr. Bernhardt had given him a libretto to take along with him for his time at the castle: *The Enchanted Rose.* He casts only a cursory glance over the pages, then he lays them aside. He is not in the mood for that sort of work, although his friends still expect him to write a successful opera, even after the unfavorable criticism of *Rosamunde.*

He arranges with the countess the timetable for his lessons, and also his fee. For each month he receives a hundred florins, making a total of five hundred, of which he will be able to save the greater part.

Each morning at about ten he meets Albert for an hour's lesson, in which the two countesses often take part as well. Albert has made considerable progress, and Marie too. She not only delights him with her clearly produced soprano voice, but especially with her piano playing. Karoline, the "playful child," as she is called in a gently protective way by her mother, plays as she always did, in a dexterous but oddly mechanical way, which from time to time annoys him.

"Couldn't you display some feeling as well, when you get to this crescendo, countess?"

"But how, Herr Schubert? I do feel what I'm playing."

"Then it's not reaching your fingers."

She holds her hands at a distance like foreign objects, spreads the fingers, and scolds them. "Will that help, Herr Schubert?"

"We'll teach it to the fingers somehow, countess, since the heart already knows."

Probably it is the very contrariness in her nature that attracts him so much, making him crave to be near her, to hear her voice, and her often arbitrary and sometimes tactless laughter. She is a good-looking young woman, who can appear uncommonly arrogant. Yet, when she thinks that no one is watching, she falls back into the role of a child, creating dolls by animating wooden sticks or beating a colored wooden hoop round the courtyard, and shaking with laughter when it rolls away, stamping her foot if she does not succeed at something or get her way, and hiding behind her mother when someone asks for her, or is looking for her.

"Karoline will never grow up." Marie repeats this as a daily excuse for surprising whims.

He goes walking even more than he did on his first visit. Albert often goes with him. He seeks out the old paths with their familiar views and prospects. But nothing is the way he remembers it. It is as if the colors had lost their intensity, the contours their clarity. He ascribes the change to his condition. He is still feeling the effects of the illness, and he now is certain that it has seared his soul.

One June evening he has escaped down to the River Gran after supper, brushing through the long grass, when suddenly Josefine bobs up, as if he had summoned her by his thoughts. Here she does not pertly keep her distance. She reaches for his hand. For a time they walk side by side. She presses his hand, sending an unspoken message of what she will be unable to say aloud.

"We've hardly had a word together yet," he said.

"Well, this time you have grander quarters," she said.

"Yes indeed, I've been given that."

"There's been a lot of gossip about you," she said.

"What is there to gossip about, then," he asked.

"Not just about your music, Herr Schubert." She lets go of his hand, puts her arm carefully through his, pulls him toward her a little.

"Have you found a future husband, Josefine?"

"If I have, he doesn't know it yet," she said, and after a pause: "People say you've been terribly ill."

He frees himself from her hold, takes a step aside: "What a lot people know. They weren't wrong. I have been really ill."

"I know why," she said.

"My hair fell out, like a mangy old donkey."

Now he reaches for her arm, but she's not having any of that, she faces him squarely, throws her arms round him, she is taller than he is and she bends over him, virtually drawing him into herself, he closes his eyes, listens to his breathing, feeling hers, and so they remain for a little while until she pushes him away gently: "Go back to the castle and get well, and teach Her Grace the Countess Karoline to play the piano properly, and be careful of anything that might make you ill again, Schubert. Goodbye."

She disappears so quickly that he can even save his farewell, only waving helplessly toward the dark thicket where the grass is rustling and the Gran rippling.

He retraces the same walk to the Gran with Karoline and Marie during the daytime. He continually watches the two young women in profile, hot from the summer's sun, living images against the good green and the evil green.

"Pepi got on my nerves terribly this morning with her chatter when she was helping me dress," Marie says.

He waits in vain, his impatience growing, for the fourth and fifth volumes of *The Lovely Maid of the Mill* which Leidesdorf, his publisher, was going to send on to him for proofreading. Leidesdorf can plan ahead with great enthusiasm, certainly, and is understanding in discussion, but when it comes to doing the work he is far more unreliable than Schubert's former publisher, Cappi. Schubert hears from his father that Leidesdorf has left the volumes with him for proofing to save time.

"We are all extremely glad about your good health," write his father and his second mother in a joint letter, "and about your good reception from the count's household. Do, therefore, endeavor to conserve and maintain your health, the greatest of our earthly gifts, and make it your concern to be worthy of the love and respect of all who wish you well.

"You know, of course, that as a teacher of the young I am inclined to moralize. . . ."

He can hear his father while he is reading the letter in small sections, his attention continually wandering as he listens to the voices outside, he can hear his father speaking. As ever, he fights with his body and his soul against this "moralizing" tone of voice that regards him as an object to be educated, and yet his attitude toward his father has changed in the course of the past months, even in the time in which he was living at Roßau. The older Schubert may have behaved in as self-righteous and bad-tempered a way as he ever did, but there were moments when vulnerability and exhaustion were evident.

Now he is amused at how his father even constructs the letter like one of his lessons. First, as a precautionary measure, the concentrated moral, and then the necessary information. After he has insisted on "inner convictions" and invoked Almighty God with "grateful heart," he can finally unburden himself of the news in staccato sentences. The Döbling apothecary Jeckel has died of apoplexy, and the innkeeper at the "Linden Tree" of a stroke. None of this affects Schubert much as he does not remember Jeckel, and the innkeeper only a little. Another piece of information, however, stirs up his memory and his feelings: "You will already know that Herr von Salieri has been retired on full salary, and Herr von Eybel has been promoted to be First Court Musical Director in his place." No, he didn't. He knew from visiting Salieri that he was preparing to withdraw from active life, but now, as Schubert learns the news, it is as if a bright, resounding space in his memory had been emptied and gone dark. He had always dismissed all evil rumors about the maestro. Salieri was his teacher, and he had learned a great deal more than just counterpoint from him.

He vows that he will visit Salieri on his return to Vienna, and like a rattling echo there come back to his mind all the job applications, supported to a greater or lesser extent with testimonials from the master—in vain.

In general, his brooding on the past conjures up forgotten ghosts: Hugelmann, for instance, that emaciated pianist who chose in the end to become a bureaucrat, and from whom three years ago he had borrowed Mozart's Piano Quintet in the André edition, but which is described in Ferdinand's fraternally boisterous letter as a quartet. Hugelmann, well, well! How can Hugelmann pursue him to Zseliz too. "Apart from these two gentlemen, Herr·Hugelmann came as well with the demand that I should return to him his score of the Mozart quartets which you were supposed to have given me for safe-keeping. But, as I could not find them after searching three times, I was unable to fulfill his request. He came to me again twice, once in the corridor at the school, and once at my home, and there he annoyed me quite considerably by letting out his feelings on your thoughtlessness so forcefully, with such a lot of noise and shouting and bad language, that I much regretted the honor of his acquaintance. Be so good then as to tell me where these particular musical works could possibly be, so that I can pacify this raging monster."

He chooses to leave Hugelmann (and his brother) dangling for a while. Why does he act that way? What use to him is Mozart, in his dusty chambers? He has the music with him, he brought it to Zseliz, so that he wouldn't be deprived of Mozart while he was away.

He replies to Ferdinand in the more even tone at which he usually arrives, but which can become unexpectedly shrill, or fall into a stubborn silence. "The quintets (not quartets) belonging to the stupid Hugel-beast made the journey with me by mistake, and by God, he shall not have them back until he has atoned for his rude and coarse behavior with a written or verbal apology. What's more, if there should be an opportunity of giving a harsh scrubbing to this unpolished pig, then I shall not miss the chance to administer it in plentiful doses myself."

He presents Hugel-man, the Hugel-beast, the unpolished pig, to the count's family at table, too, for the amusement of them all, clasping the Mozart quintet to his chest as proof, and with his pretense of fury at the Hugel-jerk, the donkey-head, he involves the little Count Albert so much in the mood of the game that for the next few days he only appears accompanied by an invisible but quite excessively and swinishly behaved Hugel-monster.

From time to time he has fleeting conversations with Karoline, which are scarcely begun before they break off again. He accompanies her to the bakery, or to nibble berries, or they are alone together for a few minutes in the music room, or she has jumped down from the carriage and wishes to walk back with him to the castle—quite out of breath, she starts by saying: "But tomorrow, don't favor Marie when we play the *écossaises*."

"I wouldn't dream of doing that."

"But perhaps when you're awake."

He searches for an answer and rubs his hands in embarrassment: "I'll take note of it, countess."

"Yes, do just that." She laughs and runs away.

He is sitting on the chaise-longue, sorting his music. She skips into the room, looks around, is about to go out again, stops. "Do you like me, Herr Schubert?"

He is not prepared for this question. He hides behind a music book. "How should I . . ." he stutters finally.

"What?" The little word pierces him like an arrow.

Silently she hurries out, banging the door behind her, opens it again and appears with Marie, deadly serious as if nothing had happened.

One evening, after he has played the new *écossaises,* she brushes past him: "How do you get your ideas," she said.

"It's my profession."

She stares at him, open-mouthed: "All the ideas are your profession?"

"And that I can perpetuate them in musical notation."

"And what is my profession, Herr Schubert?"

"To be Countess Karoline."

Blood rushes to her face. Her bright eyes grow dark. "You are horrid."

"No, I'm not!" he says, putting his hand on his chest, looking so vexed that she bursts out laughing.

He will no longer admit his love for her even to himself. He desired the thirteen-year-old child, in retrospect he cannot explain why, but he loves the young woman like an image.

To be near her, and yet to preserve the distance between them, he invites her to play duets with him. As if to make sure her childlike hands would cross with his hands, she chooses first of all the German dances with their two trios and country dances that he composed in 1818 and which she liked so much. "Please." She pulls her chair just a little closer. He thumps out the three-four rhythm so hard that she cannot hear his heart beating.

"Bravo," cries Marie, who has crept in.

"Bravo," he says softly, and Karoline asks just as quietly, "Haven't you any new piece for piano duet this summer?" At which point he replies on the piano with a theme like a very simple song. "The duet might begin like that, in unison."

It takes him two weeks, no longer. The sonata develops. Sometimes he wants to bring in more voices, instruments. He is hoping for a symphony. When Schönstein appears in August—much too late, he moans—Schubert and Marie can already perform the Sonata for Four Hands in C Major (the Grand Duo); Karoline, who had been defeated by its complexity, is immediately consoled with four country dances for piano duet.

On one of his first evenings Schönstein sings *The Lovely Maid of the Mill*.

The countess had invited the servants so that he would not have just the family and their friends for an audience.

In a good mood, Schubert lets his eye wander over the bright mixture of the assembled company, the count's family, the lackeys in livery, the others in their best clothes, Josefine in a light muslin dress, Karoline entirely in white, sitting by herself, her hands in her lap.

Nothing is over-familiar. Every bar strikes him afresh. In several passages Schönstein has trouble in keeping his voice calm, as if it were constantly overcome with gentle emotion.

After the ninth song, "Then tears flowed from my eyes, and the mirror became blurred" ("Da gingen die Augen mir über, da ward es im Spiegel so kraus"), there is a rustling, spluttering disturbance in the hall whose cause Schubert cannot immediately recognize, then he sees how Josefine is disappearing, a handkerchief pressed to her lips. Schönstein had just sung: "She said, 'It will soon rain, Farewell, I am going home'" ("Sie sprach: es kommt ein Regen, Ade, ich geh nach Haus").

Attacks of fatigue and nausea cause him to fear that the illness is gaining ground on him again, and the bouts of melancholy especially wear him down until he cannot fend them off.

"He's just being a mope," scolds Albert. His sisters agree.

In order not to be a burden to them, he pleads work as an excuse and shuts himself away in his room. Then he lies down on his bed, breathes a heavy sigh at his lot, and wishes that he had a submissive girl by his side.

Schönstein and Esterházy ask him to join them in a game of tarot. He is not concentrating, muddles his cards, and is promptly scolded by both of them. He had done Josefine an injustice. What's he doing concerning himself with a countess?

The words of his father intrude on this bad mood in a letter that is as encouraging as it is inane: "I am all the more pleased to hear of your present well-being, because I assume that you are chiefly looking forward to a cheerful future as a consequence of it."

He closes his eyes, repeating the words in his father's cadences, louder and louder, seeing himself both here and there, and thinking to himself, there are two people calling to one another over a very high wall that they are still alive.

They have sent Karoline along: "Come on, Herr Schubert, don't be difficult."

But he had done his duty and given a lesson.

"We could go walking together."

(*Ritardando.* Why does she not say, "We could go riding together?" That would fit in a scene with the country gentry. Why didn't I think of that? The Esterházys have plenty of horses. Schönstein describes their breeding and their strength. It doesn't say anywhere that Schubert can't ride. He just can't. I've been around him for so long now that I can feel his body, small, agile, and short of breath. "I can't ride," I can hear him saying, and the countess says, because there is no other way, "We could go walking together." In defiance of all those laws of propriety that govern their lives, I let the two of them go out alone into the greenery. "My darling is so fond of green" ["Mein Schatz hat's Grün so gern"]. On the way Karoline will surprise him with a remark that I don't have to invent, for it is is authenticated: "If Heaven is not as beautiful as Zseliz, then I don't want to go to Heaven." I shall refrain from inventing a reply for him, since my impression of Zseliz cannot measure up to the paradise of Karoline's childhood.)

Once again he receives a commission.

They are sitting at breakfast. The count is making preparations with Schönstein for a little expedition to the mine.

September announces its presence with changeable weather, the days are beginning to cool down.

The countess is turning the pages of a little book. Suddenly she asks Schubert across the table, "Do you know this poem by Fouqué, 'Thou art my source of loving-kindness' ('Du Urquell meiner Güte')?" She hands him the book. He reads, evidently reading it word by word. Schönstein watched him doing it: "He smiled to himself as he mostly tended to do when something had spoken to him, he took the book and withdrew immediately."

That same evening he brought down the manuscript, a quartet for soprano, alto, tenor, and bass. They sing the song through several times, more securely each time. And it gradually develops into a hymn. The count sings the bass, Schönstein the tenor (with his "high baritone"), Marie the soprano, and the countess and Karoline the alto parts.

The voices were still echoing in this song from Zseliz, when Schönstein and Schubert took leave of the castle and its inhabitants on October 15, 1824. The count had put a coach and four at their disposal. They traveled at a good speed. Only in the dark, as they had chosen a shorter route, were they afraid that the carriage might overturn. Schubert, the sad sack, had caused an upset right at the start, which bothered Schönstein throughout the journey and about which he complained in a letter to Esterházy: "To cap it all, Schubert in his carelessness broke the window at the back of the carriage as soon as we left Dioszeg, as a result of which the most horrible cold wind played freely around our ears."

Schönstein had no idea that Schubert was listening to another melody. On the eve of their departure he had discovered on the card table in the salon a little volume of poems by a poet whom he did not know, with the colorless name Ernst Schulze. The poems spoke to him. He packed the book with his things without asking leave. Now he was reading words that were already resounding, with Schönstein wrapped in a traveling rug by his side:

O heart, be calm at last!
Why do you beat so restlessly?
It is indeed Heaven's will
That I should leave her.

O Herz, sei endlich stille!
Was schlägst du so unruhvoll?
Es ist ja des Himmels Wille,
Daß ich sie lassen soll.

Schwind will be expecting him. Schober has promised to return soon from Breslau.

"Where will you be living?"

Schönstein has jumped down from the carriage. The coachman heaves down the baggage.

The city has quite different sounds from Zseliz.

"I am going to Roßau first, to the school, to my parents."

"Goodbye, Schubert."

27

Moment musical no. 9
(Not too slow)

*S*chubert never confessed his love to the little countess, as his Wanderer did, never kneeled before her, never dared to challenge the conventional attitude, how would he be able to find a true love from among the nobility, he never carved the name of his love in the bark of trees, nor sowed a message in fast-growing cress-seeds that his heart belonged to her, he did not betray himself in his songs, for the little countess would not have understood these as billets-doux or messages, but he did just once speak aloud of the thing that he had forbidden himself, and not in secret but in front of the assembled company at table in Zseliz. Schönstein tells how just once he set his childish sweetheart straight with a confession of his love:

He has dedicated the quartet on Fouqué's "Prayer" to the countess.

For which she thanks him graciously.

The count applauds.

Countess Marie warbles her part.

Schönstein praises him for his artistry.

But Karoline reproaches him for never yet dedicating a composition to her.

Which does not surprise him, does not make him ashamed.

Which, to the astonishment of all present, he corrects out of love.

He says, "My dear countess."

He says, "Why should I, since everything is already dedicated to you anyway."

Whereupon she does not, as is prescribed in old-fashioned novels, blush deeply, but is silent.

And the count dismisses them all from table.

"Go outside. Enjoy life."

28

Summer Holiday

*H*e is surprised how little he must argue with his father, who is no longer so upset as he used to be to find his son just settling into his room temporarily, and looking for an apartment. He has also given up the idea of trying to win him back to being a teacher.

They talk about the dead Napoleon and how the world is transforming his image; about the Greeks who will not stop fighting for their freedom; about the father's plan that he will still find a school in the Inner City.

Schwind regularly comes to visit him and takes him out. They meet friends, drink moderately or immoderately, and Schwind boasts that he is more diligent than Schubert, he is drawing and painting far more than Schubert is composing. Which is true for the first months of the year 1825. Schubert is not working so much, but taking stock. The German dances and *écossaises* appear with Cappi & Co. as his opus 33, the Trout is published by Anton Diabelli and Co., and Sauer and Leidesdorf bring out as his opus 35 the "Variations pour le Pianoforte à quatre Mains," the piano duet played with Karoline, a souvenir of the summer at Zseliz.

He does not see Karoline, but he does bump into Therese, quite by chance, near the Roßau schoolhouse.

He is not prepared for her to appear. She comes unbidden. He sees her on the street before she sees him. For a moment he considers disappearing into the nearest doorway.

She is obviously deep in thought, taking no notice of what is going on around her.

The old, long-forgotten feelings sweep over him with such force that he has to clutch at his breast. He watches her, and she is attractive to him, but she attracts him as a memory unexpectedly revived. While he is looking at her he hears her voice. She is singing the Kyrie from the Lichtental Mass. Her voice has remained the same—pure, hardly distinguishable from that of a boy.

He would probably have been able to walk past her without being noticed. He stands still, letting her approach. She runs straight into his soft-spoken greeting like a transparent wall.

She looks up, blinded by her thoughts, which he would have liked to know. "Yes?" Now she takes in who it is. "You did give me a fright, Franz."

"I didn't mean to."

Now, close beside her, retreating a few years, a seeming eternity, to a time on the glacis between childhood and independence, now he can feel his childlike body.

"How are you, Franz? People talk about you a lot. Are you living with your parents?"

She asks everyday questions and he gives everyday answers. That he is well, that he is working a lot, that many of his compositions have been performed.

But then she says, "Just the other day I sang the Gretchen song again, with my brother accompanying me."

That goes beyond the quick pleasantries, that strikes home, and hurts.

"Do you still remember our concert in the courtyard at the Himmelpfortgrund for my parents and your mother?"

She smiles to herself, growing serious and busy, not wanting to be pinned down. "I'm in a hurry, Franz, I've spent too long chatting."

He bows and kisses her hand.

"Farewell, Therese."

"Farewell, Franz."

This is a parting that anticipates no repetition.

He watches her go. She walks a little awkwardly, her arms swinging. Maybe, he thinks to himself, she is expecting a child. He watches her as she finally steps out of his life.

Farewell, Therese.

At the beginning of February, with the snow piled up all around, he moves out, farther away into the suburb of Wieden, to the house of Johann Fruhwirt. This is a spacious property with a beautiful courtyard that holds promise for festivities in the summer months. His landlord, the oil-maker Keller, knows of him, and regrets that he cannot put a piano at his disposal.

The room is large, sparely furnished, and pleasantly warm from the tiled stove.

If he looks out of his window he can see down into the spacious courtyard and beyond it to the Karlskirche.

What he most likes about this lodging is that Schwind is nearby. That dear region "Schwindia" is what the friends call the Schwinds' apartment in the beerhouse which stands right next door to Fruhwirt's house.

Schwind immediately sends Schober a report (the connection between the friends is maintained despite prolonged absence). "Schubert is well and busy again after a period of inactivity. He has recently come to live in the house next door to us, where the beerhouse is, on the second floor, in a very pretty room. We see each other every day, and as far as I can, I share his entire life with him. . . . Every week there is a Schubertiad at Enderes' place, in other words, Vogl sings."

Schubert owed his meeting with Eduard von Bauernfeld to Schwind's fondness for companionship and relationships. It is not long before they are sealing the bonds of friendship in sugared water, as there is nothing better to hand. It is the last close friendship he initiates and which he takes seriously.

Bauernfeld is five years younger than Schubert and two years older than Schwind. He is still studying law, but has already notched up a small success with the comedy *Der Magnetiseur* (*The Mesmerist*).

In conversation he is inclined to be long-winded and grave, which can infuriate Schwind as much as it does Schober later on, but he is way ahead of all the others in his resolute attachment to freedom, particularly of verbal expression and in the arts. In his portraits he bears a remote resemblance to Heinrich Heine with his clear, slightly pinched facial features.

They do not have much time for their friendship. They take what there is. At the weekly Schubertiads it is not now a question of repeating songs and piano pieces as they did for a time, but new compositions are always played and sung.

Bauernfeld's loquaciousness stimulates Schubert. Naturally he hopes that his new friend, the comedy writer, will give him a libretto. They consider *The Count of Gleichen,* which the censor will later assassinate.

"Often with Schwind and Schubert. He sang new songs at my house. Recently we slept at his house. As we were short of a pipe, Moritz improvised one for me out of Schubert's eyeglass case."

This was just a quick bit of fun. Bauernfeld had forgotten his pipe and Schubert did not own one. They considered this way and that, whether they should go or stay put. They had some tobacco, but no pipe. "Let's go, then." "Please stay." "We've only just arrived." Schwind was about to leave, Bauernfeld hesitated, Schubert lay down on the bed and stared at the ceiling, Schwind, reined in gently by Bauernfeld, looked around the room, weighing various objects in his hands until he found the case, and without hesitating began to work it into shape for a pipe.

"I beg of you, Schwind, where am I going to keep my glasses?"

"But you sleep with your glasses on, Schubert."

They drank his health, and for a moment he felt like rebelling, tearing the transformed case away from Schwind, but he withdrew into his black no-man's-land, which in the long run protected him from such silliness. "And you, Schubert?" "What are you asking me for?"

A few days before this he has composed a song that lingers in his head in a different way from usual. He often forgets what he has composed almost as soon as he has finished it, a strange trait that his friends cannot comprehend. This song, however, with its melodic invention, fills his mind for a time, singing in his head in a way wonderful even to him, singing a hymn to an evening landscape certainly animated more by the music than by the poetry. He had read the verse in a magazine: "Im Abendroth" ("At Evening") by Karl Lappe.

> Oh how lovely is a world,
> Father, when it gleams with golden light.

> *O wie schön ist eine Welt,*
> *Vater, wenn sie golden strahlet!*

No impulse was necessary beyond the first two lines. The fact that the poem does not say "your world," but "a world," strengthened the mood of a hymn. It is a world-creating phrase, between the temporary and the permanent, which also absorbs the end of the poem as something to be taken for granted:

> And this heart, before it breaks
> Still drinks the glow and savors the light.

> *Und dies Herz, eh' es zusammenbricht,*
> *Trinkt noch Glut und schlürft noch Licht.*

Josefine Fröhlich sings the song at one of the next Schubertiads. Mayrhofer, who is present less and less often, bursts into tears on hearing it, but Schubert makes his escape, he does not want to receive congratulations, and does not want to speak.

Schwind follows him. They look for a quiet place to sit at the "Crown" and drink a silent toast.

"I should go away again."

"Why? You've only just arrived."

"I'm going with Vogl to Steyr."

He shouldn't have said that. Schwind loses his temper.

"I would just like to know, Schubert, what you see in this painted singing machine. All right, he has helped you, he introduced your songs to people—but now . . ."

He does not react, sinking into himself and watching unmoved as Schwind pays, and throws his overcoat round his shoulders. "You just go on sitting there and hatch your horrible Vogl-bird."

Schubert, unsteady on his legs, reels after him, bumps into the door, falls in the snow, and gets up.

He does not know how he got home.

When Schwind wants to pick him up in the afternoon, he will not at first open the door. "You stay outside, you gallows blackbird, you crumpled crow, I don't want to see you."

Schwind won't be driven away so fast, threatening to set up camp outside the door, which Schubert manages to talk him out of doing. "Please, Schwind, I'm composing, I need my peace and quiet."

"I want to hear what you've written as soon as you have finished it. Otherwise I won't believe another word you say."

"You don't have to anyway, Schwind."

Schubert was not making excuses. He is working on a sonata in C major, but can't get the last two movements right, or he lets himself be distracted by the preparations for his journey. Vogl sets off ahead at the end of March to his "country estate" in Steyr. Schubert has promised to follow as soon as possible.

What is still keeping him? Who?

He starts the Sonata in A Minor. He goes walking a great deal with Ignaz and Ferdinand. In the evenings he lets himself be invited to Schubertiads, especially at the Fröhlich sisters' house, or to "Schwindiads," where pictures come alive: Schwind is spreading out in thirty drawings Figaro's wedding procession, accompanying with his own art the finale of the third act of Mozart's opera, and Schubert responds in song to what he sees, and to the many allusions before his eyes. At such moments he is approachable again. Schwind grabs at the opportunity and tries to persuade him to remain in the city—Schober will be coming soon.

In fact, Schober arrives in Vienna in June 1825 with the firm intention of staying, but Schubert is already gone at least for the time being, having followed Vogl in May to his summer holiday place, which has not only been promised to him by Vogl (and his memory of his first stay in Upper Austria puts him in a cheerful frame of mind anyway) but it will also be the last station on his life's journey at which he can draw breath.

He is received by everyone with warmth. His music accompanies him wherever he stays. Nothing inspires him more than perceptive appreciation of his work.

He puts out of his mind the ever-recurring worries about his illness, and the slight pains wandering around his body, and forgets them.

He is busy at first in Steyr, assisted by Vogl, and repeats something that on the first occasion ended for him with a humiliation. He sends Goethe a volume with poems that he has already dedicated to him. It has just been published by Diabelli and Co. after a delay of two years, and contains settings of "To Coachman Chronos," "To Mignon," and "Ganymede" with the inscription "Respectfully Dedicated to the *Poet* by Fr. *Schubert.*" This time Spaun cannot write for him. He is no longer in Linz anyway, but has been transferred by his government office to Lemberg. So Schubert writes himself, briefly and without too many flourishes:

> Your Excellency,
>
> If by the dedication of this composition of your poems I should be successful in demonstrating my unbounded veneration for Your Excellency, and perhaps in gaining some small measure of recognition for my humble insignificance, then I should regard the favorable outcome of this desire as the greatest event of my life.
>
> With the greatest respect, I remain,
>
> > Your most devoted servant,
> > Franz Schubert

He felt himself encouraged in this second approach also by Anna Milder, the great singer, who loved his songs and frequently performed them. From Berlin she sent him a critical notice that had appeared in the *Berlinische Zeitung*: "Franz Schubert in Vienna is a sensitive song-composer, a lover of modulation, who has set "Zuleika" from the *Westöstlicher Diwan (East-West Divan)* especially for Madame Milder, and dedicated the manuscript to her. Although this musical work exceeds the bounds of the Lieder form, and the five verses of the beautiful poem are set as a single piece of music, its oriental spirit is still successfully captured and conveyed in the music." She wrote in addition: "I cannot refrain from giving you news of a musical evening. . . . The 'Erl-King' and 'Zuleika' were an enormous success, and it gives me great pleasure to be able to send you this news. . . . How is Vogl? Well, I hope, and I would wish him very well. . . . Farewell to you, and do not forget, when you compose, Your devoted Anna Milder."

He takes this exhortation with him into his wintertime, and later, when the organ-grinder is already casting his shadow, he will compose for her a song that produces a summer atmosphere, in which creation itself begins to sing: "Der Hirt auf dem Felsen" ("The Shepherd on the Rock"), once again to a poem by Wilhelm Müller.

There is nothing he likes to be involved in more than a cheerful hustle and bustle. The area is laid out to please the travelers, the loveliness of the hills, the lyrics of the landscape: from Steyr to Linz, from Steyr to Gmunden and back, and then to Gmunden again and on to Steyregg.

"In Upper Austria I find my compositions everywhere, especially in the abbeys of St. Florian and Kremsmünster, where, assisted by a gallant pianist, I performed my four-hand variations and marches with considerable success," as he writes to his parents. He embellishes, in order not to upset them. But he is more and more horrified at *how* the public receives his songs, how it treats them. How the obvious, which is actually only apparent to him in retrospect, is what makes an impression and how the tentative, difficult music is dismissed. His songs to texts by Walter Scott become the great triumph of the summer season.

> Ave Maria! gentle Virgin
> Listen to a maiden's entreaty,
> My prayer shall float up to you
> From this wild and hardened rock.

Ave Maria! Jungfrau mild,
Erhöre einer Jungfrau Flehen,
Aus diesem Felsen starr und wild
Soll mein Gebet zu dir hinwehen.

"They also wondered greatly at my devoutness, which I expressed in a hymn to the Virgin Mary, and which apparently touches all their souls and promotes a religious mood. I believe that derives from the fact that I have never forced myself to devotion. . . ."

In this way he discreetly but precisely gives his father an answer to their countless arguments, often ending in shouting, about the true faith and proper piety. At the same time Schubert is voicing a situation that is causing increasing confusion in his circle: his indifference, when he withdraws, distancing himself, and from which he only breaks out a few times, here in the openness of summer, as in a letter to Josef von Spaun, whom he reproaches for allowing himself to be sent so far away, and whom he comforts at the same time with the thought that the citizenry, still maintained by Metternich in a state of complacent indolence and submissive prosperity, is becoming increasingly vulgar, and that it is more beneficial for an intellectual to stay "at the limit."

"Altogether it is a really miserable situation now, where everything is everywhere ossified and becomes insipid and prosaic, where most people look calmly on or are even comfortable with it, where they slide quite comfortably down through the mud into the abyss. It is indeed more difficult to climb upward. And yet this mob would be quite easily driven apart if only something could be done from *above*."

This is not the Schubert they know. With Anton Ottenwalt, Spaun's brother-in-law, at whose house he is staying in Linz, he debates far into the night on the subject of the inner courage of art which is opposed, and must be opposed, to a reality ruined by tyranny and cowardice, by greed and miserliness; on the joylessness of the rulers and the listlessness of the subjects; on the fickleness of many friends, among whom he, though lovingly, even counts Schober, but not Spaun.

Vogl and the others stare at him as if he has been transformed before their very eyes, a situation he enjoys and on which he plays. He has the feeling, in this bright and warmly lit salon where they are standing and sitting in casual groups around the piano, expecting him to make music with Vogl, the feeling that he himself is no longer entirely among them, but present only in the memory of the others.

As Ottenwalt writes to his brother-in-law:

> We sat together until almost midnight, and I have never seen nor heard him in this mood, serious, profound and as though inspired. How he spoke of art and poetry, of his youth, of friends and other important people, on the relationship of the ideal to life, and the like. I was more and more amazed at this mind, of which it is said that its artistry is so unconscious that it is often hardly apparent or intelligible to the man himself, and so on. And how simple it all was—I cannot speak of how far his convictions extend or whether they form a unity—but these were glimpses into a view of the world that had not just been acquired, and the part that his noble friends might have in it does nothing to detract from the singularity that is evident therein.

Maybe it is in one of the gardens in Linz, on a terrace before a facade draped in ivy, that Vogl sings *The Lovely Maid of the Mill.* Then he could join in, already hearing the rhythm of wandering, would move away again with the miller's lad and the brook, unrecognized by the listeners, intoxicated as they were with the wine and the summer sun, and hearing nothing beyond his beautiful songs, not the insistent stride, nor the beating of his heart, nor the eager pursuit of the evil "green" nor the knocking of the bird of death.

They cry "Bravo," want him to play so they can dance, and at the same time they feel an inexplicable inhibition as they approach the little man hunched over the piano, who looks up now and again, watching them, and blinking behind his thick glasses as if the light were blinding him.

"It is very nice here with you," he thanks them all around.

His friends announce that he is writing a symphony in Gmunden and Gastein. "By the way, in Gmunden he was working on a symphony that is to be performed in Vienna in the winter," Ottenwalt writes to Josef von Spaun. It is merely a question of which winter, is it the coming winter or his own winter, or winter for us all, for the Gastein Symphony is a puzzle, composed or not as the case may be, a "music in the air," created in summer, accompanying him on his journey from summer, is it finally the great symphony, or at least its opening, this unheard Gastein symphony, that he recalls in his head, keeping it to himself, or is it the other one, the Great C Major, which he completes in March 1828, and which is supposed to be performed by the orchestra of the Concert Society, but which is rejected by the musicians because they maintain that the piece is too long and too difficult for them, though in actual fact it is because they are afraid of this musical landscape, of its breadth, its sky, and its freezing chill.

The Gastein Symphony that Robert Schumann discovered and which Mendelssohn performed in the Leipzig Gewandhaus for the first time in 1839, the Symphony in C Major, is a message, still far from being deciphered in its entirety, from the journey that he will not break again.

He leaves Vogl, who wants to continue to Italy, and returns to the city, to Vienna.

29

Moment musical no. 10
(*Fairly fast, but powerfully*)

He learns from Ferdinand that Salieri has committed suicide, poisoned himself in his great distress,
bringing against himself the terrible accusation
that he was responsible for Mozart's death, but that was a rumor, nothing but malicious slander, and he is beside himself, pursuing Ferdinand
into the corridor, screaming and beating his breast, it couldn't be true
that the maestro, his teacher Salieri, had murdered the heavenly
Mozart, "Why and how, could that be true, I ask you, brother, my
teacher has for some reason died of a poison, as Mozart died too, and
I'm telling you, Ferdinand, I'll shout it out so that the ears of the great
may hear it, Salieri has died of a poison that is the poison of the age,
and I learned from Salieri, just as in all humility I learned from Mozart
and from Beethoven, but Salieri taught me counterpoint, and if he died
of a poison that he gave to Mozart, then I, too, shall perish from a poison, brother, I'm telling you," and he runs down the stairs and locks
himself in his room. There I leave him to shed tears the whole day
through until the terrible news can no longer cause him hurt.

30

Winterreise

chober and Schwind take him noisily in hand. He drinks with them, gets drunk, and gives up.

"Tell us," they beg. Hesitantly, he talks about the summer, then he asks about them. Schwind is still hurt that he refused to come and live with him and Bauernfeld. "I just didn't feel up to it," he explains.

He sleeps with Schober. It is a sort of love that means nothing to him, but Bauernfeld jokes about it from time to time.

They are friends, but no longer fellow travelers.

Now he orders time, everything moves faster, and yet seems to stand still. At this point I shall stop retelling his life story and spelling out its various stations.

At first he lives in Fruhwirt's house, then at Bäckerstraße 6, then on the bastion near the Karolinentor, then he moves in with Schober on the Tuchlauben and is more comfortable than ever before, with two rooms and a music room plus piano.

He wanders through the city, through the salons, and is feted. The Schubertiads grow into celebrations, and yet have scarcely anything to do with his music. Sometimes he annoys his host by leaving the festivity without explanation, or, when he has finished making music, by spending the whole evening brooding in a corner.

He might have started a love affair. It would have been about as foolish as Grillparzer's love for Katharina Fröhlich.

"You could see him once more, I beg of you." Josef Hüttenbrenner invites him to visit the dying Beethoven. Schindler knows about it.

It is a scene that his friends might have imagined. He is let in to the room on his own, not with Hüttenbrenner.

Beethoven is lying in bed, motionless, as if laid out on his bier. He hears nothing. He can hear everything. Schindler measures the time he spends looking. Now he is nodding, almost imperceptibly. It is enough. He must withdraw.

At the funeral on March 26 he is one of the thirty-six torch-bearers, together with Grillparzer and Raimund, and also Randhartinger, his fellow student from the Konvikt, whom he never could abide and who later becomes conductor of the Hofkapelle, and after the burial at the Währing Cemetery he sets off with him to a bar, gets drunk, and says next to nothing to him, as if he had anything to say anyway, but in his head he is trying out sonata openings.

With Bauernfeld he almost ends up one day in the talons of Metternich's police, which would have been amusing rather than anything else, but he can feel the frosty clutches. They were both invited to visit the Ludlamshöhle nonsense society, a group of citizens and artists who had to demonstrate their worth to the society as prime examples of idiocy and clairvoyance, and were now brought before the police, accused of being members of an illegal organization.

"'Run, Schubert, run,'" I shouted to him," commented Bauernfeld in retrospect.

"Run, Schubert, run."

Once more there is no proof of where and when he first turned the pages of the *Urania* in which twelve poems from the *Winterreise*, the *Winter Journey*, were to be found. The almanac is devoted to the year 1823, so it had appeared four years before. It was probably well worn, with bookmarks between the pages.

It may have been like this: He has come home with Schober earlier than usual. They talk about people they know and people they don't, people they have met in the course of the evening, while Schober does suggestive impressions of them. Schubert wants to withdraw but Schober persuades him at least to come in and have a glass of wine.

They chat. In the meantime he has learned to feign being present. Schober, for his part, is not concerned at his absence.

"You're right there," he said.

"How nice," he said.

"Oh, go on," he said.

"Yes, Huber is a bit common," he said.

On the table lies a little volume that Schober has obviously had with him on his travels. Schubert reaches out for it, inquiring silently of Schober if he may, leafs through it without any great interest, the book remains open as if of its own accord, he reads the name of the poet, Wilhelm Müller, he reads on:

> I arrived as a stranger,
> I depart again as a stranger,

> *Fremd bin ich eingezogen*
> *Fremd zieh ich wieder aus,*

then he gets to his feet, excuses himself to Schober, crosses the corridor to his room, sits down, draws the chair close up to the table, lays the book in front of him, smooths the open pages with the back of his hand and reads, "I arrived as a stranger, I depart again as a stranger," and taps out the eighty notes, this pacing figure that denotes neither running nor walking, but impetuous footsteps on the spot: "I arrived as a stranger."

(*Ritardando*. They walk toward each other, two complicated characters, introverted, tired before their time, and yet neither catches sight of the other. It is some time ago now that I wrote this opening to a short description of Wilhelm Müller's life. Now, rereading it, I am all the more amazed that Schubert never bothered more about the poet of *The Lovely Maid of the Mill* and the *Winterreise*, he never inquired about him and sought no knowledge of him. Müller was deprived of Schubert's answer, he never heard it. It would no longer have been of help to him, but it might have given him a moment's happiness. Müller was three years older, born in 1794 in Dessau. He grew up in humble circumstances, and, like Schubert, he lost his first mother at an early age. His father enabled him to make extensive studies in law and philosophy. He traveled and became a soldier. In Berlin he was the delight of the ladies and gentlemen in the salon of Luise Hensel; stimulated by Goethe he wrote the cycle of poems *The Lovely Maid of the Mill* as a "game," he married Adelheid Basedow, yielded to his feelings of restlessness, traveled about, intending to go to Athens but arriving in Rome, he was horrified at the curtailment of liberty decreed by the authorities and the press censorship, he became a loving father, and a respected librarian in his native Dessau. Heine praised him, and the Swabian Romantics welcomed him into their circle. But by this time he was already on his way, he had published his long and not entirely successful poems on behalf of the Greeks, who were fighting for their freedom, and from then on was known as the Greek Müller, he was on his way, and the bark in which he had carved his love had turned to ice:

My heart, do you now recognize
Your own image in this stream?
Beneath its crust is it also
Seething and tearing its bonds?

Mein Herz, in diesem Bach
Erkennst du nun dein Bild?
Ob's unter seiner Rinde
Wohl auch so reissend schwillt?

In the year 1827, when Schubert started out on his winter journey, setting the twelve poems from the *Urania*, Wilhelm Müller died. Maybe he took his own life, weary from his wanderings. I ask myself whether in fact none of the Viennese newspapers carried this news. That is scarcely credible, but it seems to have been the case. Schubert did not discover that the companion of his wanderings, the man who knew as much as he about the shivering cold among people and the cooling of the earth, had gone on ahead of him.)

226

He departs again as a stranger.

Nobody is allowed to disturb him now, not even his closest friends. He does not tell them what he is working on.

In the evenings he lets himself be taken along with them, to the "Anchor," to the "Burgundian Cross," to the "Golden Lamb," to the "Blackamoor," to the "King of England," to the "Red Hedgehog," to the "Red Cross," or to the "Red Crawfish."

Schwind asks him if this composing business isn't making him shrink. He seems even shorter.

"Don't overdo it," begs Bauernfeld.

He's better than he's been in a while. The distance from which he replies frightens him.

> The wind plays with the weather-vane
> On my dear love's house.
> In my delusion I thought it was mocking
> The departure of the poor fugitive.

> *Der Wind spielt mit der Wetterfahne*
> *Auf meines schönen Liebchens Haus.*
> *Da dacht ich schon in meinem Wahne,*
> *Sie pfiff den armen Flüchtling aus.*

At one Schubertiad in the house of a count, the hostess showers Schönstein, who is singing, with the highest praises, and overlooks the composer, who accompanied him. He spends the evening sitting behind the piano, and it would not have taken much for him to have disappeared inside it.

Schober occasionally brings admirers to his room, staying with them and making sure that they do not get on his nerves. "I visited him in his sparsely furnished room at the top of the house. I can still see a fairly wide desk, natural and simple, of the sort you stand at to work—there were freshly written manuscripts on it. 'You compose so much,' I said to the young maestro. 'I write for a few hours every morning,' he replied most modestly. 'When I have finished one piece, then I begin another.' Obviously he really only did music—and his life was something secondary."

And his life was something secondary.

While he is writing he is constantly thinking of the Lovely Maid. At the same time it is clear to him in every bar, in every melodic idea, that he is crossing a frontier with the nameless Wanderer. The summer, the green earth, and the whispering stream have all afforded the Wanderer a death beneath the starry heavens,

> And the heaven up above,
> how spacious it is!

> *Und der Himmel da oben,*
> *wie ist er so weit!*

On the other side of the frontier, where he wanders now, there is no more green, the world congeals under ice and snow, love is no longer personified, it appears in the Wanderer's memory without concrete form, as a reproach to his warmth, and the brook, his restless friend, congeals and abandons him.

> You wild, bright river,
> Which rushed so merrily,
> How still you have become.
> You will not bid me farewell.
> You have covered yourself over
> With a hard and rigid crust.
> You lie cold and motionless
> Stretched out in the sand.

> *Der du so lustig rauschtest,*
> *Du heller, wilder Fluß,*
> *Wie still bist du geworden,*
> *Gibst keinen Scheidegruß!*
> *Mit harter, starrer Rinde*
> *Hast du dich überdeckt,*
> *Liegst kalt und unbeweglich*
> *Im Sande ausgestreckt.*

The sequence of poems in the *Urania* closed with "Einsamkeit" ("Loneliness"), not with "Der Leiermann" ("The Organ-Grinder").

After he has finished composing the first twelve poems in the *Winterreise*, and has discovered a further twelve poems in the enlarged edition of Müller's *Posthumous Papers of a Traveling Horn-Player*, he calls a halt to his wanderings, taking a leap back into reality, which from now on he will view with the eyes of the Wanderer.

He is invited to Graz by the lawyer Pachler and his wife, the pianist Marie Pachler. He composes for her the *Twelve Graz Waltzes*.

This is not just a conventional thank-offering. During the three weeks of September he is taken seriously by friendly and knowledgeable people and is able to gather strength for the last stage of the journey. He knows that he will return to a winter that will never end, and he hints at this in his letter of thanks to Marie Pachler. "Already I am aware that I was too well looked-after in Graz, and I can't quite stand the idea of Vienna yet, which is, to be sure, rather large, but it is lacking in cordiality, candor, true thought, sensible words, and especially in wise deeds. One really has no idea if one is being clever or stupid, there is so much chattering confusion, and one seldom, or never, attains to a heartfelt cheerfulness. Of course, it is quite possible that I myself am much to blame for this with the slow way I warm up."

With the slow way I warm up:

> Here and there, some colored leaves
> Are still to be seen on the trees,
> And I often stand by these trees
> Lost in thought.
> I look up at the single leaf
> And pin my hope to it.
> If the wind plays with my leaf
> I tremble, as much as I am able.
> Ah, and if the leaf falls to the ground
> My hope falls with it,
> And I too fall to the ground
> And weep on the grave of my hope.

> *Hier und da ist an den Bäumen*
> *Manches buntes Blatt zu sehn,*
> *Und ich bleibe vor den Bäumen*
> *Oftmals in Gedanken stehn.*

Schaue nach dem einen Blatte,
Hänge meine Hoffnung dran;
Spielt der Wind mit meinem Blatte,
Zittr' ich, was ich zittern kann.
Ach, und fällt das Blatt zu Boden,
Fällt mit ihm die Hoffnung ab,
Fall ich selber mit zu Boden,
Wein' auf meiner Hoffnung Grab.

He has scarcely returned from Graz when he begins the second part of the *Winterreise*. Every song elates him and weakens him. He needs more time than usual, he pauses, diverting his mind with other compositions. His journey becomes in its eternal repetition an artistic portrayal of disaster, and the handwriting on the wall:

Strange old man,
Shall I go with you?
Will you turn your barrel-organ
To my songs?

Wunderlicher Alter,
Soll ich mit dir gehn?
Willst zu meinen Liedern
Deine Leier drehn?

He cannot escape him any more. He does not struggle against him either.

Before he traveled to Graz, he had invited friends to Schober's music room and had sung them the first part of the *Winterreise*. He was sure that the songs would terrify them. But first he succumbed to his own feelings of terror: "We went to Schober's where we met Spaun, Schwind, and Bauernfeld . . . because Schubert, Schober's lodger, had invited us to hear his new compositions, but our friend Schubert did not come. In the end Schwind undertook to sing a few older songs by Schubert, which delighted us."

He had fled to the "Crown," keeping out of sight. They would hear the message soon enough.

In the following autumn he repeated the invitation, and appeared. As expected, the friends were disconcerted.

"In a voice full of emotion, he sang the whole of the *Winterreise* through for us. We were quite amazed at the somber mood of these songs," remembers Spaun.

And Schober said that he had only liked one song, "Der Lindenbaum" ("The Linden Tree"). Schubert said at this point, "These songs please me more than any others, and they will also please you in due course."

In Schober's opinion he will recover from the strain. After all, he has his blackamoor's curls back again as he used to.

After all, he no longer complains of the wandering pains.

After all, he has one success after the other, even music publishers from Berlin and Leipzig show interest.

Does this concern him?

A bizarre guest makes his appearance in Vienna, presenting music as a balancing act, as magic. Now he enjoys such daemons. With Spaun he attends the first of the fourteen concerts given by Paganini.

"There is only one voice within our walls, and it cries: Go and hear Paganini."

A fleeting shadow, as close to fire as to ice, and a fellow traveler too.

> The frost has spread a white sheen
> Over my head.
> Then I thought I was already an old man
> And was greatly pleased.

> *Der Reif hat einen weissen Schein*
> *Mir übers Haar gestreuet;*
> *Da glaubt ich schon ein Greis zu sein*
> *Und hab mich sehr gefreuet.*

Sometimes he manages to escape from the watchful care of his friends. He goes after the girlies again, not by the Danube this time, but in the *Heurige* inns where the new wine is celebrated. They do not expect much there, and charge even less. And if he stays by himself, no one takes any notice.

The lights from the lanterns dance in the trees.

He drinks a lot. Then it is easier for him to talk, to invite one of the young women to his side, casually.

Mostly he goes to Grinzing, to a winegarden where an old man, down on his luck, plays the fiddle amazingly, Mozart for preference.

"Come on."

She presses herself against him.

He kisses her, holds her.

"What's your name?"

"Franz."

"Franzl."

A chance guest, Hoffmann von Fallersleben, a visitor from afar, curious and eager to see Vienna's famous sights, crosses his path beneath the trees with their autumn coloring: "The old fiddler played Mozart. . . . We caught sight of Schubert and his girl from where we were sitting. He came over to us, and kept out of sight from then on," disappearing from the suburban picture, with or without a girl, but with his curls again, and dressed "in a clean coat, with a shiny hat."

> And when the cocks crowed
> Then my heart awoke.
> Now I sit here alone
> And remember my dream.
>
> I close my eyes once more,
> My heart is still beating so warmly.
> When will you leaves on the window grow green?
> When will I hold my love in my arms?
>
> *Und als die Hähne krähten,*
> *Da ward mein Herze wach;*
> *Nun sitz ich hier alleine*
> *Und denke dem Traume nach.*
>
> *Die Augen schließ ich wieder,*
> *Noch schlägt das Herz so warm.*
> *Wann grünt ihr Blätter am Fenster?*
> *Wann halt ich dich Liebchen im Arm?*

He sends a message to the noble Fräulein Nanette Hönig, one of those who adorn the Schubertiads, to be delivered "into her own hands": "I very much regret to have to inform you that I will be unable to have the pleasure of being of your company this evening. I am ill, and in such a fashion that I am quite unfit for any society. With the repeated assurance that I am extremely sorry to be unable to be of service to you. . . ."

> Again today I had to walk past
> In the depths of the night.
> Then, even though it was dark,
> I closed my eyes.

> *Ich musst auch heute wandern*
> *Vorbei in tiefer Nacht,*
> *Da hab ich noch im Dunkeln*
> *Die Augen zugemacht.*

On January 14, 1828, the music publisher Tobias Haslinger announces in the *Wiener Zeitung:* "*Winterreise* by Wilhelm Müller, Set for Solo Voice with Piano Accompaniment by Franz Schubert. Opus 89. Bound in a Colored Cover."

It makes him proud to read this. His mood lightens somewhat, whereupon Schober immediately gets busy planning and reactivating something that had been active once before: the friends should meet for reading evenings again. For reading matter he suggests books by the "New Generation," for instance Tieck, Kleist, Schlegel, and Novalis. One last time Schober manages unintentionally to further his friend on his journey. There are still a few stations to come, a few movements.

They read together Heine's *Buch der Lieder (Book of Songs).*

Now at last the figure can join him that has been his companion in its many guises: the doppelgänger, his double.

He appears (in a deep dream that begins to turn into music) at the point where the Wanderer arrives and departs as a stranger. It is the same scene, the same inhospitable reception, which cannot be dispelled:

The night is still, the streets at peace,
My darling used to live in this house;
She left the town long ago,
But the house still stands in the same place.

A man is standing there too, staring upwards,
And wringing his hands in anguish,
I shudder when I see his face—
The moonlight shows me my own features.

You my double! You pale companion!
Why do you mimic the pain of my love,
That tormented me here in this place,
Many a night, in times long past.

Still ist die Nacht, es ruhen die Gassen,
In diesem Hause wohnte mein Schatz;
Sie hat schon längst die Stadt verlassen,
Doch steht noch das Haus auf demselben Platz.

Da steht auch ein Mensch und starrt in die Höhe,
Und ringt die Hände, vor Schmerzensgewalt;
Mir graust es, wenn ich sein Antlitz sehe—
Der Mond zeigt mir meine eigne Gestalt.

Du Doppelgänger! Du bleicher Geselle!
Was äffst du nach mein Liebesleid,
Das mich gequält auf dieser Stelle,
So manche Nacht, in alter Zeit.

The ostinato with which he opens this song, a melodic cross-rhythm, bears the marks of the Passion, and is the counterpart of the increasing weight in the eighth notes for the Wanderer:

I cannot choose the time
For my journey,
I must find the path by myself
In this darkness.

A shadow cast by the moon goes with me
As my traveling companion,
And on the white alpine meadows
I seek the tracks of wild game.

Ich kann zu meiner Reisen
Nicht wählen mit der Zeit,
Muß selbst den Weg mir weisen
In dieser Dunkelheit.

Es zieht ein Mondenschatten
Als mein Gefährte mit,
Und auf den weißen Matten
Such ich des Wildes Tritt.

On a sudden whim that he explains neither to himself nor to the others, he explores the city, goes out to the Himmelpfortgrund and to Roßau, strolls through the Inner City, collecting memories of places where he lived, climbing staircases and running down again without having knocked on any door, burnishing his memory of inns and tables where he regularly sat with his friends. Everyone whom he chances to meet he takes with him for a little way, time permitting, and entertains them with anecdotes or recites poems like a schoolboy. And he enters, like a pilgrim, churches that he knows from his childhood.

On March 26, 1828, he gives his first private concert, "at seven o'clock in the evening in the Hall of the Austrian Music Society, Unter den Tuchlauben 558." He has programs printed on the finest paper, and although Paganini is again appearing that same evening, the hall is full to overflowing. Four gentlemen, Böhm, Holz, Weiß, and Linke, play the first movement of a new string quartet, probably the allegro from the String Quartet in D Minor which was later called, after the variations in its second movement, *Der Tod und das Mädchen* (*Death and the Maiden*). Vogl sings four songs including "The Wanderer's Address to the Moon" ("Der Wanderer an den Mond"):

A stranger, I wander from land to land
So homeless, so unknown.

Ich wandre fremd von Land zu Land,
So heimatlos, so unbekannt.

Tietze and Loewy sing, Josefine Fröhlich and Katharina's pupils perform Grillparzer's "Ständchen" ("Serenade"), and last but not least, a "New Trio for Pianoforte, Violin, and Violoncello" is played, the Trio in E-flat Major. He has a tumultuous reception, is hugged and kissed. The whole evening long he is borne along on a tide of admiration.

After this, Schober hardly ever succeeds in tempting him from the house. He is composing a Mass, making notes not just for one sonata but for three at the same time, and for a great string quintet.

"I need time, and I haven't got it," he said.

Schwind calls him a fool, and himself behaves like a matchless one. For three years now he has been courting Anna Hönig, whom they call Nettel. It was she who, on the first occasion, turned him away with an embittered speech about his agnosticism, at which point he, enraged at such great and glowing piety, advised her to fall in love with the pope, that would stand her in better stead.

Now he is trying again.

Schwind is invited as fiancé punctually for eleven o'clock. He oversleeps, searches for his frock coat, not even a black one but purple with yellow lapels. It tears at the back as he puts it on. Bemoaning his ill-fortune high and low, he stops en route to see Schober and Schubert, who send him packing without consolation. He is soon back, dejected and close to tears. Once again he has suffered rejection, this time also as a scoundrel.

"I'm off, I'm leaving Vienna, I want nothing more to do with her, I have to get away."

Schubert, too, moves out once more and changes his abode.

"Listen," he begs Schober, and sings for him what he has been writing, one of the Heine songs, "listen."

> I, unfortunate Atlas, must carry a world
> The whole world of sorrows.

> *Ich unglücksel'ger Atlas! eine Welt,*
> *Die ganze Welt der Schmerzen, muß ich tragen.*

Schober leaves the room without a word.

Schubert, startled, looks towards the door, and calls softly: "Schober."

And he actually comes in and says after they have had a long and profound discussion: "You're exaggerating, Schubert. You're even using your music to help you exaggerate."

"No, I'm not doing that."

"Oh, Schubert."

"Oh, Schobert."

That night he slips into Schober's bed. They lie side by side in silence, listening to each other breathing. They embrace one another.

He says: "I'm moving out, Schober. Ferdinand has a new apartment in a new house, and I've asked him if he can take me in."

Schober lies for a while as if paralyzed, then he suddenly pulls Schubert close: "Why? Am I getting on your nerves? Am I disturbing you?"

Schubert breathes hesitantly, as if he were testing his words: "My illness. I can feel it coming back. I've even been to the doctor already. Not to Bernhardt, to Rinna."

"Why didn't you tell me? Am I not your friend?"

"You are, Schober, it's just that . . . "

"What?"

He doesn't say.

Ferdinand picks him up the following day. He makes himself at home in a narrow little room. It is damp, and will grow damper. The house has only just been plastered. Summer no longer was able to dry the walls.

"Don't neglect yourself," Ferdinand warns him. "Don't work too hard. Relax."

He might have done so. He meets Marie Pachler at the theater. She is really pleased to see him and invites him to Graz. He must come as soon as he possibly can. He does some figuring and thinks that it might just be possible with the fee that Haslinger will pay for the second part of the *Winterreise*. But it is still not enough.

The soles of both my feet are burning,
Although I am walking on ice and snow.
I would rather not stop for breath
Until I can no longer see the towers.

Es brennt mir unter beiden Sohlen,
Tret ich auch schon auf Eis und Schnee,
Ich möcht nicht wieder Atem holen,
Bis ich nicht mehr die Türme seh.

Now he writes out in quick succession the three sonatas, the C minor, the A major, and the B major, which he had already prepared. In the first movement of the B Major Sonata he forgets the inexorable pacing rhythm and creates space for the Wanderer, strangely tranquil, wide-ranging, and calmly sorrowful.

"I like November," he says, "it's my month," and adds cheerfully and inexplicably for the benefit of Ferdinand's children who are listening to him: "November city, November world."

He corrects the string quintet.

And once again he recalls the joy of duet-playing, writing a Fantasia in F Minor, dedicating it to Countess Karoline, and sending her a message in his own way by taking a motif from the *Winterreise*, from the tenth song:

I realize now for the first time how tired I am
As I lie down to rest.
Walking kept me in a cheerful frame of mind
Along the inhospitable path.

Nun merk ich erst, wie müd ich bin,
Da ich zur Ruh mich lege;
Das Wandern hielt mich munter hin
Auf unwirtbarem Wege.

Schwind bids farewell. He is leaving Vienna.
"Stay, dearest friend."
"You have no further use for me, Franz."
"Stay."
"Farewell."

His tears fall on his music like the November rains.
"Go then. Farewell."

> Frozen teardrops fall
> From my cheeks;
> Did I really not notice
> That I was crying?

> *Gefrorne Tropfen fallen*
> *Von meinen Wangen ab;*
> *Ob es mir denn entgangen,*
> *Daß ich geweinet hab?*

He must learn more about composition. This decision surprises
Ferdinand.

"You?"

"I'm going to study fugue."

He has made an arrangement with Simon Sechter, and has his first
lesson immediately.

"There is so much that I still don't know."

On October 31 his brothers, Ferdinand, Ignaz, and Karl, invite him
to the "Red Cross" inn. At the Himmelpfortgrund. He retraces his
steps into the region of his childhood.

They could have been noisy but they are not. They talk about Father
and about their plans for the future, moaning a little about their situation.

"You're saying absolutely nothing, Franz."

The meal comes, fish from the Danube. They drink each other's
health. He eats, then lays his fork aside. "I can't," he says, really to
himself. "It makes me ill. The fish tastes poisoned."

It tastes like a rumor, a premonition, it tastes like the memory of
Salieri, and of Mozart, poisoned, just like poison.

"Take me home."

> There is one signpost that I can see
> Constantly before me,
> A road that I must follow
> From which there is no return.

Einen Weiser seh ich stehen
Unverrückt vor meinem Blick;
Eine Straße muß ich gehen,
Die noch keiner ging zurück.

On November 11 he takes to his bed, never to get up again. He follows the prescriptions of Dr. Rinna exactly. He sets up an hourglass so that he will under no circumstances forget to take his medicines at the correct time.

He cannot eat, and drinks very little.

Bauernfeld and Lachner come and talk gently with him, wanting to give him strength with memories.

"You're so kind."

The proofs of the *Winterreise* are brought for correction from Haslinger's. Despite his weakness, he travels again from one station of his Way of the Cross to the next.

He asks for Schober, who best knows the tortuous paths of his journey, but he hears nothing.

He writes him a letter.

Dear Schober,

I am ill. For eleven days now I have eaten nothing and drunk nothing, and I wander between my chair and my bed and back again, exhausted and unsteady. Rinna is treating me. If I do eat something, I have to throw up immediately.

Would you be so good as to help me with reading-matter in this desperate situation. I have read Cooper's books, *The Last of the Mohicans*, *The Spy*, *The Pilot*, and *The Pioneers*. If you should have anything else by him, then I beg you to leave it with Frau von Bogner at the coffeehouse for me. My brother, who is a model of conscientiousness, will most conscientiously bring it to me. Or something else.

Your friend Schubert

It is not known whether Schober brought the requested literature to Frau von Bogner.

Schober did not visit Schubert. Probably for fear of infection.

Even his father stayed away.

On the afternoon of November 19, 1828, Franz Schubert dies of the illness that has plagued him in his last years and been his companion.

He is lying there now, waiting to be picked up. He is being watched over by his brothers and by his friends. Anyone who sees him, far and near, anyone who has walked for a time at his side, suddenly glimpses in the Wanderer the little boy who sings and listens to voices, near and far.

Now, my Schubert, the organ-grinder is waiting.

31

Moment musical no. 11
(Rather slow)

An organ-grinder stands over there
Beyond the village,
And he turns the barrel-organ as well as he can
With numbed fingers.

He staggers on the ice
With his bare feet,
And his little plate
Remains ever empty.

No one wants to listen,
No one looks at him,
And the dogs growl
At the old man.

And he lets things take
Their course
Turning the handle,
And his organ is never still.

Strange old man,
Shall I go with you?
Will you turn your barrel-organ
To my songs?

Drüben hinterm Dorfe
Steht ein Leiermann,
Und mit starren Fingern
Dreht er, was er kann.

Barfuß auf dem Eise
Schwankt er hin und her,
Und sein kleiner Teller
Bleibt ihm immer leer.

Keiner mag ihn hören,
Keiner sieht ihn an,
Und die Hunde knurren
Um den alten Mann.

Und er läßt es gehen.
Alles wie es will,
Dreht, und seine Leier
Steht ihm nimmer still.

Wunderlicher Alter,
Soll ich mit dir gehn?
Willst zu meinen Liedern
Deine Leier drehn?

32

Moment musical no. 12
(Very slow)

The scene used to be a drawing. A picture. Not any longer.

I find myself in a room and I do not know how I have come to be there. And I do not ask why.

The floor is sloping, as in a lecture hall. A few chairs stand scattered about.

It is Schwind sitting on one of the chairs if I am not mistaken, and Schober on another.

Josef von Spaun, who is standing directly in front of the stage, leans on the back of his chair for support.

Schubert is sitting on a stool attached to the piano by the edge of the stage.

Only now can I hear the piano.

Schubert is playing triplets, pacing figures, as if from far away.

Unsure of myself, I turn to Franz von Schober and ask him if he can hear anyone singing. He watches my mouth as if he cannot understand me at all, and turns away, but not at all in an unfriendly manner.

Schubert has stopped playing.

He is silent for a long time, and then asks, without raising his voice, "Shall I start again from the beginning?"

And very softly he replies to himself, "There is no point."

It grows dark in the room.

I would be glad to turn away now.

Finis

Acknowledgments

I thank my wife, who has been my companion in my work on this book, both in discussion and with her advice and her criticism. I thank Mitsuko Shirai, Hartmut Höll, and Tabea Zimmermann for their ever-stimulating practical introduction to playing Schubert. I thank all the musicians who taught me to hear Schubert, most especially Artur Schnabel, whose interpretation of the Piano Sonata in B Major (D. 960) is the foundation, in every meaning of the word, for my enduring preoccupation with Franz Schubert.

I am grateful to the authors whose works listed below were stimulating and helpful:

Adorno, Theodor W. *Moments musicaux.* Frankfurt, 1964.

Brusatti, Otto. *Schubert im Wiener Vormärz: Dokumente 1829-1848.*

Deutsch, Otto Erich. *Franz Schubert—Thematisches Verzeichnis seiner Werke in chronologischer Folge.* Kassel, 1978.

—, ed. *Franz Schubert—Sein Leben in Bildern.* Munich and Leipzig, 1913.

—, ed. *Franz Schubert—Briefe und Schriften.* Vienna, 1954.

—, ed. *Schubert—Die Dokumente seines Lebens.* Kassel, 1964.

—, ed. *Schubert—Die Erinnerungen seiner Freunde.* Wiesbaden, 1983.

Dürr, Walther, and Arnold Feil. *Franz Schubert: Reclams Musikführer.* Stuttgart, 1991.

Eggebrecht, Hans Heinrich. *Musik im Abendland: Prozesse und*

Stationen vom Mittelalter bis zur Gegenwart. Munich, 1991.

Einstein, Alfred. *Schubert.* Zurich, 1952.

Feil, Arnold. *Franz Schubert: Die schöne Müllerin; Winterreise.* Stuttgart, 1975.

Fischer-Dieskau, Dietrich. *Auf den Spuren der Schubert-Lieder.* Wiesbaden, 1971.

Fröhlich, Hans J. *Schubert.* Munich, 1978.

Gal, Hans. *Franz Schubert oder die Melodie.* Frankfurt, 1970.

Georgiades, Thrasybulos. *Schubert: Musik und Lyrik.* 2 vols. Göttingen, 1967.

Gülke, Peter. *Franz Schubert und seine Zeit.* N.p., 1991.

Hilmar, Ernst. *Schubert.* Graz, 1989.

Kolb, Annette. *Franz Schubert.* Zurich, 1947.

Kreissle von Hellborn, Heinrich. *Franz Schubert.* Vienna, 1865; repr. Hildesheim, 1978.

Metzger, H.-K., and R. Riehn, eds. *Musik-Konzepte: Sonderheft Franz Schubert.* Munich, 1982.

Müller, Wilhelm. *Gedichte.* Leipzig, 1868.

Reed, John. *Schubert: The Final Years.* London, 1972.

Reininghaus, Frieder. *Schubert und das Wirtshaus: Musik unter Metternich.* Berlin, n.d.

Rissé, Joseph. *Franz Schubert und seine Lieder,* vol. 1, *Müllerlieder.* Hanover, 1872.

Schneider, Marcel. *Schubert in Selbstzeugnissen und Bilddokumenten.* Hamburg, 1958, 1989.

Schochow, Maximilian and Lilly, eds. *Franz Schubert — Die Texte seiner einstimmig komponierten Lieder und ihre Dichter.* Hildesheim, 1974.

Schubert, Franz. *Winterreise: The Autograph Score.* New York, 1989.

Spaun, Josef von. *Erinnerungen an Schubert.* Berlin, 1936.